THE VISIBLE SPECTRUM

THE PAINTING AND THE CITY
ROBERT FREEMAN WEXLER

Robert Freeman Wexler was born in Houston, Texas, and lives in Yellow Springs, Ohio, with the writer Rebecca Kuder. *The Painting and the City* is his second novel, and was previously available only in a limited, long out-of-print UK edition (PS Publishing, 2009). In the intervening years the novel has acquired cult-classic status; this new edition marks its US debut.

Wexler's other books include the novella *In Springdale Town*, the novel *Circus of the Grand Design*, and a story collection, *Psychological Methods To Sell Should Be Destroyed.* A new collection of short stories, *Undiscovered Territories,* will be published in 2021 by PS Publishing; his third novel, *The Silverberg Business,* will be published in 2022 by Small Beer Press.

www.robertfreemanwexler.com

PRAISE FOR ROBERT FREEMAN WEXLER

"Wexler's control of his prose, the careful delineation between characters, the ease with dialogue, the purposeful pacing (deliberate but not slow), the precise description of the setting, are all in the service of a sudden, sharp shock, a bizarre interface within the real world. Don't call it North American Magic Realism—call it North American Surrealism."

—Jeff VanderMeer, *Locus* (review of *In Springdale Town*)

"He's one of those writers who travels his own country, for whom the terms *science fiction* or *fantasy* or *mainstream* are pointless appelations . . . There are instances of the fantastic in all his major works, but they are inextricably linked with the "realistic" concerns of the everyday . . . It's just there, like any other aspect of the world. This restraint of reaction in the face of the surreal . . . creates a very dream-like quality to his fiction. Wexler is willing to live with mysteries not revealing their secrets, and because of this his fictional realities become more believable, more solid."

—Jeffrey Ford, from the introduction to the 2009 edition

ROBERT FREEMAN WEXLER

The Painting
and the City

THE VISIBLE SPECTRUM

THE VISIBLE SPECTRUM SERIES 007
the-visible-spectrum.com

Copyright © 2009, 2021 by Robert Freeman Wexler

This edition published in 2021 by The Visible Spectrum
under license from Verse Chorus Press

FIRST U.S. EDITION

Previously published in the UK by PS Publishing, 2009

Philip Schuyler's journals appeared in somewhat different form in *Polyphony*
4 and *Polyphony* 6.

The quoted text on page 219 is taken from the foreword by Tony Hiss to
Manhattan in Maps, 1527–1995, by Paul E. Cohen and Robert T. Augustyn
(Rizzoli International Publications, 1997), © 1997 Tony Hiss.

Portions of Charles Dickens's dialog are adapted from his *American Notes*

Cover and book design by Steve Connell | *steveconnell.net*

ISBN 978-1-953835-07-9

Library of Congress Control Number 2021934092

We've got the normals squinching.
    —Randy "Biscuit" Turner (Big Boys), *The Wreck Collection*

New York . . . is a city and it is also a creature, a mentality, a disease, a threat, an electromagnet, a cheap stage set, an accident corridor. It is an implausible character, a monstrous vortex of contradictions, an attraction-repulsion mechanism so extreme no one could have made it up
    —Luc Sante, *Low Life: Lures and Snares of Old New York*

For Rebecca and Merida

1

THE CITY

Tonight, for all its magnificence, the city projected a claustro-phobic attitude in which barren and cheerless buildings huddled for companionship, creaking across streets and alleys to confer with their neighbors. The sky had the brittle look of overripe fruit, all lumpy apples and oozing bananas, while the air felt more July than May, sodden and heavy, attacked by the aroma of uncollected refuse that overflowed its containers like some rain-swollen tropical river, and the faces of the homeless shone with brown light.

In summer, rancid haze clings to the buildings, a coating of torpor that drives out all who are able to leave, for a weekend, for a month, two months, all who own the means of leisure, while the rest take what ease they can, shunning the subways, avoiding the lifeless underground air weighted with the bones of past generations, whose inability to speak shackles the city, at its worst in the dead time of heavy summer. Breezes of shaved concrete crumble through the open windows of anyone unfortunate enough to lack air conditioning, and nightfall carries no release, as the trap laid by the day clamps down, vengeful and loathsome.

But Jacob Lerner always remained in town and worked, his sculptures gaining life from summer's breath.

Returning to the city from his Friday sculpture seminar at Rutgers, he had slept, miles of train-sleep, and dreamed a dream of which he could remember only disconnected scraps, forests of monolithic ferns with grasping, rubbery leaves; the dream had resumed on the F train, more confining—the ferns grew higher, closely packed, trapping him; he woke when the train stopped, and left the car without thinking. He emerged at 2nd Avenue and Houston, one stop from his intended destination of Delancey.

Outside again, the thick air of the city enveloped him. Dusty hands of brick applauded his passing, hissed their approval. Arches opened to allow unimpeded passage. Fountains emerged to quench his thirst and send sparkling drops into the air, drops that darted among the moonrays, careening and laughing. He hitched a ride on a droplet of iridescent green, sending it off into the depths of darkness, using its stored moonrays to light his path, a trail that wound in geometric randomness past alcoves and minarets, along streets of glass and towers constructed from grains of sand, until, satisfied, they dropped him at the door of his friend Gary Freed's apartment and the party it contained.

Lerner worked alone, hours in the studio bending and pounding metal or shaping clay. The solitude eventually filled him with a craving for contact, but the suffocating press of people in a small space, after his time alone, was a difficult transition. Tonight he felt sociable. Though his sculpture seminar had tired him, it had also left him craving more human interaction.

He pressed Freed's buzzer a few minutes before 10 p.m. He would be at the party for at least an hour before seeing the painting. Though not a memorable party, everything that happened prior to that moment crystallized, as if his first sight of the painting merged both immediate past and far future into one ineradicable memory.

"Hey Jacob, have a mojito," Freed said at the door. "It's Cuban. Hemingway drank them."

Lerner thanked him and took the drink. Freed looked the way he always did: sleek, healthy seal nicely groomed and dressed in something stylish and appropriate, suitable and proper appearance for a successful plastic surgeon. Seeing him, Lerner remembered that he had planned to go home and change before the party, but hadn't even gotten on the right subway to do so. The train-dream had thrown everything off.

A man and a familiar-looking woman stood nearby. The man was talking with his mouth close to the woman's ear, his gaze moving from her face to her breasts, not large but well-exposed by the cut of her top. Lerner caught a few words about sweet locations and options to buy.

"Seminar Day go okay?" Freed asked. They chatted for a minute, then Freed moved off to join a woman standing in front of a series of black and white photographs showing the steel frames of skyscrapers under construction. Freed, an art collector, also owned an early piece of Lerner's, a small bronze with the appearance of a distorted cage, burst open at the top from the inside, as though whatever it once housed had tired of captivity. (Lerner had done cages years ago, moved to other themes, and returned.)

"Did I hear you say something about making clay things?"

Lerner turned toward the familiar-looking woman and recognized her—Foul-Mouth Juliet—an actress he had seen in a modernization of *Romeo and Juliet* (now with black hair, which had previously been red). He had met her several times but she never remembered him. Once, he told her that he worked as a zeppelin pilot in Tanzania, bringing supplies to remote regions, and was in New York recovering from surgery after a near-fatal attack by airship pirates.

Showing unexpected interest, she asked Lerner about his seminar, but the man interrupted. "Did I just hear you say you only have to work one day a week! I had no idea teaching was so lucrative. You artists have it made, government grants, teaching gigs. If you worked *two* days a week you could buy a vacation home in East Hampton. I'm in the wrong fucking business!"

Lerner stared at the man's face for a moment, then responded: "That isn't what I said. I teach one day a week. I work more than that. A lot more. I'm working right now, talking to you . . . there's a shadow on the wall behind you, I don't know from what, that's not important. The shape is the important thing. What form would that shadow take in three dimensions?"

Without waiting for a reaction, Lerner turned away. While crossing the room, he intercepted a man carrying a tray of drinks and exchanged his empty for a new one.

Two women stood near his old sculpture; one of them had set her empty glass in the middle of the cage. The base of the cage was a thin layer of concrete. Lerner had cut down an assortment of plastic tubs, using them as molds for ready-mix concrete, in which, after drying, he would drill holes for the bronze rods. For his current work, he used a bronze disk as the base, welding the rods to it.

Groupings of random syllables rose from the women, growing ordered and distinct as Lerner drew closer. Their voices inter-twined, sometimes repeating the same phrase as though each was talking to herself.

"Up a quarter point. Not advisable. Too much for too little. We told him but he wouldn't listen. We told him. After the market closes. Always after the close."

One of them said something else, and both laughed, identical laughs, a crackling that sounded forced and studied, as if, lacking a natural means of expressing mirth, they had taught themselves to approximate. The duo had the coppery-hair, dark suit-dress look of financial advisors. They hovered, leathery-winged, between Lerner and his art. Their too-white skin stretched along unsmiling faces that expressed no welcome.

"I . . . excuse me," Lerner said. "I was just coming to see the art." He indicated the sculpture, and the women glanced at it.

"Is *that* what this is?" one of them asked.

"Of course. Don't you remember that seminar we went to? What was it, 'Art Investment through Market Fluctuations.'"

"Right right. I see, there's the name, Jacob Lerner. Is he blue chip?"

"I wonder if he's blue chip?"

They spoke in identical, flat voices that vacuumed oxygen from the room.

"I hope this is appreciating at a commendable rate," the first speaker said. She directed her attention to Lerner. "Are you thinking of investing in art?" Though her glance at his frayed khakis said she had doubts.

"I made my investment years ago," he said.

"Oh look," one said. "He must be an artist. Gary always has a few around."

"You're so correct, look at the hole, there, just above the knee." She pointed. "No one else would come to a party dressed so ... "

"Indiscriminately," the other said, finishing. They laughed their dry, tinderstick laugh, and left Lerner alone with his sculpture.

Emblems of migratory impulses collide amidst the ruins of unimagined civilizations. Paths overgrown by decay, blanched by summer heat, yet never obliterated. Remnants. If found, they bring quite a price at auction. But what of art? Art binds, art guides. The leaders of nations understand this. Even Hitler was a painter. Perhaps the source of the problem lies there, for if an art lover could also be a monster, then far safer for the world if its leaders reject such things. Business is the Lord, art is what remains after vultures pick the carcass of society.

He abandoned the graceless curves of his immature metal.

Across the room, Freed pointed out a painting to several guests, including the financial women. Obviously a recent acquisition—whose would it be, *this* new banner of wealth and taste?

Wishing to avoid the group viewing Freed's new painting, Lerner entered the kitchen, a modern, magazine feature of steel and stained concrete. Freed's caterers had been using the oven and restaurant-quality stove; the temperature change hit him a few feet in, but he found the heat pleasant after the chill of the other rooms.

And, even more pleasing, he saw his friend Buddy Drake, talking to a woman wearing an Admiral Horatio Nelson hat.

"Truckstop sentimentality," the woman said.

"I know, I know, but I'm a sucker for twang and pedal steel," Buddy Drake said.

"Buddy likes anything that sounds like Mississippi," Lerner said when he reached them. Buddy Drake was a photographer; they had met in art school, and over the years had shared a series of East Village and Lower East Side tenements.

"Hey Jacob, have you met Liz Crandell? We just finished shooting some publicity photos for her new novel."

"That's why I'm wearing make-up. Though, turns out, women are supposed to wear it all the time."

"I was just telling Liz that this band, Blind Revenant, wants me to go with them, take pictures. Their first European tour. And why not? It gives me a good excuse to get out of the city this summer."

They talked about their work. Lerner described his recent twisted metal cages. Liz Crandell's second novel was due out in the fall, but she said she wasn't expecting much of a response from critics. "My problem is," she said, "I'm a hopeful surrealist in an age of neo-conceptualism and irony." She laughed. "Sorry, I've been practicing lines for interviews."

Freed tapped Lerner on the shoulder. "Hey, I want to show you guys the new painting. Come on."

They followed Freed to the hall where Lerner had seen him with the investment women. Lerner couldn't have known, as he took those first steps toward the painting, that time would stop, would become an inconsequential monolith dedicated to its own absence. Depths of forgotten dreams, years traced in lines on faces, the maze of lines, maze of minds, maze of bodies on the street, walking without listening, without seeing, all oblivious to the suffering beneath the surface.

Closer to the painting, coils of frosty air tugged at Lerner. A warning, perhaps an attempt to save him. He stood at the wide end of a long, dark funnel. Nothing existed outside the tube, and its tapering walls directed him to a scene so delicate that at first all he could see was the glow of a painterly candle. His breath stopped. Water covered him, clear water that didn't distort the canvas. In the foreground a woman sat facing the viewer; a candelabrum on the low table before her illumined the darkened room. Lerner floated, alone, no one in the world but himself and the painting. The eyes of the woman met his. He smiled, for her face bore the beauty of Diana, of Athena. But what was that in the doorway?

Walking, walking, but mud ensnared his feet . . . he looked down; the mud, a brilliant blue, blocked his way. It mounded in front of him, a thick wedge dotted with stiff peaks. Mounds of other colors and hues lay nearby. A hum filled the air, and Lerner glanced up to see a shape descending, a vast wedge of stiff fibers. The fibers enveloped him, scooping him up with the blue mud. He rose and rose, to an impossible height. Then the fibers dashed him against a fabric wall. From there, he looked out at Freed's apartment, looked out from the painting, his body flattened into the web of canvas.

Freed's voice broke through the buffering muddy layers that surrounded Lerner. "Philip Schuyler. Dutch-English. I'm told it's quite rare, that he usually painted outdoor scenes, markets and such."

From his perch within the painting, Lerner sensed unrest. In a doorway behind the woman, a man stood, so indistinct he might have been a shadow, save for the candle he held, his hand shielding the light so that it exposed no more than his face. His expression displayed such malevolence that Lerner had to force himself to look elsewhere, at the velvety red drapes, Oriental rug. The woman—her serenity implied she carried no sense of the presence behind her.

Voices mingled. Clinical discussions of imagery, or technique . . . but . . . what of the woman, the sweet, unsuspecting woman?

"Jacob. Jacob . . . are you okay?"

He found that he had slumped against Buddy Drake. His collapse, or whatever it was, had turned him from the painting, and outside its influence, calm resumed.

"Tired," he said. "Long day. Got up early to teach my class. Guess I should be getting home."

2

LESSONS IN URBAN PLANNING

In the morning, Lerner's clay—solidified rivers packed in neat plastic bags—waited to be transformed. Shapes, concepts, the honesty of dirt and metal, a churning lump moving onward . . . davits of circling swollen bronze, in the night forlorn, silent, but they crash, monumental. Foreshortened renderings that convey a misplaced sense of development. Furnace howls, raging, committed to nothing but its task. Entrusted with the primal elements, fragments of journal entries revolve, evolve. Incoherent streams glow and vibrate. Which of these breaks the barriers of hate, of racist fear? On the street, a deathwatch, flesh and fantasy interweave in a stupendous dance. Homeless vagrant immigrant nonentities prowl the nightmares of the inheritors, who fortify themselves in opposition to the encroaching swarms. *Their* sidewalks accommodate only the new and the shiny. Vinyl circles rage against stultification . . . you make me nervous and I crawl the floor . . . a fight without end, a fight always co-opted, forcing the revolution to lie dormant before one day, one distant day metamorphosing anew. *The Shelf Life of Revolution*—that would be the title of this piece.

Heat pulsed through his loft. Having fired a group of clay figures shaped earlier in the week, he shut down his electric kiln and moved away from the circular mold that he had just filled with molten bronze.

Most of his bronze he commissioned from a foundry in New Jersey, one- and two-foot strips that he could bend and hammer into the shapes he fancied. But on occasion, he needed something special, a disk to use as the base of the cage, or a ring. These he made himself, melting bronze ingots with a blowtorch, then pouring the metal from the crucible into rough molds of clay. Hot and dangerous work (on the floor near his worktable, hardened splotches of bronze illustrated the need for care).

The rush of activity and concentration ebbed, and fragmentary images of Freed's painting drifted through the stale air of Lerner's studio. Saturdays, he didn't usually work, but the need to complete his current piece had overtaken him. Now that he was finished, he couldn't stop thinking about the woman, and the man's threatening pose. What had that artist intended? Looking at his new clay figures, he saw the faces from the painting.

His loft occupied the third floor of a former garment sweatshop at Crosby and Howard, a narrow space, but with windows on three sides (though the rear windows opened onto an air shaft, providing negligible light). His door, a steel slab wide enough to allow passage of sweatshop machinery, opened into the studio, which he had set up in the corner with the best light. Past the studio was a sitting area, then the kitchen, and the bedroom and bathroom in the rear. With the help of friends, he had laid sheets of plywood over the existing concrete floor, sanded them smooth, and stained them a light golden color. As was common in the city, he paid for all renovations himself.

Garment sweatshops still flourished around him, on the floor below his and in the neighboring building; mornings and late afternoons Chinese workers jammed the sidewalks. Every morning on the corner, a woman sold thousand-year-old eggs from a cart. The determination and honesty of the garment workers, Lerner's conception of it anyway, formed the basis of his current sculptures, a series of twisted metal cages surrounding clay figurines.

When Lerner first discovered his neighborhood, he had been captivated by the way workers moved finished clothes from the third- or fourth-floor sewing factories by stringing a cable from the window to the waiting truck. Walking east on Grand Street, he had first seen the fluttering dresses, heard them swoosh down the cable. The sight continued to thrill him.

Tired, satisfied with his day's work (before the questioning and doubt that always lurked beyond his sight pushed its way forward), he stood gazing down at the sidewalk, a moment of indecision, of rest, between what has been and what is yet to be, idle time, drift of thoughts, of vision; afternoon passage of Chinese school kids, tourists, workers loading and unloading delivery trucks. A boy—ten years old? Twelve?—stopped to cross the street. On his back he bore another boy, smaller, but not a real boy, a strange doll made of reddish glass, which gazed up at Lerner from its perch, blank eyes reflecting the sun.

Deciding he had to see the painting again, today, Lerner called Freed to set up a visit. Lerner and Freed had known each other since sixth grade, meeting at Zionist summer camp in the Texas Hill Country, during the 1970s of their youth. They had lost touch sometime during high school, intersecting again briefly during Lerner's one year of college in Texas, then again in Manhattan, drawn by their shared past, needing each other's contact in some instinctive, unspoken way, as a touchstone in a city where natives were the only ones admitting to a prior history.

Like many, Lerner had come to New York to attend art school, where he found a congeniality of creation rare in less concentrated cities. Art, music, and literature entwined. And after the usual succession of group shows and independent exhibits, he had found Rezinsky. "The arch-devil," as named by one of her long-time artists, the nearly blind painter Claus von Sem. Rezinsky always referred to Lerner as "that Jew from Texas" because she hadn't thought it possible for there to be Jews anywhere in the U.S. but New York, especially from someplace as distant and exotic as Texas. She had been good to Lerner for a time, before alcohol and indifference drained her motivation. During

Lerner's final exhibit, the gallery's one remaining assistant disappeared while Rezinsky was in Europe. She closed the gallery a few months later, instead showing art out of her Upper East Side apartment.

Lerner had found his current gallery because of Gary Freed's patronage, liberating him from his enslavement at Rezinsky's.

Lerner strolled east on Grand, passing through what had once been Bunker Hill. Instead of following the terrain, along curving depressions, sharp rises, or streams, the city had always ploughed itself level, eating inconsistencies and shitting them out the sides to increase the island's girth. Leveled long ago, the hill's banished earth called out to deaf passersby. Sometimes, when traffic stilled in one of the rare, uncanny gaps amongst the flow of citystreetnoise, the amputated hill could be heard, a wheeze and grumble like shifting sand.

Beyond Bowery, Lerner stopped to eat at a Vietnamese noodle shop, then continued east, past the Kosher bakery. On the next corner, he overtook a man and woman. They were about Lerner's age. The man wore a yarmulke. Lerner caught the end of what the man said: "It was so good it was like eating *trayf*!"

The *Village Voice* had recently run an article about the younger generation of orthodox Jews moving into the Lower East Side, reclaiming territory once inhabited by their immigrant ancestors.

One of Lerner's summers at Zionist camp, the counselors had organized a theatrical production, a musical about immigrant life in the late nineteenth-century Lower East Side and the growth of labor unions; young Freed had been the star. For Lerner, camp had meant softball, hiking, and later, girls. The other aspects had washed off, no re-awakened religious fervor for him. Others had absorbed the teaching and moved to Israel. Lerner's parents were functionally religious: they attended a suburban Houston synagogue, mostly for bar and bat mitzvahs of relatives or the children and grandchildren of friends, abstained from pork, lit candles on Friday nights. Lerner's disinterest in both religion and money troubled them. They would have preferred that he had taken Freed's path: why not a doctor *and* an artist? But he disdained such divisions.

Nearing Freed's, a modernized tenement building dating from 1887, Lerner came upon an old and failing structure. A distended belly of a place, its walls bulged, groaning with a wet slurry sound.

All buildings in Manhattan, all old ones, possess a unique voice. In 1997, a structural engineer named Reginald Meisner studied the voices of buildings, using listening devices originally developed for Cold War espionage. Meisner arranged a dozen of the devices in a building for a month, recorded, then moved on to the next. Meisner's team worked its way through locations generated randomly by a computer that had been fed the addresses of all buildings at least 125 years old. Initial setup involved isolating and identifying all human and mechanical noises, then eliminating them. Something found to be common was a low, dry chuckling, an old man or woman's rasp, the laugh of a vaudevillian weak with age and illness, yet with humor intact.

Lerner stopped and pulled his sketchbook from his satchel so he could capture shape and detail. Grayness clung to the afternoon air, to the sickly building, a sullen ocean gray that made breathing difficult, and with each breath, the odor of gray, like potatoes left too long in a cellar. The building's windows and door were blocked by plywood sheets, and he wondered how long before it would be demolished in favor of new condominiums, stifling its laugh forever.

And later, reconstructing the painting in his memory as he walked along the gray-choked sidewalk, past the gray man sprawled face down on a stoop, past a boutique selling $500 designer handbags in neon colors . . . the woman: her dress a rich wine, her skin and hair dark. Of the room, he remembered little. The horrid face of the man in the doorway—he was the fulcrum that swung the attention. Discrete random variables intruded on his review of the painting. He needed to see it again, commit its shapes to memory.

"I'm going out," Freed said. "When you're finished, make sure the door is closed all the way. It'll lock automatically."

Lerner stood in the entryway, suddenly apprehensive about viewing the painting again. His stomach jumbled, as though he was about to greet a new lover, still in that bloom of early romance, before repetition dulled the excitement.

The woman leaned forward, a gentle tilt to the chin that spoke of expectation, of patient waiting for the return of a devoted companion. But the figure in the doorway—he was *not* the expected one, and his unknown advance indicated danger. The man's posture was that of one accustomed to devious acts accomplished in shadow. Their surroundings, the cushions and drapes, indicated comfort, a lifestyle of repose.

Something about the composition was off, though, an object misplaced, an element added later perhaps, which canted the balance in a disturbing way. But that sort of mistake seemed unlikely from this artist; his grasp of technique was impressive.

The red of the drapes—had it been so bloody before? Like pillars of rich, flowing blood, the drapes framed the darkened window. They had a moist quality, a hue sickening in its accuracy, as though the artist meant to convey the full flood of life within the woman, thereby magnifying the hidden threat of the shadowy figure. Lerner knew this truth with a startling certainty, though interpretation of scenes had never interested him.

But there it was, in such painterly detail he found himself sucked into the complexity of brush stroke and daub, the foundation on which the scene took shape. The role of each player, though ill-defined, formed a moment frozen for over 150 years. Lerner arched forward, letting his gaze dissect the shadowy figure. Close in, the face became a blotch of competing marks and colors. Stepping back, Lerner could see the suggestion of something under the man's coat, a bulge signifying the hidden threat, handle of gun or knife. Though would this man take such a messy approach? His type was more that of a garrotter.

Nausea pounded at Lerner, and he lurched backward, finding himself, with a confusing suddenness, seated on an oak bench in Freed's hall. He remained there for several minutes, inhaling and exhaling, a purposeful, regulatory breath. The painting still called, and from the bench, out of the canvas's direct line, he dared a glance. From this angle, he couldn't see the shadowy figure, and its absence calmed him. The woman appeared serene, a goddess of her parlor. Perhaps she had vanquished the intruder.

Lerner got up and navigated his way to the kitchen; on the pad by the telephone, he jotted a note for Freed: "Call me. Let's meet for lunch tomorrow. I need to know more about the painting."

He would find out where Freed bought it, trace it to previous owners, and research the artist, Philip Schuyler, discover who the woman had been, whether portrait study or merely a model used to enact a scene of the imagination.

At the library, Lerner found a book called *Art in Manhattan: A Look Back at 150 Years*, published in 1938, that referenced a journal by Schuyler. The author had a dubious opinion of Schuyler's journal, dismissing the (as he put it) erratic descriptions of secret societies, kidnapping, and intrigue (including aid from Charles Dickens, in New York during his 1842 trip to America) as "the ramblings of an unstable mind." And the author could find no record of the portrait that Schuyler allegedly had been brought to New York to paint.

The library didn't have a copy of the journal itself. Lerner wrote a note and asked a librarian to leave it for Simon Hoff, who oversaw the New York Public Library's art and architecture collection. As an undergraduate, Lerner had taken art history classes from Hoff, and they had become friends. If an accessible copy of the journal existed, Hoff would be able to locate it.

Lerner checked out a thin book, printed in 1948, called *The Candlelight Paintings of Philip Schuyler*, which showed a series of dim streets dotted with market stalls, women carrying baskets of produce, mothers holding their children's hands, everything depicted at night among glowing candles.

A day of exchanged notes and messages—on returning to his apartment he played back a call from Freed: "So yeah, I'm leaving in the morning, going away for a week with my new lady friend. Why don't you join us for dinner tonight. . . . "

The offer of dinner presented a conundrum; he picked up the phone and called Tansy Jenkins. "Hey . . . would you mind coming here instead of me going to Hoboken?"

Tansy was a costume designer on the faculty at Rutgers. They had met through friends, had become friends themselves over a three-year period. Then, during a week spent at a rented house on the Jersey shore with a group of several others, they had sex for the first time, an event that surprised them both and had since continued, though neither were interested in living together or even seeing each other more than once or twice a week.

"You never want to come here unless it's from Rutgers—you Manhattan types can't seem to leave your island."

"You're probably right."

"I'm always right."

He told her about the painting. "Something about it has gotten into me. I have to talk to Freed about it some more. So there's a legitimate reason. It's not just my phobia about stepping off the island."

"A painting? It's not going anywhere, even if Freed is. I don't appreciate being stood up for your obsession."

"Come on," he said. "I'd love to see you. You can charm Freed's 'new lady friend' while I get what I need from him."

"Fuck you. I'm not your wife. I don't have to help you with social engagements."

"I didn't mean it that way . . . I know you hate crap like that."

They had both been married once, Lerner to Beth-the-cellist, a condition that had lasted less than a year, and Tansy to Jonathan-the-fake-writer—who did actually write, and had received considerable attention for it recently—but fake because of the way he scammed himself into Important parties, where he expected Tansy to supply the charisma he was incapable of and which, for a time, she did. When Lerner and Tansy first met they had talked about their marriages; neither wanted another, but Tansy said she wanted a child at some point. Lerner didn't, and he knew that this would eventually cause a rift.

"Maybe I can come over later, Lerner said. "I don't want to spend the whole evening with them. When I'm done I'll go to the PATH."

"Your loss, sweetie. I have to be somewhere in the morning anyway. It's actually better this way. I can get to bed early."

"I'm sure this won't take very long. I'll call you after dinner."

"No. This is better."

He knew that tone—no swaying her decision now. Tansy Tansy red-headed Tansy. . . . "I'm beginning to think I'm making the wrong life choices," he said.

"Make it up to me next week. We've got the thesis plays. Run along to your obsession then."

3

CATHERINE VANADIS

The restaurant Freed chose was called Delta, one of those shiny new overpriced bistros appearing on the fringes of the neighborhood below Houston Street and above Little Italy and Chinatown (given the trendy name NoLita, for North of Little Italy). Blame it on the popularity of SoHo, but now all would-be hip neighborhoods needed a name, something for the marketeers to flash in business meetings. Propelled throughout its history by the drive of commerce, this city continually reinvented itself, sowing new industry and architecture in fields of concrete, brick, and stone.

Lerner arrived first and took a table toward the back. Most of the tables were full, colonized by the young and fashionable who kept the city's money river flowing. Lerner and his friends looked with scorn on this younger generation filling the trendy bars and restaurants, enacting their idea of grand lives in the big city, despite high rent and low pay, inhabiting assistant positions in publishing, finance, fashion, and advertising. Older residents had likely felt the same about Lerner and his friends, filled back then with art school pomposity, attempting to emulate artists of earlier ages. Many of Lerner's college friends had left long ago, returning to their places of origin: Texas, Wyoming, California, Indiana. But some stayed. Despite the eternal noise, and grime, and crime, and desperation, no other city would serve.

Freed entered, followed by a woman wearing a tight wrap-around dress and the glitter of income; Freed wore the heterosexual male equivalent, and both blended well with the surrounding diners. Though Lerner had showered before going out again, he wore the same faded jeans with the hole on his right hip, where the keys in his pocket had rubbed the denim thin. He rose to greet them.

"Hi, I'm Stephanie Gaines," the woman said. Lerner recognized her from Freed's party. Over the ensuing small talk, he discovered that she had an MBA from Harvard and was the youngest vice president at one of the publishing conglomerates. Lerner doubted that she was Jewish. As a youth, Freed had been an active Zionist who rarely socialized with anyone outside their religion, but he had long ago discarded those sentiments. When they first reunited in the city, Freed's changes had amused Lerner—this reinvention of self was something he had seen in others who, moving to a new place, created personas to represent their fresh lives. He had probably done it too, transforming himself from Houston high school kid to New York art school sophisticate.

They examined the nouvelle-southern menu and ordered. Group dinners made Lerner uncomfortable. Though he had been able to support himself without a regular job for the last eight or so years, the precarious nature of his finances kept him frugal. Art supplies were expensive. He rarely paid a lot for eating out, preferring the lower-priced restaurants in Chinatown or the East Village. And he never ordered wine in a restaurant. When dining with people who either had more income (or merely spent as if they did), he usually set firm limits to keep from subsidizing other's habits.

Dining with Freed, he didn't have to worry about the expense. Freed was the sort who always insisted on paying, for whom paying was as necessary as breathing. What would happen, Lerner sometimes wondered, if Freed dined with someone equally adamant? Lerner was unsure whether Freed's generosity was true, or an aspect of his reconstructed city persona. He hadn't been particularly generous at summer camp, but at thirteen, who is?

Lerner's frugality made the art possible. Though never far from debt, he always managed to find money when he needed it, through teaching, occasional carpentry work for museum exhibits, and sales of his art. Once, soon after graduate school, he had received a grant. Once, but never again, and he had long ago discontinued what had been an annual ritual of assembling slide packets and statements. Three times he had attended public panel discussions of the works, and after the third experience, he stopped submitting. The grants were always juried by dried-up, scabrous unimaginative husks of pseudo-artists, always looking for either the most sensational or most mundane, depending on the surrounding political environment. Lerner's art depended on being able to transport the viewer outside their conscious, rational self. His work didn't fit into a category that could be reduced to a blurb. So he produced art. Produce instead of reduce, he said, until his friends tired of hearing it.

The waiter brought the wine and poured. They clinked their glasses. "Cheers," Stephanie said.

"I've been researching Philip Schuyler," Lerner said. "Where did you find that painting anyway?"

"Did I tell you about the Kreunen's new bond package?" Stephanie asked, turning Freed's attention to finance.

"You should meet with them, Jacob," Freed said. "They manage at least twelve percent growth a year no matter what the economy does."

"I don't know who you're talking about," Lerner said.

"They're self-taught," Stephanie said.

"Always both of them in meetings," Freed said. "They're like Siamese twins without the connective tissue. They cut me out of a plan that just wasn't performing." He reached for Stephanie's hand and smiled at her, as if seeing his rising investments written on her forehead. "We met because of them. Now we're limited partners on a property development in the Bronx."

"I came here to talk about your painting, not your stockbrokers."

"They're not stockbrokers," Frees said. "They're investment wizards. Dora and Denise Kreunen. Twin dynamos of financial power. Sisters who act as one. I've never heard them disagree on an investment."

"I did once," Stephanie said. "And it tanked completely. Some kind of software start-up. If those two are ever not in agreement, look out."

Lerner remembered the two cold-faced women at the party and knew those were the sisters Freed was talking about. Perhaps he *would* approach them. He had just sold a pair of sculptures to the new museum at Antioch College. He could see how the sisters did with the money. But . . . the painting . . . he was after the painting, not investment advice. "I'm looking for a copy of Schuyler's journal," he said. "It might not have anything on your painting, but I need to know more about him."

"You're always obsessing about your own art," Freed said. "But what's with this painting?"

"It's special. It's—"

"I don't like it," Stephanie said.

"We're going dancing later," Freed said. "A newish place on Houston, between Eldridge and Allen. You're not dressed properly, but they would probably let you in with us."

"Sure," Lerner said, though he had no intention of going.

"Catherine Vanadis said she'd be there," Stephanie said.

"She's the one," Freed said. "Her place is where the painting was found. Old row house on Bond Street. The ground floor and basement are being renovated for her new restaurant. They found a room down there that no one had touched in decades. The door had been blocked by paneling and a century's worth of junk. She was there. You can ask her about it."

Freed excused himself to go to the restroom, leaving Lerner and Stephanie. "Gary says you've known each other since you were kids. Got any cute stories about him?"

Cute wasn't one of the words he would ever have used for junior Freed. "You guys met through these investment sisters?"

"It was at the clinic, and somehow we figured out we both went to the Kreunens."

Lerner stared at her face, sharp cheekbones, slightly flaring nose, lips neither fat nor thin. He wondered which feature she had engaged Freed to mold. He glanced down at the improminence of her breasts beneath the tight fabric, finding no answer there. Weren't there rules about involvement with patients?

"Not at *his* clinic," she said, seeming to catch Lerner's thoughts. "I volunteer at the Livdahl Clinic's soup kitchen. I couldn't believe his generosity."

Unclear what any of this had to do with Freed, Lerner gave her a blank look.

"Tattoo removal?" she said, forming the phrase into a question. "I guess he doesn't publicize these things. He does laser tattoo removal for ex-cons, ex-gang members, people trying to turn their lives around who don't want the stigma keeping them from getting decent jobs."

These places always had velvet ropes at the entrance, guarded by men of a size that deterred argument. Lerner doubted that entry requirements were strict (bodies in = money spent), but they needed to retain the illusion of exclusivity. The music was probably crap. Even if they found this Catherine Vanadis woman, he doubted that they would be able to talk beneath the blasting sound system. But on entering, he found an entirely different scene. Down a short hallway, the club opened into a warehouse-sized room shrouded in silky light. Plush chairs and sofas lay scattered about, with dancers weaving among them. Like the light, the music was muted, subdued vocals and soft guitar, keyboards. No disco beat.

"Not what I expected," Lerner said to Freed.

"You don't get out much. Living Room is in. For a kinder, gentler party crowd. The city is brash enough. We need graceful diversion."

Stephanie led them back toward a far corner, a choice that relieved Lerner. The sofas in the middle of the immense floor felt oddly exposed. He liked the idea of having at least one wall near.

A man waved, and Stephanie paused to speak to him. While they waited for her, Lerner glanced around the club. A few feet farther on, two women occupied an arrangement of 1940s-style chairs and a sofa, all nubbly green fabric with curved, wooden arms; one sat on the chair, one on the sofa, leaning toward each other, faces close.

" . . . market fuel pretty much used up," Stephanie said to the man, speaking in hushed tones, as if afraid of being overheard.

Lerner gazed toward the women, wondering if one of them was who they were looking for. Though the murmur of their voices reached him, he couldn't distinguish any words. The one on the sofa spoke with broad gestures; the other wore a sleeveless black dress, exposing thin, meatless arms—the woman they sought, Catherine Vanadis was . . . owner? . . . chef? . . . of a restaurant—those arms would not be hers.

"Not here. We'll go over it after my trip," Stephanie said. "Or, I can call from there if you need me too." The man moved on, and they continued toward the pair of women.

"This is Jacob Lerner. The sculptor," Freed said, and Lerner shook hands with the women. The one on the sofa was indeed Catherine Vanadis; the other was named Deneba or Geneva-something. "Jacob wants to know about that painting you found."

"Oh! I saw your show last spring at Ventricle Savage's," Catherine Vanadis said. "I really liked it. I'd love to buy something of yours for my new restaurant."

"That would be great," Lerner said. He sat beside her.

Ventricle Savage carried Lerner's art at his uptown gallery. Doubtless an invented name. The rumor Lerner preferred was that Savage grew up in rural North Carolina, with a father in the salvage business, which he, through either typographical error or ignorance, spelled "savage." Lerner's recent show there had been his most successful yet (in both reviews and sales).

"Vermont," Freed said from somewhere behind Lerner.

"A bed and breakfast up in the White Mountains," Stephanie said. "For maybe a week. I have to get out of this heat."

Lerner turned around in time to see Freed kiss her. "Gary," he said. "Can I get a key? I may need to look at the painting while you're gone."

"Oh just let it go," Freed said without looking toward him.

"You really *are* interested in the painting. I get obsessed with things too, like finding a good source to smuggle in Sichuan peppers," Catherine Vanadis said.

She repeated Freed's story about the sealed room.

"The paneling obviously hadn't been nailed over the door by accident. My workers had been pulling it down so we could see what kind of shape the wall was in, then—zap—there it was, this black recess. The guy who shined a light in screamed and dropped his flashlight. Everyone laughed at him. I went over there when I heard the scream.

"The painting was on a marble-topped sideboard—I'm keeping that for the restaurant. In front of the painting, five burned-down candles arranged on the marble in a U-shape. The appraiser who looked at the painting thought it was pretty remarkable. He said there wasn't a lot known about the artist."

Lerner sat back in the saggy-bottomed sofa—he had been leaning stiffly forward while she spoke, as if trying to receive her words sooner. Freed and Stephanie danced nearby. The Geneva-Deneba woman had disappeared.

Catherine Vanadis said the building had been constructed as a home by Paul Bookman, one of New York's wealthy elite of the time. "There are references to him in Philip Hone's diaries and elsewhere. Hone says Bookman's ancestry was Dutch, that his family Anglicized its name from Beekman. Hone and Bookman both moved uptown about the same time—hard to believe Bond was once uptown—but after some point, Bookman is never mentioned again, not by Hone or anyone. A later deed showed the house registered to a Martin Lilley, with no mention—"

Freed approached holding two glasses of amber liquid. "Williamson 15-year-old," he said.

"I accept," Lerner said.

"Me too, me too!" Catherine Vanadis said. She raised her glass. "Thanks Gary."

Freed drifted back to Stephanie, and Catherine Vanadis gazed off into the depths of the club, perhaps looking for the Geneva-Deneba woman. She turned back to Lerner.

"Maybe they're doing the marionette acrobat show again. You should see it sometime."

"Puppets?"

"The whole thing with that painting was kind of creepy. I didn't want to keep it. I was going to put it up for auction, but ended up selling to Gary."

"Why would someone wall up a painting like that? There must be something else in the building's history. How did you find out all that stuff?"

"The owners know everything. They're kind of amazing people. They—"

The Geneva-Deneba woman reappeared. She extended her hands toward Catherine Vanadis, who reached to grasp them and got up. The couple moved a few feet over, to dance near Freed and Stephanie.

Why *was* he so fascinated by the painting? Its style, yes, the colors employed, and the brush strokes, but more the overall composition. The innocence of the woman inspired his sympathy for the threat aimed at her. A painting of such Gothic presentation was unusual for that period.

The couples danced. Lerner sipped from his glass of Scotch. The music here, though pleasant, did little to inspire him. He preferred something with teeth, either sonic or lyric. Punk was the folk music of his generation (or, at least, the segment of his generation that interested him). "This is Bob Dylan to me," the

Minutemen said, and Lerner agreed. Lerner had drummed with inept enthusiasm in several ephemeral bands in an era of ephemeral bands, augmenting a small kit with wood and metal "sonic sculptures" as he called them, long lost, stolen with the van that contained the band's instruments. He sometimes wondered where his pieces had found a resting place, whether they might appear someday in an East Village junk shop. If they called to him, the city's cacophony drowned their plaintive cries.

Lerner decided to go home.

On the way out, he reminded Freed to send him a key, and Catharine Vanadis gave him her card. She wrote the name of the art appraiser on the back.

There was little he could do until Monday. Hoff wouldn't return to the library to find Lerner's note until then. He could call him at home, but what was the rush? Though when he reached his apartment, he decided to call the appraiser and leave a message—that would make him feel as if he had Accomplished (his mother, when she called him, always asked "Did you Accomplish today?).

A recording guided him to the appraiser's extension; he left his name and number, mentioning Freed and Catherine Vanadis, and asked the man to call him as soon as possible.

Before going to sleep, he leafed through the library book of Schuyler paintings and read the introduction, which said little was known of him and compared him to Petrus van Schendel, and others of the period. The writer didn't mention the journal.

4

HOMAGE TO THE FALLEN
DEITIES OF COMMERCE

Then as the fearful millennium neared, rabid doomfinders proclaimed the downfall of man (with woman expected to partake as well) and dug pits in the streets, foxholes for a war no one could win or lose. Then now, as the dreaded date passed, as no calamity sprang forth to justify the purchase of gasoline generators, crates of bottled water, batteries, and ammunition, new groups raised the flag of forgetfulness, hoping to export opium calm; commerce gods transformed consumption into novel configurations, and from a branch high in their old growth forests, corporate leaders smiled. Fearmasters feted the left and right, pitting everyone against the middle, allowing only yes or no as an answer. And a pretender took the throne, not by force but by apathy, regaining the seat abdicated by his father.

Dissonance submerged and blandness crept out in everbroadening waves, co-opting everything it touched, turning surrealism into advertising, counterculture into commodity. Enclaves of the arts, ever more insular, turned on themselves, tearing and rending in self-destructive voluntary compartmentalization, marginalized and irrelevant.

Despite the preponderance of the gods of commerce and their minions, art fought back, some days with more vigor than others, the never-ending battle that would only be won in increments so small that the corporations couldn't see them, and one day they—the artists—would reign again. Only art holds the magic necessary to recreate the world.

Lerner stepped back from his worktable. This piece then, with its five columns of bronze (the middle column thicker than the rest) arranged on a broad curve, like the portico of a broken temple, he would call *Homage to the Fallen Deities of Commerce*.

Jacob Lerner Mr. Sculptor withstander of hype, pure of popular culture (the self-made artistic person), took up a hacksaw and cut off a length from one column and glued it to the base, as if it lay where it had fallen from decay or cataclysm. He shaped clay into three genderless figures. The first he left whole, but with a wire he severed the head from one and the arms from the other. After drying and firing, he would cement the figures and their amputated parts in the semicircular base behind the columns, forlorn statues abandoned by the ages, their identity lost.

And so, as the new century eased from its first spring into summer, he recalled a birthday party that Freed's parents gave — taking several boys to a movie theater to see *2001*, a year that carried the mythical aura of incomprehensible distance, as remote in young Lerner's mind as the Pleistocene or Devonian. This trade that they had made — dreams of moon bases and space travel exchanged for panic and greed — pleased no one but corporate executives and their financial advisors. Or was this merely jealousy? For art as commodity had boomed in the 1980s, ending soon after Lerner finished his MFA, leaving his generation desperate to find gallery representation and recognition.

Lerner laughed aloud at his ramblings, and at his ruined temple he called art. The hands of the clock over his kiln neared 1:45. He had worked without stopping since getting up at seven, but now that he had finished, his mind turned back to Philip Schuyler, his painting and his obscure journal.

Every morning, to avoid distraction, Lerner turned off the phone's ringer and his answering machine's volume. Now, his day's work complete, he approached the phone, hoping to have heard from Hoff or the appraiser. But the answering machine message indicator displayed a zero. He stared down at the red numeral but, as it refused to change, he decided to take action.

This time, a receptionist routed him to the appraiser's voice mail, but he didn't bother leaving another message. Sometimes he wanted to scream at the difficulty of reaching people, the endless stream of exchanged messages.

The appraiser's office was in Midtown, not far from Ventricle Savage's gallery. Curious about the place where the painting had been entombed, he thought he would walk up to Bond to look at the restaurant site, then take the subway uptown. He hadn't even asked her about the restaurant. Too muddled with thoughts of the painting. Was she chef, or merely owner? Recalling her strong and acrobatic fingers, chef was the likely answer.

The day turned out to be the swirling kind, not windy, not rainy, but enough suggestion of each to make walking a discomfort. Disrespectful shadows squeezed the light, a grip so tight that narrow ribbons of luminescence oozed from the edges, faint and ragged. Walking up Lafayette, Lerner tried to surround himself with the New York that Schuyler would have known. The city had surged with constant transition, older buildings demolished for newer ones, streets pushed through the recent grazing lands of cattle to reshape the cityscape into its present form. Something his New York shared with the historical one was noise, the clang of humanity and commerce.

As he passed the restaurant supply store just above Houston Street, Catherine Vanadis appeared in the doorway. She smiled and called out. "Hello Jacob—isn't it funny how in this huge town, if you meet someone new, you always run into them again within a week? That's the Vanadis theory anyway." They shook hands and gave each other perfunctory kisses near their cheeks. Scents of ginger and citrus clung to her, prompting Lerner to ask about her restaurant.

"Come see the site!" She grasped his arm and pulled him to the crosswalk at Bleeker Street, where she plunged in without waiting for the light or his response. She held his arm and told him about her restaurant. "I run Gingerleaf?" She said it as a question, paused to wait for Lerner to recognize it, and continued when he didn't. "It's a multi-Asian noodle place. Upper East Side. The new one is Fresh Ginger. It'll be similar, but more casual, less pricey."

"Sounds yummy," he said. "I eat a lot of Asian noodles. I live down on the edge of Chinatown, so there's no shortage."

Living where he did, with access to authentic noodles, Lerner had little use for the current neo-noodle phenomenon. At least her restaurant wasn't something obviously trendy, like tapas. And he had no doubt that her restaurants served a quality product (product being the correct term for food-as-commodity). Even her *moderate* version would likely be priced beyond his budget.

They entered a cloud of moaning saws and hammering. "They're building counters and cabinets today," she said, talking over the clatter. She waved a hand toward the back. "Counters against the walls and tables in the middle. Bar in the back, kitchen behind it." A sawdust-clothed woman approached them; she was introduced as Handy Mandy, architect and contractor.

"I want to see where you found the painting," Lerner said. Catherine Vanadis pointed him toward the basement stairs, and he left them to their business.

Downstairs was a jumble of drywall, lumber, and electrical cable. Filling one side, the frames of embryonic cabinets and counters, gestating skeletons shaping the promise of future flavor. He went straight to the rear, drawn toward an open doorway. Five spots of waxy residue splotched the sideboard's marble top. The positions . . . they matched that of the columns on his newest piece.

The basement lights flickered.

Five figures had gathered here, robes and hoods hiding gender. Low voices sounded, like the thrum of flapping wings. Again, the lights flickered, in time with the rhythm of the voices. The murmurs of the figures drifted into the corners of the room, like dust motes, adhering to the molding, one atop another, thicker and thicker, soon rising to the hems of their robes. Twice more the lights flickered, then darkness commandeered the room. Lerner floated along passages never-ending. Far below, the candles burned, casting their light all together at first, then alternating, a complex ballet, one candle, then another, and another, left to right, rear to front, and with each burst the middle candle, thicker than the others, flared brighter, as though accessing the released energy. The middle candle grew so bright, blasting through Lerner's eyelids, through his hands clamped over his eyes, that he had to turn his face.

Images of light grew monumental, but their shape remained ill-defined, solid yet not, reaching toward him yet motionless. Lerner joined the light in a frantic ritual, leaping into a void constructed from a black so deep it regurgitated itself, as if a subterranean blackness took solid form and invaded the world above. He danced through the void and out the other side, where the light, with one last mammoth flare, died.

Lerner . . . lone prisoner in his cell of darkness . . . throat raw from the screaming light, sprawled face down on the floor. Underground . . . darkness dank and vicious—light, sweet light banished, never again to warm leaves and soil! He rolled onto his back and sat up. His head throbbed. Once on his feet, he slipped up the stairs and out of the building to seek comfort in familiar sidewalks and urban chaos.

Outside the restaurant, a shadow made him glance upward, over his shoulder. A man stood in an open, third floor window, staring down at him, his expression one of dread, a silent plea for rescue. The window frame that surrounded him shimmered in and out of focus, and the man's clothing and appearance looked odd, fashions long out of date. Lerner stopped, turned all the way around to see the man straight-on, but somewhere in the act of turning, the man vanished, replaced by a closed window, with a green shade obscuring the interior.

That man—he had projected such hopelessness and despair—how to answer his summons? Unable to help him, Lerner abandoned the blank window and walked toward the entrance to the uptown number six at Bleeker. But he couldn't go back underground!

Instead, needing to remain in the daylight, he boarded a bus.

The swirling day had become somewhat less so, but it still carried a layer of distortion that made the buildings passing outside the bus windows appear remote and shimmery. This street in Schuyler's time had become a dirt track after passing 14th, leading out to dairy farms and corn fields. Fragments of them remained, protruding ghosts of trees, barn, and cow, embedded within the surrounding walls and pavement.

Like the rest of the country, New York was born of desperation, and when the desperate gain wealth, they lose the capacity to perceive justice. They become arrogant. For if they made their fortune from nothing, then others would have to do the same, with no help from the social body. This was, of course, felt the most in the arts. Art as art was swiftly dying, replaced by art as commodity. And for all his brave words and thoughts decrying this trend, he didn't know how to reverse it. Seeing his glum face reflected in the grime-streaked bus window, Lerner smiled. He always sank into moods like this when visiting the Midtown gallery district. There, more than any other part of town, art represented accoutrements for the wealthy.

Several times during Lerner's earliest years in the city he had contemplated leaving. The blank-faced rushing people on the streets enervated him, his classes enervated him; he longed for views not blocked by brick and steel. A woman he had been seeing, a fellow art student who played guitar in a band that had begun to receive some attention, suffered a breakdown and moved to Lawrence, Kansas. Lerner felt himself drifting toward a similar fate. He withdrew from classes and found work on a fishing boat based in Greenport, Long Island. The forced discipline of rising early, the grit of physical labor, served to inure him to the trivialities of art school. Though not of art itself, not trivial that, nor did the labor turn him from his path. No, his time on the boat made his future a possibility. Without it, he might not, would not, have forged the persistence, the willingness to continue no matter the difficulty.

After a season of working on the boat, he returned to class. For several years, his friends called him Captain Lerner, or The Captain (a name he sometimes still used when signing letters).

He had recently fashioned a piece that recalled his nautical period, curved metal arranged like the skeleton of a ship, staves to which no planks would ever be fixed. He had called it "The Captain's Husk," and likened it to a desiccated chrysalis from which a butterfly had sprung.

Lerner entered the art appraiser's building and took the elevator to the 23rd floor. The receptionist buzzed him into a boxy but sunny space bordered by a window, the reception desk, and thick Plexiglas walls, likely bulletproof, to guard the rear, which he supposed housed valuable artwork. Outside the window spread the green of Central Park. When he gave the receptionist the reason for his visit, she said that the appraiser hadn't come in to work that day.

Stymied again, he returned to the street. A black limousine eased to the curb near him, and a man staggered out. From the angle of Lerner's approach, he could see two women on the back seat, sitting so close they looked like Siamese twins. The man grasped a bus-stop pole to keep from falling, and the car drove off.

Lerner reached to steady the man, who appeared dazed, not comprehending his position or Lerner's presence beside him.

"Can I help you to a cab?" Lerner asked.

Ignoring him, the man limped to the door of the building Lerner had just exited.

In Savage's gallery, Lerner encountered an exhibit of Are No's iridescent flop.

"If you'd like to know more about the artist, we have information handouts at the desk."

The speaker was a thin, youngish man. Some new imp-hireling of Savage's. He smiled at Lerner, the measured smile of someone judging the likelihood of Lerner's being able to purchase art. He had obviously started working there sometime after Lerner's most recent show. When was that—September? Already nine months. Long enough for him to have gestated a new body of work. Savage likely wouldn't give him another solo exhibition so soon. His general rule was every other year. And if someone's work didn't sell adequately, even more time passed. Lerner was eager for his recent sculptures to be seen. Sometimes Savage would arrange a group show of one or two new pieces by his main artists. Lerner asked the young man to get Savage, and waited, focusing on an area of floor rather than Are No's rancid shapes.

An inescapable fact: he had to share the same gallery with mindless crap. Are No's pieces—made using spray cans of insulation foam, the kind that expanded and hardened in the air, which he then painted in neon colors—sold well, and sales drove any gallery's list. Fortunately, Lerner liked and respected most of Savage's other artists, Joyce Harkness, Scott Eagle, Jane Andrews, Olaf the Wise.

Savage came out to greet Lerner. He was a tall, gaunt man with a wobbling gait that made him appear continuously in peril of toppling. Always the tallest in the room at art openings, he floated among the crowd, buoyed by the closeness of the bodies, and Lerner often wondered what would happen if the crowd parted, leaving Savage without support. Savage spoke to his artists as though they were his esteemed subordinates and treated most gallery patrons with condescension and sometimes the exaggerated conviviality of theater people: "Oh . . . dah-ling, we MUST have lunch on Tuesday!" But his business sense was impeccable. He had an uncanny way of knowing which tone to apply to a person within seconds of their first words to him.

He introduced Lerner to Kirk, the new gallery assistant, who began to fawn when he realized that Lerner was one of the gallery's artists. Leaving Kirk, they walked down a narrow hall toward Savage's office.

"Do you know Gingerleaf restaurant?" Lerner asked, and Savage nodded, his body swaying with the motion. "I met the owner recently and she's interested in buying something of mine for her new place on Bond. I'll have her come to my studio to pick it out." Even if Lerner sold something on his own, in his studio, the money always had to go through Savage. Lerner could likely do it without Savage ever knowing (and therefore keep Savage's percentage), but the long-term maintenance of their relationship was more important than the occasional extra money (and the consequences—violating his contract and leaving him without a gallery—were not worth risking).

Savage proved receptive to Lerner's suggestion of a group show, which they tentatively set for November. "Okay and fine, I'll call you next month to set up a studio visit," Savage said. An expert at defining the end of a conversation, Savage floated to his feet and extended a hand for Lerner to shake.

Lerner stopped to use the phone at the front desk to check his messages; Buddy Drake had called, saying he would be at Geraty's Tavern later. Back on the street, Lerner walked toward the subway stop, but when he passed the appraiser's building, he decided to try again. This time, the receptionist said the man was in.

She buzzed him. A thin voice sounded from the speakerphone: "Please . . . I asked to be left alone . . . no calls . . . no—"

Lerner leaned toward the phone. "I need to talk to you about the Schuyler painting. The one that was just found." A light on the phone console extinguished.

"Musta hung up," the receptionist said. "He came in all pinched and shaky looking. He said he didn't want to be disturbed."

"I really need to find out about this painting," Lerner said.

"You a collector?" She asked the question in a bored way, but Lerner took it as an invitation for further conversation.

"I'm an artist. Sculptor." He told her his name, not expecting the woman to have heard of him but wanting to be friendly, wanting her to help him. "My friend bought a painting. It was found in a closed-up room. Catherine Vanadis, the woman who found it, had it appraised here. I'd like to know more about it." Lerner hoped he didn't look fanatical. He had showered after working, hadn't he? Sometimes he forgot, and would later find smears of dried clay on his face. But Catherine would have mentioned it.

The receptionist smiled, and pointed to her computer screen, a wide LCD set in a clear plastic frame. "Database," she said. "We don't need *him*. Come around to this side." Lerner rolled a chair closer to her. "I'm Adele," she said. "Nice to meet you Mr. Artist. Just give this a minute to open." The firm pose of her mouth, its air of competence and self-assurance, set him at ease. She seemed unperturbed by the appraiser's near-hysteria, had even contributed to it by defying his demand to remain undisturbed.

"I don't know computers," Lerner said. "The university gave me an email account but I never check it. I should take a class so I can get comfortable with it. Right now all I can handle is the library card catalog."

"Spell the name of the artist you want me to look up." Adele typed the letters as he spoke, then waited. "Nothing here," she said. "You sure you have the right place?"

The door leading to the interior of the office opened, and Lerner looked up, ready to ask the man about Schuyler, but it was a woman wearing a dark suit-jacket and skirt. "Bye now," she said to Adele, and left.

"That's the other appraiser. I'd ask her but she doesn't know crap about anything."

Adele's voice reminded him of some of his Rutgers students. She was probably from the same part of New Jersey. He described what he knew about the discovery of the painting. Fog encircled him, a thick, clinging gelatin that constricted every attempt at discovery, as if some remnant of whoever had sealed the painting in that room still worked to keep it hidden.

"I remember," Adele said. "The owner of Gingerleaf. That's one of my favorite restaurants." She tried something else with the computer.

"This is odd. See, I'm running a data recovery program. When you delete things, they're actually still on the computer, but the computer has been told to ignore them. They stay where they are till something new gets put in their place. This program should be able to find something, but it's like the information was never there. But it was. I entered it myself."

She swiveled her chair around to face him. "I'm sorry, that's all I can do. Tomorrow I'll try to get him"—she pointed to the glass panels—"to call you. The paperwork is probably in his office."

Lerner exited the subway at Spring and headed west, toward Geraty's on Charlton. The swirling day had softened with evening, forming lace curtains through which the air moved with greater freedom. Geraty's was a relic, an early nineteenth-century tavern that had resisted the endless, repeating crush of reconstruction and revision that ravaged lower Manhattan. It stood near stalwart fellows, Federal-style row houses of an even older vintage. Perhaps Schuyler had walked these streets, passed these same houses. Geraty's dented and patched walls were painted a dull color, or perhaps a once-bright color dulled by ages of cigarette smoke, though a few years ago the owner had instituted a ban on smoking until after 8 p.m. Some long-time patrons had complained, but they adapted, knowing that a city-wide smoking ban was inevitable. Entering, he spotted Buddy Drake at the bar with Stacey, his sister Eleanor's girlfriend.

"I've been uptown, consulting with the dark forces," Lerner said.

"Ventricle Savage?" Buddy Drake asked. "Then you need

something stronger than beer." A nearby table emptied and they claimed it.

"I went to talk to the guy who shows my work," Lerner said to Stacey. "It's always a little depressing. But not as depressing as having no gallery."

She asked about his art, and he described his current obsessions. She was a botanist, teaching at New York University, though she worked several months a year in Peru, which was where she had met Eleanor, an anthropologist.

Seeing Eleanor framed in the dark wood of Geraty's doorway, Buddy Drake waved her over. Eleanor was three years younger than Buddy Drake, and had moved to New York only a couple of years ago, after finishing her PhD and teaching for a time at a small college in New Hampshire. Lerner had first met her when he and Buddy Drake were in college, during a summertime visit to the Drake family home in Mississippi. He always enjoyed her company, and had several times said he wished she was straight, to which she replied that she wished he was a woman.

"Hi baby," Stacey said. They kissed, and Eleanor gave Buddy Drake and Lerner each a quick hug.

"Hey Jacob, haven't seen you in ages," she said.

"He's been busy. Some mania over an old painting," Buddy Drake said. "Doesn't have time for his friends."

Lerner told them about meeting Catherine Vanadis and his lack of success with the appraiser. "Not sure what to do next. I want to see the painting again—if Freed would just send me the damn key."

"I know someone who could get you in," Stacey said. "One of my teaching assistants. He claims to have been an amateur burglar."

"Is that something where you have to reach a certain amount of gross dollars stolen before you have professional status?" Buddy Drake asked.

"I think I'll pass," Lerner said. "Hopefully won't be much longer."

"I have an actual date later," Buddy Drake said. "Dinner and a movie with a nice girl."

"You met a nice girl?" Eleanor said.

"I was out with Creasey and those guys Saturday night, and Creasey's wife had her friend Petra along. I don't think it was supposed to be a setup, but there I was, there she was, the only un-paired of the group except for Jerome and he's gay. We're going to try that new Moroccan place on Avenue C."

"My Christian cousins are visiting," Stacey said. "Eleanor and I are taking them someplace safe later."

At a nearby table sat a lean man with a shaven head that made him look even leaner. The man was familiar, and Lerner's attention shifted back and forth from the man to his friends' conversation, trying to place him. Timelines converged, college, the dank interior of the Pancake Club on Avenue B, its ragged sound system and stage the size of a kitchen table. The man pushed back his chair and rose.

"That guy reminds me of someone," Lerner said.

The others turned to look; the man made his way toward the door and out.

"That's Warsaw Lorca," Stacey said. "He runs the Action Foundation. We got a grant from them."

"For a project in Peru," Eleanor said. "Mostly they try to encourage self-sustaining lifestyles, agriculture, etc."

Buddy Drake glanced at Lerner. "That's not what Jacob and I know him from," he said. "He was the guitarist and singer for Section 32."

"Can't believe I didn't recognize him," Lerner said. "We saw them two dozen times, at least, 1980, '81, '82."

"They put out those two albums, *Complete Control*. . . . "

"And *S*," Lerner said, finishing Buddy Drake's sentence. "*Complete Control* was 34 minutes of high-speed attack-guitar, bass, drums. Vocals high in the mix, clear despite the rush, the rough production."

"*S* was like being strangled by velvet," Buddy Drake said.

"Lush, textured, the same message but delivered with thoughtful phrasing, polite determination. Ending with 'Wall,' spoken: 'We are not safe / we are dependent / corporations forge walls / of comfort anesthesia.'

"It sold maybe 500 copies," Lerner said. "They broke up. The other members resurfaced here and there, but I never heard anything else about him. I'm glad someone I admired kept his principles—I would've hated to have found out he was CEO of a pharmaceutical company."

"I think he started the foundation after he came into a load of money from his family," Stacey said.

"I wish he'd make some new music. I'd like to think we can combine art and activism," Lerner said.

"You should go after him, Jacob," Buddy Drake said. "Maybe he knows *your* work. He's got money. He could be your patron."

Lerner let his gaze drift to the door as he considered Buddy Drake's words. "That's not how I'd want to do it," he said, turning back to his companions. "It would be great if he saw my work and liked it, but I'm not going to chase him. I don't want patrons."

"Send him a card," Buddy Drake said. "Now that you know how to find him. Next time you have a show, send a card to him at the Action Foundation. There's nothing wrong with that." Buddy Drake fiddled, as he often did, with the glass bead of his gold earring, turning it round and round from the front of his lobe to the back. "Shit, I'll send him a card. I've got a show in December."

5

A MAZE OF BOOKS

What makes a person an artist? Talent? Perseverance? Yes, impossible without those, but what socio-environmental confluence makes a person *choose*? Lerner had endured a semester at the University of Texas in Austin, a wasted interval before transferring to Parsons School of Design. In his Texas dormitory he had known artistic people. One guy had an electronic keyboard in his room, played along with his art-rock records and, Lerner was told, sat in for a song or two with bands playing at his fraternity's parties. But Lerner doubted he had ever done anything with the music, hadn't formed his own band or joined another's. He had talent. His upbringing had been similar to Lerner's. What then? Desire? Art had always been available for Lerner, as a child building model airplanes, constructing dioramas for his army men and model tanks, drawing and painting. His parents had encouraged him. But when the time came for college, their advice turned toward the commercial—advertising, architecture, even engineering.

Cannot a person be a doctor or lawyer first, an artist evenings and weekends?

Though perhaps art is not a choice, no more than breathing is a choice. Each a life-giving act, instinctive and undeniable.

Lerner, making a choice, began college as an architecture major, and he learned two things: he had to be an artist; and he had to go to art school. Instinct, bodily need, defeats choice.

True, the university had a decent art department, but the

overall environment of the school didn't inspire him. Having to share space with members of fraternities, sororities, and football teams detracted from inspiration. And he had the luxury of an upper middle class background. He could change schools, go from an inexpensive, state-supported school to a private one. For him, the struggle had been to break from the promise of comfort, but there had never been a question, even from his family, of art's importance.

He had a friend, an award-winning writer, who had encountered a succession of obstacles—family with little education or money, had quit school pregnant at sixteen, married, divorced at twenty, but persevered. Compared to her, his path had been easy, impediments low and easy to step over.

When Lerner reached home after Geraty's, his answering machine light was blinking. Two new messages. Hoff, finally, saying he hadn't found the journal yet but would keep trying. And Catherine Vanadis, suggesting a meeting to look at his recent sculpture.

He sat on the edge of his bed and pulled off his shoes. A sock had a small hole forming in the heel; he tossed the pair into the nearby trash basket and flopped onto his back. The rotating ceiling fan over his bed stirred a dull rhythm of breeze. An air of expectancy punctuated his thoughts. Seeing Warsaw Lorca brought him back to a time when all futures appeared possible, when action and art would take the world from the fearmasters and their corporate stooges. He felt on the verge of something, though was unsure what. Breakthrough in his work? Personal relationships? The painting, the painting, the painting.

Those Siamese twin women he had seen in the back of the limousine—Lerner was certain that they were the investment sisters from Freed's party. The Kreunens. And the man who had staggered from their car—the art appraiser. Lerner should make an appointment to see them, perhaps with Freed.

And Freed. Where was he? Away, and no key had appeared in the mail, no way for Lerner to view the painting again. He went to his desk to dig out his address book, called Freed's mobile phone and left a message.

All these inter-connections, bound by the painting.

He called Catherine's home number, assuming that she would be at the restaurant, and told her answering machine that afternoons were best, as soon as she liked. "My newest piece," he said, "has five columnar shapes, just like the positions of the wax residue on that sideboard. It's called *Homage to the Fallen Deities of Commerce*. Once the sideboard is moved upstairs, I'd like to put my piece on it. If you like it, of course."

Where is foresight? Where is self examination? Unwanted, unneeded, a populace with no desire to look past their immediate surroundings, their velvet walls. If someone hits you, hit them back. Never ask why. Real study, real solutions, are inconvenient, taking far too long to maintain the public interest. Act-React-Act could be the title of the history of the world. Lumpen lines, form-less shapes, nothing flowing inward or outward, nothing but the resistance of clay to fingers. Brick everywhere, brick windowsill, and below, wet street and sidewalk, clingy-moist drizzle—not rain but sweat—and out in the sticky damp, humanity on its ceaseless mission, a script written in the seconds before birth by playwrights versed in the arts of destiny, the sort that can never be articulated until the mirror emerges: *The Reflection of the Beginning Is the End*.

Lerner spent the morning at his worktable that overlooked the street, shaping clay, watching the passage of dozens of Chinese men and women, including a girl who carried on her back another of those odd, reddish glass dolls, or perhaps the same doll, though this one had a bowler hat perched on its head.

Though he was gripped by a rampant desire to finish the temple piece, the previous day's deliberately broken figures were not yet dry enough to fire. He had moved on to another piece, sustaining the creative flow as always. Before him on the table, a new group of clay figures now numbered nine, and he stopped, satisfied with the number, an asymmetrical reflection. But for the structure in which to place the figures . . . he pulled a pad from the cabinet beneath his table and began to sketch: girders of bronze, the skeletons of buildings. Buildings in construction or decay?

He hadn't made a large piece in years, but as the pencil moved across the page, he saw the final work occupying the dimensions of Savage's front room. What he made here would merely serve as maquette.

Later, under the spray of his shower, he continued to visualize his installation, estimating the time and materials needed for completion.

Lerner toweled himself and pulled on clean clothes. For lunch, he assembled a sandwich of cheese and cucumber. He wanted to go out, but having begun a mental budget for his installation, an immediate start to saving money was the best option.

Perhaps he would offer *Homage* to Catherine in trade for food.

That rare thrill of the first meeting, its intertwining branches of infatuation and yearning . . . years since he had last experienced something like that. For a while, after graduate school, he had become addicted to the feeling, had filled his calendar with interaction: art openings, parties, dinners, weekend retreats, meeting and engaging in brief, intense relationships with many women, more for the thrill of new social contact than for sex (though there was no lack of it). Beth had been one of those women. Sudden infatuation leading to marriage and even quicker divorce. After Beth, he hadn't returned to his frenzied social calendar, deciding such behavior deterred commitment to his art.

Meeting Catherine reminded him of those days. The difference now, of course, was that nothing could divert him from his art, but he might re-integrate more social activity. He had never shunned parties and such, but he had rarely moved beyond talking to those he already knew. Fresh sensations, new activities, new places, all (if treated with care) served to stimulate the artistic side as well as the social.

He didn't believe his art had grown stale, but if he had more life outside his art, maybe he wouldn't be so damn obsessed about Schuyler and his painting. Meanwhile, he was embarrassed to talk to Catherine after fleeing the restaurant site. What had possessed him? He'd never had a claustrophobic attack like that. The choking mist, the columns . . . he shuddered, remembering, and was glad to be home, his safe and secure home.

The phone rang. He swallowed a bite of sandwich and gulped water before answering.

"This hasn't been easy," Hoff said. "None of the usual places, not art school libraries, not the Library of Congress. There was only one place I could find it. Not someone I like to bother often, but I figured he was the last chance. And lucky for you he's even in your neighborhood."

"Thanks, Simon," Lerner said. Realizing he had been pacing the entire time Hoff spoke, he sat again at the table and idly tore off a strip of crust from his sandwich.

"Now I want to see this mystery painting myself."

"Freed's still out of town. I'm waiting for him to send me a key. It should've come already, but I don't guess it's as important to him as it is to me. I'll let you know."

Hoff gave Lerner the information and hung up. Lerner had never heard of an antiquarian bookstore on Bowery. Schuyler's journal had all this time been sitting nearby, lingering, patience waning, while he fumbled his way closer.

Quality Brothers Restaurant Supply occupied the building one up from Hester, on the west side of Bowery, one of many restaurant supply stores strung along both sides of the street. Lerner had been in several over the years, buying mugs, metal shelving, frying pans, a carbon steel wok. He had possibly bought something at Quality Brothers, but the places all merged into one giant warehouse of glass, ceramic, and steel; they all carried the same scents, a metallic flatness, though if he concentrated, he could detect traces of the restaurant equipment's future: garlic, ginger, peppers, coffee, duck, scallops, the cloy of sugary drinks.

A man sat at the counter, waiting, and from his appearance—gray hair and lined face—he had carried out this activity of waitfulness for many years, a waiting from which he could have observed the riot of changes that passed through the city, from inception to futures unimagined.

The man looked up when Lerner reached him, a movement of his neck and eyes so economical that Lerner was unsure whether it was actual movement or merely the suggestion. Lerner presented the name that Hoff had supplied, and the man gave another economical tilt of his head, and one low sound, which, combined with the descending staircase that lay in the direction of his head tilt, said: "basement."

From below came impressions of depth and darkness. On the bottom step, the journey to which seemed to have taken far longer than the actual distance would have indicated, Lerner found himself standing on the periphery of a maze. His eyes adjusted to the dimness, and the maze became a vast library, rows of bookcases cast about like dice, standing everywhere with no two aligned.

Stacks extended deep into the shadowy room, which bulged with print, the repository of several oceans of ink. Lerner had once met a woman who claimed to have developed a process for reclaiming ink and paper from discarded books. She would attend library sales and buy piles of hardbacks by romance and other popular writers, which she would process, lifting ink from paper in some secret alchemical method. Divorced books, ink and paper once thought joined for eternity, separated into their premarital state. The dead books she sold to a maker of journals who bound on new covers; the ink, vented into the air, spread across the city to shape new words.

A man who could have been twin to the upstairs-waiting-man emerged from the shadows and beckoned to Lerner. Come outside, the man said, but there *is* no outside, only this basement of books never-ending, no fields, no breeze. Holding fast to this belief, Lerner followed. Through the buzz of light, light years pass, organic modules of incandescent fluid, seeping through the gouged bark, golden in the sunlight, beside the brook. Hum of grass that soothes the rawness of diesel and fills the crevices of this haven, a home for bright things, lost things, soft things, hidden in the open and unseen. All around, all sides, stacks of brick formed into blank walls withholding secrets. Bricks and mortar, mortar shells casting ruin, but not here, not in the refuge.

The air—where the man had led him—the air held only freshness, carrying a breeze of early spring, the many-fingered kind in which winter and summer struggle for control. Out here, humidity and heat, all banished.

The man, librarian, caretaker of books, of brooks, of the oasis, guided Lerner to a bench placed at the edge of a pond. A ribbon of water flowed out from the pond, passed over a rocky bed for a few feet, then plunged underground. "The water persists, but now it must be secret water, expelled by progress, they say. But the springs remain, the springs which once fed the Collect, lost even to memory."

A breeze furrowed the pond's surface, wavelets ran and faded; a cloud slithered past, showing its belly to the water. But the pond didn't reflect the surrounding brick, as though the structures were unworthy of disturbing its mirror. Lerner had read about the Collect, a large pond that had formerly existed in Lower Manhattan. Difficult to picture now, amidst concrete and diesel. But so it had been, until growth and industry polluted it. Then it was drained, filled in, and forgotten, the drainage canal covered to become Canal Street.

The caretaker held out a book, slim, leather-bound, old yet

unravaged, preserved in the library maze; its cover—smooth, sweet leather—bore no title.

Lerner accepted the book, leather soft and glowing with a warmth that made him smile; he opened the cover to the title page—

—and ... between the title and subtitle ... Schuyler ... a portrait—Schuyler's face ... the face that Lerner had seen in the third-floor window over Catherine's restaurant.

THE JOURNAL OF
PHILIP SCHUYLER.

ON THE OCCASION OF HIS VISIT

TO THE ISLAND OF MANHATTAN, 1842.

LONDON:

SAUNDERS & OTLEY, CONDUIT STREET.

1844

Sunday, February 6 (Mid-Morning)

I came to this wretched shore willingly, yet after disembarking, my first thought was to retrace my way to the ship, which during the tedious trans-Atlantic crossing had assumed the familiarity of home. How I was soon to wish that such had been my path! But I had accepted a commission. And as I am the son of a Dutch father and an English mother, the history of this settlement calls to both sides of my heritage.

Indeed, my Dutch heritage was the reason for my commission—the man who wrote to me, one Hendrick Stuyvesant, explained that he, and others, were descendants of the city's Dutch founders, and desired a portraitist of the Dutch school. The fact that I had spent my youth in both England and Holland made me ideal for the commission, as I was equally fluent in both languages.

Though the details he presented were scant, the monetary offer was quite handsome, an unexpected windfall at a time when such were becoming limited (owing to a fall in demand for my style of candlelight painting, and to indiscretions with the wife of a former client, involving her desire for a nude portrait and what arose subsequent to that).

Stuyvesant had given me an address for lodging—the Carlton House Hotel, Broadway—some distance from the South Street docks. The hansom cab carried me along cobbled streets, past multitudes of wood and brick buildings. Everything in this Manhattan is in motion, everywhere noise and bustle of shopkeepers, drivers. Swine snuffle through garbage in the streets. Ships arrive and depart in a constant flow, to and from every part of the known world.

I had heard of the jumbled condition of this city, as it

raced vainly to catch up with its elder European sisters, and had been warned that neighborhoods of squalor stood alongside those of the respectable classes. Others have told me that however obsessed with commerce the inhabitants of Manhattan may seem, they are not devoid of romantic notions, but after my initial impressions I find it no surprise that its citizens need to import artists from Europe, for New York has not the atmosphere for creative endeavor.

At the hotel, I supervised the placement of my trunks. Unsure what I might find here, I had brought my own art supplies, pigment jars wrapped with care to prevent breakage, brushes, canvas, oils, and glazes.

A simple room, with a bed, desk, washstand, bureau.

My employers had instructed me to send a message on my arrival. I composed a short note, but instead of calling for a messenger, I began this journal, using a notebook small enough to keep in an inside pocket of my jacket. I had purposed each evening to add to my account; now, I augment and annotate the entries with the reflections of knowledge and events that have since occurred.

But more of those anon.

Outside my windows, Broadway, chief thoroughfare, with a sun warm beyond the season casting a healthy shine upon passing ladies in their colorful silks and satins, parasols held high to block the rays. Vehicles crowd the streets, cabs, coaches of myriad size, many thick and boxy, sturdy enough to traverse the wild country lanes which this city becomes some few blocks north.

I decided to venture out to find a barber, for I urgently needed a shave. Over the last several days of the voyage on the ever-rolling, never-stable platform of my journey out, I had given up the practice. Though the ship's barber was an experienced hand, I had no desire to bare my face to his blade until the seas subsided!

Before leaving the hotel, I paused in the lobby to give my arrival note to the concierge, that he might have it delivered on to my employers.

And, after a pleasing shave, with most of the day yet before me, I set off to explore the surrounding streets. Out among the gaily dressed men and women, I found myself drab indeed, with my scuffed shoes and jacket still marked by ocean travel.

I walked the surrounding blocks in fascination, careful to avoid the area known as Five Points, a den of crime and disrepute, I had been told.

East of the dazzle of Broadway is another large street called Bowery. Here everything was more humble, the houses smaller, the taverns darker, the passersby dressed in a rougher style more to my liking. Passing a one-eared swine, I stepped into a place advertising "Oysters in Every Style."

Sunday, February 6 (Evening)

When I returned to the hotel lobby, a man confronted me, a well-dressed, somewhat portly figure with hair fashionably curled over his ears, who addressed me by name. He introduced himself as Mr. Lilley. Retrieving a watch by means of its massive chain, he glanced at it, then looked to me. "We have no time to tarry," he said. "Why did you not contact us? The project at hand requires exacting coordination of schedules and means. We must depart immediately."

"I merely took a turn through the neighborhood," I said. "To acclimate myself to my new locale."

Indicating that I should follow, he strode out to the frenzied avenue. A carriage awaited. The man opened the door, and I mounted.

He told the driver: "Colonnade Row," then followed me inside, taking the opposite seat. The carriage set off. Once in motion, Mr. Lilley's agitation left him and he became more friendly.

"It is understandable that you felt the need to wander about," Mr. Lilley said. "There is not another city on this earth like New York, nor a land like our United States. Your Old World, for all its finery, is passing on." He extended his arms as though embracing the sky, including it in his territorial grasp. "This is the land of dreams. The profits to be made here are astounding." He lectured me for some minutes on the pastime of land speculation, and the risks of boom and bust, of which only men of courage may partake.

"My commission," I said. "The details. . . . "

Mr. Lilley interrupted, telling me that another would be informing me as to the particulars.

The carriage traveled gracelessly through the streets, stopping here and there as the driver struggled his way around various obstacles—piles of building materials, crowds of workers. A fire brigade stalled our progress. "Fire is our ever-present companion here," Mr. Lilley said. "Much has been lost, but much gained, as the blazes sweep areas clean for new construction."

As we progressed, the buildings grew fewer, and Mr. Lilley informed me we were nearing the northern edge of the town, reaching quieter neighborhoods of grand residences, constructed far from the bustle of the commercial center. The carriage turned down an alleyway, pulling up behind a block of houses.

"You will have to view the residence from the front another time. This is one of the grandest new row houses in the city. Great columns line the front and the entry ways are magnificent. But for now 'tis more expedient to enter from the rear."

57

The carriage stopped and we alighted. Mr. Lilley took me into a parlor, then up a flight of stairs to a sitting room, where another man waited. This individual was introduced as Mr. Vanderkemp. He bade me sit, and ordered refreshments from a servant.

"Will Mr. Stuyvesant be joining us?" I asked.

Neither answered for a moment, then Mr. Vanderkemp explained that Stuyvesant was merely a name they used for correspondence, that it represented the interests of their group. His tone began mildly enough, but escalated as he delved into a topic that was obviously dear to him, that of the varied history of his nation and his city.

"You may not know the segment of Dutch history that pertains to these shores, but Petrus Stuyvesant was the great leader who brought New Amsterdam into the modern world, setting the stage for the America that was to come. Though the honorable John Brodbent has lately been ridiculed for daring to say that America's origins exist elsewhere than with those ridiculous Puritans, such reaction is nothing but base nostalgia for a Puritan world that never existed. It was the Dutch who brought the twins of tolerance and commerce. It was the Dutch who brought Democracy, not the rigid Puritans!"

Mr. Lilley touched Mr. Vanderkemp's arm and they moved to the door, where they spoke briefly in voices too low for me to overhear, then shook hands. While they spoke, I examined my surroundings. The furniture— chairs, end-table, settee—was of plain, yet expensive appearance, dark wood with cane bottoms; the carpet, a rich weave, brown and tan of an Oriental design. A doorway framed by Ionian columns separated the parlor from the dining room. Several daguerreotypes adorned the walls, portraits of family members. They fascinated me, for I have seen few. Their power to capture likeness was most impressive, but the flatness grew monotonous after extended viewing.

The servant soon returned with a decanter and filled two glasses. Mr. Lilley departed. On leaving, the servant pulled sliding doors from their recess in the wall and shut them.

"I understand that you would like made plain what your commission entails."

Mr. Vanderkemp spoke in a firm, authoritative voice, as one accustomed to giving orders.

"It is quite simple, as was said in the original letter. The aspect of secrecy is merely that the portrait is to be a surprise for a lady's husband. Therefore, we must act while he is distant, conducting business in the West Indies and other points.

"You need not know her name, or the name of her husband. The less you know, the easier to keep the secret intact.

"Their residence is nearby. Mr. Lilley will take you in the morning to meet her, and you will begin your work. Supplies, if you need them, can be procured by others. Priming of canvases and other menial tasks can be undertaken for you. It is best that you spend the entirety of your time at work on the portrait itself."

Some while later, Vanderkemp announced that our meeting was at an end. The butler returned and escorted me outside, where the carriage and Mr. Lilley awaited, and I was anon transported back to my hotel.

Monday, February 7 (Evening)

Mr. Lilley joined me at breakfast, dressed smartly in a smoking jacket of figured velvet, and I went with him in the same carriage (or one similar) to the home of my subject. On the way, I enquired whether Mr. Vanderkemp would be joining us, and Mr. Lilley replied that he had other engagements.

"We are meeting the woman in her own residence, but the actual work of portrait-making will be carried out at Mr. Vanderkemp's. It will be easier to guarantee surprise, should her husband return unexpectedly. And meeting first at her own residence will prevent servants' gossip from touching on the 'impropriety' of her repeated visits to the residence of Mr. Vanderkemp."

I agreed that the plan was a sound one. In our efforts at secrecy, it would prove ill if the husband interpreted the innocent surprise of the portrait as something less than honorable.

The carriage drew up to a grand, colonnaded front, and I remarked on the architecture. Mr. Lilley's face fairly glowed with pride, as though the design of the structure had been his. "This is what I spoke of last evening. The finest yet, in this city of finery. Designed by the great Alexander Jackson Davis and built by Seth Geer. It is meant to be a New York version of London's Regent's Park. Astor lives here, as do other luminaries. There are nine magnificent residences in all."

We were met at the door by a butler, who escorted us to an upstairs parlor much like that of Mr. Vanderkemp. I was, in fact, somewhat confused as to whose house we were in—yesterday at Vanderkemp's, Lilley had praised the magnificent columns, and today as well. Perhaps Vanderkemp lived in another of the nine residences Lilley had mentioned.

The arrival of the lady of the house caused me some surprise, for her skin, though not of the darkest hue, marked her as at least partially connected to a race not commonly found in the houses of the wealthy, save as servant (or slave, in the southern climes of this free land of America). But she wore clothing typical of the comfortable class: silk taffeta dress with embroidered over-sleeves and a pleated bodice. She appeared to be at her ease here.

The lady spoke English with a French accent, a joyous, musical inflection, so unlike the others, whose "Americanisms" had transformed their language into something base. I assumed she came from an island in the Caribbean and was likely an amalgam of races, African and French.

Mere paint would be unable to capture the loveliness of her skin, which had the quality of coffee blended with a modicum of cream.

The lady being eager to begin, we sat in the soft light of her parlor. Thinking her native tongue might set her more at ease, I addressed her in French, and noted a brief look of consternation on the face of Mr. Lilley, as though he were displeased with his incapacity to understand our conversation.

I thought little of it at the time. Later events, of course, made the reason apparent.

She proved to be knowledgeable on many topics, literature, politics, history, and we chatted amiably in both French and English while I executed a series of sketches, attempting to find the pose that best captured her lovely and regal self. I learned that she had been born into a wealthy family, in one of the few republics wholly governed by those of African descent. Her grandfather had been a Frenchman, an official with the governor's office when the island was under French control, and both parents were of mixed race. She had met her husband through his business dealings with her family. They had married secretly in her land and lived separately for a year until he arranged for her passage here.

I expressed admiration for a society which accepted her

so readily, but I surmised that this acceptance was more politeness and propriety than actual warmth. Though no one in sound mind could reject such a lovely person! I found myself disappointed when our session drew to a close, even knowing that I could rejoice at the prospect of spending long periods in her company. We agreed to meet the following morning at Mr. Vanderkemp's to begin the portrait. I would take the rest of the day assembling my materials and transporting them to Vanderkemp's house, so that all would be ready for the first sitting.

Tuesday, February 8 (Evening)

Today was much colder, and various stoves had been kindled throughout the hotel, filling the rooms with an overabundance of heat. I was glad to be spending the day elsewhere.

Again, Mr. Lilley met me at breakfast and accompanied me uptown. At my mention that I would be perfectly able to make my way on my own, thereby saving him the trouble, he demurred, stating that it was best for a newcomer to this brusque city to have a guide. The cab drivers could not be trusted, he added.

The plunge from the over-warm hotel to the crisp air on the street invigorated me, but I foresaw potential discomfort in this constant fluctuation of temperature.

Having gone into Mr. Vanderkemp's residence twice from a back entrance (my first visit and last night's, transport of art supplies, of which I have not written for there was nothing of note to report), I was surprised when the carriage pulled up to the front, and I saw that Vanderkemp's house indeed shared the same columnar façade as that of my client. In the foyer, I was pleased to see a rather charming painting of three children by the acclaimed English-born American artist Thomas Sully, whom I had met in England several years previously, when the City of Philadelphia commissioned him to paint Queen Victoria. And in the dining room an even more pleasing sight awaited me: one of my own paintings, a candle-lit scene of the Bruges market.

Mr. Vanderkemp would be at his business office downtown during the day, with Mr. Lilley remaining as his representative. We had arrived, of purpose, before the lady, so that I might ready myself and my materials. The previous afternoon (despite Vanderkemp's directive that others would do the work for me), I had prepared a canvas, though for today my plan was to create several studies of gouache on paper in preparation for the actual work. I explained this to Mr. Lilley, whose only injunction was to be sure that I informed him when I was ready to begin the actual portrait.

The light of the upstairs parlor well suited my needs, so it was there that I set up my easel and paints. However, I found the heat oppressive and asked if we might open a window for ventilation. Mr. Lilley seemed confused, as though unsure how to carry out my request. He fumbled with the latch for a minute, then raised the pane. Immediately I felt better.

Some short while later, the bell rang below, and Mr. Lilley departed to attend to the newcomer, returning with a bundle of women's clothing draped over his well-tailored arms. A maid followed, carrying a parcel of hats and scarves. As the maid and Mr. Lilley exited the room, I heard her say that she hoped she would not be expected to wait on a nigger. His reply eluded me.

Soon, the lady herself appeared, dispelling a dark current that had pooled around my head after overhearing the maid's remark. Smiling, I greeted her in French. Her dress was of a similar cut to yesterday's, though muslin rather than silk, designed more for everyday wear than for fashion.

The day's work passed well. As an artist's model, the lady was quite natural—each turn of her chin or movement of shoulder, the set of her eyes, was a painting unto itself, and I foresaw my only difficulty would be in settling upon but one of this bounty of poses.

At mid-day I indicated that we would pause for refreshment. Mr. Lilley rang for the servant woman, who, however unwillingly, brought us tea, and after we were settled upon it she unwrapped the lady's dresses and hung them over a screen so that we might view them. Some conversation followed. The lady favored a dark red silk, and Mr. Lilley seconded her. I was drawn to a pale blue cotton, the hue of which reminded me of the exquisite paintings of Vermeer, but I found myself won over.

We returned to our work. I had decided to position the lady on a particularly handsome couch that faced the front windows. "Duncan Phyfe," Mr. Lilley said with the pride of a man claiming enviable proximity to pedigree. The couch was well-suited to reclining, having one end open and the other closed, with ample cushion, and I admired the sweeping curve of wood on its back. Finding the columned doorway pleasing, I claimed it as a background and balance, and I also desired to use the red drapes which framed the windows.

Again, I thought that any position the lady took would make a magnificent portrait, had I the skill to achieve it!

A graceful silver candelabrum with three branches stood on the mantle. I transferred it to a low table in view of the sofa and asked Mr. Lilley to close the curtains so that I might view the lady's pose by candlelight. The actual work of the painting would take place in daylight, with a shadowy atmosphere and glowing candles imposed upon it.

After settling on what I felt to be the optimal pose, desiring not to over-tax my subject, I called an end to the day. I escorted the lady downstairs to the door and bade her farewell.

Thursday, February 10 (early morning)

How quaint the last entry looks to me now. Would that I might return to such a calm moment!

Yesterday evening I found myself unable to open my notebook and write of the day's events; I wanted them banished from my memory. This morning, however, I resolved to take comfort in the act of noting my experiences, reclaiming my life and dispelling my disgust and dismay at what had been presented to me.

My plan, as I had detailed to Mr. Lilley, was to commit a study in oil as a final preparation for the actual portrait.

On arriving at the house, I began organizing materials as per my habitual way. Someone had primed five 34 x 44 inch canvases, giving me six total. I told Mr. Lilley I had not the need for so many.

"Always set yourself up for eventualities," he said. "One can never possess too much of anything. 'Tis our American way."

He added that the lady would be appearing somewhat later than usual, in order that I might have more time to prepare, the which I began to do. Assorted materials having been deposited for me, I took the time to examine them.

"This linseed oil is too dark," I said, thinking that poppy would be better, or walnut, though the drying time presented a problem, given my employer's need for timely completion. "I will require poppy oil with sulphate of zinc added to speed drying."

At the sound of the bell, Mr. Lilley excused himself.

My spirits had lowered at Mr. Lilley's mention of the lady's delayed arrival, but the bell raised a surprising thrill, telling of my growing affection for her.

However, Mr. Lilley's return with a bulky parcel, rather than the lady, dispelled my eagerness, though I knew I would see her soon. Without explanation, he placed the parcel in a corner, and I took no further notice of it. I had planned to paint today on board, but there being such an abundance of ready canvas, I raised one to the easel and commenced a layer of imprimatura.

The lady entered, at last, attired in the red dress. On her head she had placed a charming straw bonnet decorated inside the brim with lace and flowers of silk, and over her shoulders was a shawl to cover her flesh where it was bared by the cut of the dress. I bade her place the bonnet and shawl out of sight. As she settled onto the sofa, I decided I would henceforth call her "Madame Burgundy," for the color of her attire and in honor of her French heritage, which elicited, when I informed her (in French), a lovely, unselfconscious sound of delight.

I cannot put into words how deeply struck I was by the effect of her coffee cream shoulder against the deep crimson fabric. I only hoped that my paint might express what language cannot.

Time passed in the steady and rewarding exercise of applying paint to canvas, bringing the fine shape and features of Madame Burgundy into appearance before me.

None of what I have expressed here is alarming, is it? A reader might wonder in what I found this disgust I spoke of, what appalling events silenced my pen for a day.

I see that I am having difficulty coming to it. But I also wish to set the stage, to tell the events in their proper order. But I must break here. I have arranged an early breakfast in my room, so that I might eat in peace, without the intrusion of Mr. Lilley, who has begun to haunt my steps and my thoughts, like some avatar of despondency.

Thursday, February 10 (mid-morning)

Having refreshed myself, I must continue, that I may complete this account before Mr. Lilley's arrival. I dread the work required of me today, but take comfort in knowing I will be in the presence of the dear lady, my subject. I must persevere!

As yesterday afternoon progressed, Madame Burgundy complained of lightheadedness. She revealed that earlier she had been bled, in order to protect against the fevers that often strike the city in the warm seasons, and she needed rest before continuing. She then departed, and I applied myself to the painting. I was dissatisfied with the coloring of the dress, having tried vermillion and carmine without settling on either. I said as much, aloud, to Mr. Lilley, who sat in an oaken armchair behind me, smoking his pipe and reading the day's news.

"Well then I believe it is time to open this package."

He retrieved the previously mentioned bundle, which I had long since forgotten, and unwrapped the brown paper covering to reveal pint jars: one full, one partially, of a dark crimson liquid.

"Having that pretty red dress makes this much easier don't you think?" Mr. Lilley said, to my consternation, for his words confused me.

"It is requested," he said, continuing in a flat tone as though reading from a note of instruction. "Nay, not requested, firmly stated, as a condition of your work, that you employ this substance in your painting. That this substance" — indicating the jars — "may become fully embodied and incorporated within the painting. Of necessity which will be revealed in more detail anon. Sufficient for now is that you know of the lady's ancestry, from a land filled with superstition and the use of charms."

A knock falls upon my door. Mr. Lilley, calling on me for today's sitting. I tell him that I am not quite ready and will meet him downstairs shortly. I have but a short way to go before reaching the end of the day's events and will not stop until I arrive.

And so, I responded to Mr. Lilley that I was fully confident in choosing my own materials and pigments, but . . .

"Must be materials of the subject herself incorporated," he said.

This statement, combined with the liquid's depth of color, and the lady's comment on her recent medical procedure explained all. Those who retained my services require that I imbue my work with Madame Burgundy's own blood!

Now I must depart. I will return to this account later, after the trials of my day. My only solace is that I will be once again joined by Madame Burgundy.

Thursday, February 10 (evening)

In the carriage with Mr. Lilley, I spoke but little, while he chattered as unconcernedly as a man on the way to a shooting party at his country estate. He talked of wealth, the wealth of his fair city of New York, the wealth of his young nation, how commerce would bring more and more wealth to these shores until all the world knew their names. His thoughts were not original. They had been spoken throughout the ages, by Greece, Carthage, Rome, Spain, England, even Holland, whose commercial enterprise, though corrupt and ill-conceived, founded this city he praises so highly.

I have always been of the opinion that such wealth manifests a corrupting influence, that excessive wealth begets the insatiable greed for more, which leads nations to aggression upon their neighbors. And in this nation, where the barbarity of slavery yet reigns, what could be the moral cost of this gold lust?

Guido Reni of Bologna in the seventeenth century wrote much on the subject of pigments, of color. He described methods for the use of blood, calling for it in combination with a preservative coat of resin, which ensured color retention. The resin must be applied while the blood is still wet, but the two will not mix. The resin sits atop, shielding the blood from the elements, from fading. I thought I had not the proper resin, but on arrival found it provided in abundance.

"The material itself is not yet ready," Mr. Lilley said. "I am told it needs to be concentrated and purified. So you are to plan your work accordingly."

With the impending arrival of the lady, I had to compose my mood. I did not wish to appear in any way disturbed, lest my disposition mar our sitting. My assumption was that the lady did not know of the proposed use of her body's elixir for the portrait, though Mr. Lilley's hints about both her ancestry and superstition spoke otherwise. I found myself not trusting him, or my employers. I had begun to fear some other reason lay behind their demands, something opposed to the lady's continued well-being. But with no evidence to support this feeling, I would need to keep it buried for the present.

And so, with poise and charm that raised my desolate spirits, Madame Burgundy appeared, and the morning passed in the joyous interaction of painter and model, painter and paint. I spoke more in French than I had previously, for I wanted to be sure that Mr. Lilley did not understand, and to accustom him to hearing it in a commonplace way, so that if something later arose which confirmed my suspicions, I could convey the information to Madame Burgundy without alerting our watcher.

It had been my intent that on concluding the daily sittings with the lady, I would work on the background, but today I was loath to do so. After a half-hearted recreation of the doorway molding, I indicated to Mr. Lilley that I had finished for the day. He seemed displeased, but made no protest.

The drapes on the side window of Mr. Vanderkemp's study, the window which would be appearing on the right side of the painting—these drapes were of a red darker than the lady's dress, of a heavy and likely expensive material. I decided that I would *not* use the blood, as commanded, on the person of Madame Burgundy. If I pursued this course, however, I would need to diminish the jar's contents. Therefore, I would incorporate the blood into the drapery.

With Mr. Lilley present more often than not, I would have to take care not to be observed.

There is a note I would like to make here—although I know that Vanderkemp has a family, and indeed have seen the children's portrait, they were never present during my days of work in their house. I cannot help but wonder whether their absence has something to do with the blood, with my commission, even with Madame Burgundy herself.

Monday, February 14 (morning)

My last entry was Thursday. I have allowed my account to lapse for a few days, not because of dire circumstances but because the days flowed without incident. Friday and Saturday, Madame Burgundy sat for me. I made slight adjustments to her pose, and I began to capture what I felt to be her true character. Enchanted by my sitter and the way the portrait took shape, filling the canvas with her presence, I became lulled, dismissing my previous unease.

We conversed, as usual, in French, and I found her intelligent and charming beyond measure. Being a woman, she was without extensive formal education, but coming from a wealthy family in a realm where the people were industrious in their desire for advancement, she had been well-educated at home, and as an adult read history, literature, and philosophy.

I could easily see how her husband had developed such deep adoration, for I found myself ascending a similar path!

This despite our differences in race. I admired the will of her husband, that he had persevered in bringing his love into a society where such was not looked upon with approval.

Yesterday being Sunday, the lady did not sit, though I was nevertheless expected to work. And so I did, taking particular care with the couch, capturing the scrollwork of its arm and the brocade cushions.

Later, I was surprised by a chance meeting with a friend, whose presence here has greatly relieved the strain of this commission. As I neared the door to my room, a man called out my name, and I was pleased when the caller turned out to be none other than the illustrious writer Mr. Charles Dickens, who had arrived in New York the previous day and was residing in my hotel.

He and I had become acquainted during my most recent stay in London, when I had been called upon to paint portraits of a certain wealthy family, a commission which led to more commissions, causing my residence to extend to a much greater length than first anticipated.

Because of the many social calls required of Mr. Dickens in New York, he had procured a private sitting room where he could escape the press of his fame (he found himself in great demand in all parts of this country, a prospect which daunted him greatly). He took me to this parlor, and a light supper was brought to us.

I sketched my commission, relaying the fabrication that my employers had instructed me to use: that I had been brought to New York to paint the children of a man named Bookman (whom I had not even met). Lying to my friend proved to be quite distasteful.

We exchanged our views of America. Mine were, of course, limited to a small portion of Manhattan. He described what he had seen in Boston and elsewhere.

As Mr. Dickens had a social engagement, we cut our visit off at this point, but planned to meet again soon.

Monday, February 14 (evening)

Madame Burgundy sat for me in the morning as usual. This afternoon, a package was delivered to Mr. Lilley. He opened it. The blood, having been somewhat altered by its mysterious purification, was now reduced to about three-fourths of a pint jar. Ample, I was sure, for the intended use.

Tuesday, February 15 (evening)

By Thursday I fear I will no longer need to have Madame Burgundy sitting. I will be finished with her. And a few days thereafter will find the portrait complete.

The thought of departing from these shores, from the noise and rot of this frantic and unkempt metropolis fills me with a shining hope. I miss my friends in Amsterdam. I miss my own studio, however drafty it may be in winter. Soon, soon, I will return. Visions of home fill me with a great sense of peace, which I was able to shape into the serene face of my subject.

Thursday, February 18 (evening)

On this day I bade a heartfelt farewell to Madame Burgundy. Having discovered nothing further about any ill intentions toward her, I have become more at ease, though I carried out my plan of enmeshing the blood with the drapes rather than her clothing.

In the evening, I was fortunate to be dining with Mr. Dickens, his wife, Catherine, and a man of their recent acquaintance, David Wadholm, who was active in the anti-slavery movement.

We settled in the private parlor, served by an attentive waiter whose girth and enthusiasm for the menu indicated his own attraction to dining.

Relief flowed through me as I sat among amiable companions, an interlude that removed from my mind the cares and conundrums of my commission. Our group chatted for a time. At some point, the waiter apologized for a delay, saying that if our food didn't arrive soon, he would "fix matters so that management knew about it."

"Here is something I have noticed in my short stay in America," Mr. Dickens said, after our waiter had departed. "There are few words which perform such various duties as 'fix.' You call upon a gentleman in a country town, and his help informs you that he is 'fixing himself' just now, but will be down directly: by which you are to understand that he is dressing. You inquire, on board a steamboat, of a fellow-passenger, whether breakfast will be ready soon, and he tells you he should think so, for when he was last below, they were 'fixing the tables.' You beg a porter to collect your luggage, and he entreats you not to be uneasy, for he'll 'fix it presently.' If you complain of indisposition, you are advised to have recourse to Doctor So-and-So, who will 'fix you' in no time."

After dinner, I told them of my commission (the truth this time, as I could not continue in the lie), though I made light of the demand for painting in the lady's own blood, attributing it to superstition and hiding my fears.

Mr. Dickens speculated on the identity of my subject, saying that these Yankee traders had amassed great wealth and pretension, and, due to the roughness of their own land, a liking for all things European.

Mr. Wadholm, having only recently relocated here from Boston, did not recognize the names I gave, though the social circumstances of the racially mixed marriage interested him.

"Such a marriage would not go uncommented upon," he said. "And I would be surprised to find it well-accepted."

"There is a wealthy man here who, I'm told, married a former whore," Mr. Dickens said.

"Eliza Jumel," Mrs. Dickens said.

Mr. Wadholm wondered aloud whether the husband of Madame Burgundy was involved with abolition, and he said he would conduct a few discreet inquiries.

The interest of Mr. Wadholm was a fortuitous circumstance, for I had not shaken the sensation that some ill was intended on Madame Burgundy, likely without the knowledge of her absent husband.

Saturday, February 19 (evening)

There is not a more divine sensation than that which arises upon completion of a work of art!

Sunday, February 20 (evening)

Today, I find I am no longer free, nor do I see myself soon returning to my home.

It was not until after I finished the portrait that the arcane nature of my commission became apparent.

I journeyed to Vanderkemp's house as usual, in the custody (I use that word drolly, though the circumstances report the opposite) of Mr. Lilley.

My intent was to carry out the final glazing of the portrait, for I believed that this was all that remained.

I had grown accustomed to the passage along the streets, but when Mr. Lilley's driver made a turn which varied from the norm, I thought nothing of it.

However, when we stopped before an unfamiliar house, I turned to Mr. Lilley with a question on my lips.

"Mr. Bookman's house," he said. "The gentleman would like to speak to you about painting his children. You will find him most agreeable. He is a collector of antiquities from far-off Greece and Rome and has traveled much in Europe."

I had no intention of executing another portrait in America, but the conditions dictated that I follow Mr. Lilley into the house, through a foyer decorated with amphorae and a marble bust of Roman origin, then up a staircase. In yet another second floor parlor, I found Madame Burgundy's portrait. Mr. Vanderkemp was there, and another I took to be Bookman, a plump man wearing an ashy coat of an old-fashioned cut.

My assumption was that the pair wished to see the portrait, one to approve, or not, of my endeavor, the other to see if it matched the expectations he held for the likeness of his children. I would have preferred that they wait until I indicated it was ready for viewing, but as I was used to the thoughtless actions of patrons I made no comment.

"I am honored to meet such an accomplished artist," Bookman said. "I dabble, influenced by my visits to Italy. I have great affection for Europe. I only wish I had greater facility with the languages. I get by with just enough to keep my belly full, but no more."

Mr. Vanderkemp indicated for me to seat myself. Mr. Lilley walked to the portrait and stood in front of it for a time. "This will serve, don't you think?" he finally said.

"Quite a likeness indeed," said the man I assumed to be Bookman. "A fine start to this," he added, and I wondered what he meant.

Turning to me, Mr. Vanderkemp spoke. "There is more to be done, much more. What you have executed is merely the first step. Six in total are required. This one"—he pointed at the portrait—"is to hang in the residence of the person you call Madame Burgundy. Five more are required."

"The purpose intended for the others is quite different," Bookman said. Vanderkemp gave him a look which I assumed meant the man should not have spoken.

"The purpose of the other portraits is not your concern" Vanderkemp said. "Mr. Beekman here will see to your needs."

"Bookman," the man said. "My grandparents, you see, my grandfather actually . . . changed from the Dutch way of spelling."

Ignoring him, Vanderkemp informed me that while completing the other paintings I would remain here, in the home of Paul Bookman, or Beekman, as Vanderkemp called him.

I said that I was quite happy with the hotel and the current arrangement, but Vanderkemp said that time was scarce, that it was imperative I finish before a certain date, and proximity to my studio would ensure this.

"This is not part of the commission I accepted," I said. "And I am not inclined towards any further work here. I long for my home in the Netherlands and desire to return."

"Your homecoming must wait," Vanderkemp said. "I consider this to be all-inclusive. By God it must be, for the process to work. It must be *your* hand that connects all six, as it is the woman's blood that ties them as well. You will receive no payment until the entire group is complete."

I saw that I would not be able to change their views, and I contemplated walking out that instant, but the prospect of losing my income did not appeal. How I hate to discuss such a gross subject, but the importance of money is an unavoidable detail.

What recourse had I if I left? Through Mr. Dickens, I was quite familiar with the lack of appreciation in this nation for the rights and income of writers, due to an absence of copyright law, which prevented Mr. Dickens and other European authors from earning one cent for their works published in America. I feared that the same would be true for artists, and I had not the funds to retain an attorney to test this supposition.

Perhaps through Mr. Dickens, through the many people of import he had met during his stay, I might find work painting portraits while I pursued legal action. I would need to find less expensive lodgings, for my current patrons were paying for the hotel and I did not think I could manage the rate on my own.

Oh, but that would mean delaying my return home! And staying here, carrying out this extra commission, caused the same delay.

Bookman and Vanderkemp conferred, their voices too low for me to pick out any but scattered phrases. They repeated "The man from Schoharie" several times. Mr. Lilley left the room.

I stood.

Better to delay my return home in circumstances of my *own* choosing than toil longer in the company of men I dislike and distrust.

Mr. Vanderkemp turned toward me.

"I am not interested in your machinations," I said. "I was hired to paint a portrait, and that is precisely what I have done. Therefore, I shall take my payment and depart this country."

I stepped toward the door.

"If Mr. Lilley's services as coachman are no longer available, I will find my own way back to the hotel. Payment can be sent to me there. I am sure you can find another, even here, to fulfill this new contract."

On reaching the door, I found a man blocking it, a lean and sallow man with a cap pulled low over his forehead. Mr. Lilley stood behind him. This newcomer—his very being disturbed me. Projected from his lined, blotchy-red face an obvious callous nature, disdain for art, for life, for anything but his own interests.

"Here is the man of whom I spoke," Bookman said.

"Splendid," Vanderkemp said. "Mr. Schuyler, you are to begin immediately." He spoke flatly, commandingly, disregarding my statement of objection, my intention to leave.

Mr. Lilley and the newcomer entered, and I backed away from them, instinctively, not wanting to be in such proximity with what this person represented.

I found myself once again seated on the couch.

Vanderkemp spoke. "This man must be incorporated. He must appear in the five, in the new paintings. You have left ample room."

The horror of my situation was now made clear—the man was to become a cancer, an eater of beauty.

Bookman told me to place the man in the doorway first and then in the succeeding paintings move him by degrees closer, closer, closer, to Madame Burgundy, until his hands encircled her lovely neck.

Monday, February 21 (morning)

I awoke on a narrow bed. A small room, a servant's quarters, in the house of this man, Paul Bookman. The door, I knew, was locked.

On awakening I was surprised that I had even slept, for I had sat up late, staring into the dark, my mind disquieted by the day's events.

Yesterday, giving in to the inevitability of my having to carry out this addition to my contract, I had them empty a room for my use, removing all furniture, carpeting, and ornamentation that I might have nothing to distract me from recreating on canvas the room at Vanderkemp's, and there I began the work of copying Madame Burgundy's portrait five times, beginning with the alla prima and ending. . . .

I did not wish to think forward to that event.

A man was sent to bring my belongings from the hotel.

First, I must sketch this newcomer, the garrotter.

I had used two of the original six canvases: one for the study, one for the portrait itself. Another had lately been provided, giving me the five required.

What was the intent of these men? Not the glorification

of my friend! I had read various alchemical sources that described the connections between blood and figurative representation, but I was surprised to find such knowledge here. This "man from Schoharie" referred to yesterday, no doubt his involvement was vital.

The reasons were clear why they wished to harm such a harmless being. A marriage of mixed race. Her husband's social position. The economic well-being of the group, these Stuyvesants.

I placed the garrotter in the doorway and sketched him, then instructed him to cross the room so that I might watch the movements of his body, a slight limp in the right leg, the swing of his arms. His facial expression rarely changed, giving me no inkling what lay beneath the ruddy skin.

Thinking on the pigments needed to match the garrotter's rutilent face, I concocted a new scheme, as a form of quiet rebellion and revenge and as a further use for some of Madame Burgundy's blood.

I tried to keep my suspicions from showing in my face or actions. I believed that my well-being depended on hiding my knowledge, and hoped that affecting ignorance of their plan would cause them to relax their guard enough for me to escape and warn Madame Burgundy.

But this morning, I found my resolve, and my health, less assured. When I rose from bed to refresh myself at the washbasin, a pervasive dizziness caused me to grip a chair for support.

Returning to the bed, I wrote in my journal, in haste, desiring to update my record before my jailors came to conduct me to the studio.

Monday, February 21 (evening)

Flushed and feverish, I paint, for that is what I do.

Wednesday, February 23 (evening)

As in Vanderkemp's house, I never saw any family members, and I saw little of Bookman.

The days passed, I painted, my body remained weak. Captivity, I find, is injurious to the health.

I hate this man whom I am crafting into the presence of the dear lady. Though he might be merely an actor hired to play the role of garrotter, I knew this was not so. His mood colored his complexion, and his flat way of speaking cast a pall on the room, dampening even Mr. Lilley's usual jocularity. And Mr. Lilley himself— he was never far, lounging outside the painting studio, sleeping in the room opposite mine. I must take even more care that he does not see my use of the blood for drapery (and the garrotter's face!) rather than the lady's dress.

These two creatures—how I long to separate myself from them!

After a while, I ceased to view them as fellow-men, seeing in their eyes the beasts they kept hidden within themselves, beak of vulture, claws of lion, skin of reptile, cold and coarse. Please, let me never see these demons revealed.

Thankfully, I will soon have no further need for this other, this garrotter. Capturing him on canvas has not been difficult, and I hope he will soon depart.

Thursday, February 24 (evening)

Today my captors allowed me to go outside for a time, into the garden at the rear of the house. The work has gone well, despite my aversion. These copies will take much less time than the original. I breathed in the free air, still chill but with Spring promising. But what will this Spring send to me?

Friday, February 25 (evening)

Today, as I sat in the courtyard, a second city, newer yet older, began to emerge, overlapping the garden wall at odd angles, lingering at the edges of my sight. I practiced catching it, first the corner of a brick arch, then the plane of an open door.

Claiming exhaustion, I returned to the privacy of my room, where I sat at the narrow window overlooking the street. Through hours concentrating on keeping my eyes turned in a leftward pose, I was able to make out across the way a window, a shop window filled with plaster figurines painted in garish reds and greens. A rush of vehicles filled the street, steel carriages in a multitude of colors, chiefly a custard-yellow. What struck me about these carriages—they lacked horses. Seemingly self-propelled, by steam engine perhaps, they darted athwart lanes of traffic, stopping here and there to let off and take in passengers.

My captors appeared not to notice this second city, and I began to hope that it, having manifested to me alone, would provide my means of escape.

I have no further need of the garrotter, yet he remains, having also become Mr. Lilley's partner in attending to my captivity. He brings my meals, and I am loath to ingest any foods his hands have touched.

Saturday, February 26 (afternoon)

This other city continues to fascinate me, though I am only able to examine it from the garden, the windows of my cell, and those of the room where I work. This morning as I looked out, I saw a man in strange dress—indigo trousers and a thin shirt, of some pliant material, which left his arms bare save for a sleeve ending inches below the shoulder—and I could have sworn his gaze met mine. He staggered, putting a hand to his head as though taken by a fit. Then—another man passed through him. This second man, by his attire, belonged to the city of my captors. The oddly clothed man—he occupies a space contiguous with my own, yet somehow separate. In another realm of time perhaps. Or perhaps I am mad!

Despite the increasing clarity of this second city, I have not discerned how it might aid me. And I know that this afternoon I will finish the paintings.

Saturday, February 26 (evening)

They have summoned "The man from Schoharie." Mr. Lilley has taken a train north to bring him hither.

The paintings are complete, save for glazing. Mr. Bookman informed me that the glazing would take place under the supervision of the newcomer, that he would advise me on the materials to be used. Then, they will present Madame Burgundy with her portrait. And after that, they will no doubt carry out their macabre schemes.

Sunday, February 27 (early afternoon)

I arose early and inspected the paintings. A few details needed attention, but otherwise all were ready. I wished to spend the rest of the morning in the garden, sketching the newly opened flowers of Spring in an attempt to quiet my apprehension. I had hoped to do this in privacy, but was not allowed to escape the company of the garrotter.

Descending the stairs, I saw in the entryway below me Vanderkemp, who had been absent since the first day. He spoke to someone out of my line of sight. I paused, hoping to catch them unawares.

"Five into one," a stranger's voice said. "That will be how you know. Success, then five into one. Failure, then five remain five."

The garrotter gave a push to the middle of my back, causing me to stumble on the stair. I seized the rail to keep from falling, but my ankle twisted. I looked back at the garrotter, whose face bore no expression, no sign of why he pushed me, and he voiced no explanation. Below, Vanderkemp, having heard my approach, moved into another room with the newcomer, who must be this man for whom they have waited.

I limped into the garden and sat on a bench, my desire for sketching banished.

Sunday, February 27 (evening)

This "Man from Schoharie," as they call him (and no name is given me) is not at all what I expected. Looking at his round, bespectacled face, I might guess "manager of a counting house" as an occupation. And his tone is soft, his manner of speaking genteel. Whatever beast might lurk within, it is far better concealed than those of my captors. Under his influence, I find myself questioning my earlier fears.

They had told me at the outset, Mr. Lilley said, that the blood, the preparations, were for enacting a protective charm. Perhaps I should not have disbelieved them. But this garrotter? His presence pointed toward the opposite of protection. But could he have been called upon merely to play the part? Could, somehow, his actions against her likeness (actions painted by me), cause some envelope of safety to surround her?

Surely this man, this kindly uncle from Schoharie would not involve himself in a murderous plot.

The material that he presented to me, the which I was to incorporate into the glazing was, he said, a distillate of sap from various plants, combining the medicinal and aromatic.

I glazed the paintings.

Tomorrow, I am to accompany Mr. Lilley and Mr. Bookman to Madame Burgundy to present her portrait.

This will be my first departure from either house or garden since the onset of captivity. If I am to escape, Monday will be my lone chance. But first, I must warn the lady!

Tuesday, March 1 (evening)

I have found Mr. Dickens! And barely in time, for he and Mrs. Dickens would have been departing today. I am presently in the home of his abolitionist friend Mr. Wadholm, where I am safe and able to rest.

But I must now relate how I came to be in this happy circumstance.

Monday morning, having slept little, I awakened early. What would this day bring? Suddenly recalling my dream, I sat upright.

I had been in the other city!

As dusk fell, I found myself riding in one of those horseless vehicles, sitting on a broad cushion of dark, stiff material. A window separated me from the front compartment, where a man sat, manipulating a wheel that appeared to be the means of steering. He pulled it violently to one side, and we veered, my stomach lurching with the motion, then we accelerated, passing quickly through an intersection only to stop with a suddenness that threw me forward. I pulled a silvery lever on the panel to my right, and it swung outward. Before leaving, I handed the driver some bills of currency.

This setting quickly turned into Madame Burgundy's sitting room, the location of our first meeting. She sat, smiling and chatting as she poured my tea, but her demeanor changed, composure soon replace by a look of terror, and a shriek as something dark an enormous descended from the ceiling. Waking, I was unable to return to sleep.

In the dream, I had been another person. One accustomed to life in this other city.

Mr. Lilley called upon me to assist in something which turned out to be the transportation of the five new paintings to the basement of Mr. Bookman's house. There, in this subterranean locale, we set them on a marble-topped sideboard, one after another, the outermost being the painting depicting the garrotter at his farthest point from Madame Burgundy.

Five into one, I thought.

Then it was time to visit the lady.

The three of us went, I carrying the portrait, Bookman and Lilley walking on either side.

This house of Bookman's was on a side street, Bond, scant blocks to the south of Madame Burgundy's.

What a relief to be away from the garrotter, whose face would be forever imprinted upon me!

But what a joy it was to see again the face of my dear lady. And the delight she showed on seeing my creation! As Madame Burgundy gazed at the painting, I spoke gently to her in French, attempting to convey urgency while maintaining a tone of normal courtesy. I entreated her not to betray anything, in words or expression, no matter what she heard me say.

"These men are not your friends, nor friends of your worthy husband." I pointed to a part of the painting, as though explaining its nature.

"They intend harm.

"After we leave, you must burn the painting.

"The blood," I said, "the blood binds you to them."

I am sure she comprehended the seriousness. Before leaving, I made one last request of her. "As we are going out, ask ... the man with the name of the flower," — pausing, I waited to read the understanding on her face — "ask if he can assist you with something, call him back."

Descending the stairs, I managed to keep Bookman ahead and Lilley behind. Bookman opened the door and stepped outside.

"Monsieur Lilley," the lady said. "My husband is soon to return from New Orleans. He sent ahead a trunk— could you come help Joseph carry it up the stairs? It is quite heavy."

Mr. Lilley stopped, then turned and followed her into the rear of the house. I pulled the door shut and shouldered Bookman aside.

I fled!

But Bookman, whose slowness I had depended on, lunged, clutching the tail of my coat, tripping me. We tussled, rolling into the street. The man's strength was far greater than I had guessed from his comfortable appearance.

I had only a few minutes before Lilley would exit the house, and I knew I had no chance of overcoming both of them.

Bookman pushed his weight down upon me. Then he screamed.

The other city had interceded!

One of the yellow vehicles rumbled toward us. I could hear it!

As could Bookman. He threw himself back in fright. While I, trusting the evidence of my days of observation, believing in the insubstantiality of these apparitions, jumped to my feet and ran straight into the onrushing machine.

Heat, quivering heat, and my vision blurred. Yet I kept moving. As though gazing up from the ocean's depths, I could see Bookman and the machine mingle, then separate, leaving the man gasping, wide-eyed yet unseeing.

I did not wait for his recovery.

Past the street on which stood the houses of Vanderkemp and Madame Burgundy, structures grew fewer in number, smaller, meaner, shacks and bits of land, no doubt soon to be devoured by the encroaching city. I came upon a wooded swath and made my way under the trees. My ankle, twisted that day upon the stairs, throbbed, its condition aggravated during my fight with Bookman and my flight. I could go no further. I would shelter here, I thought, protected by briar and branch.

My clothes were torn, one knee scraped raw and bloody.

I found a brook and splashed my face with its chill water, then dipped my knee to cleanse it. In the morning, I would set off for downtown to locate my only friend on this wretched shore.

When morning came, I found I had slept well, under the boughs of freedom.

Knowing that the island narrowed as it went southward, I kept to the trees for a time, passing a small dairy farm, then entered the zone of brick and timbers, streets leading to populated areas. I recognized Bowery. I found my former hotel.

But on entering the bustling lobby I saw the unshakeable Mr. Lilley conversing with the clerk. I slipped back through the door and set off along the sidewalk, which had seemed such a gay promenade when first glimpsed from the hotel window on the day of my arrival.

Fearing that the others were near, dreading the sight of my shadow, the garrotter, I kept my face down. I passed an alley, then stopped, thinking to try a rear entrance to the hotel, one that might take me through the kitchen or some other domestic region and, doing that, I made my way to Mr. Dickens's door and hid myself therein.

Though I deplored becoming a burden to him and his wife, I had no one else.

I explained my situation to Mr. Dickens, and he quickly settled upon the plan of requesting the assistance of Mr. Wadholm. He forthwith composed a note to the man, which he sent by swiftest messenger, asking Mr. Wadholm to hasten here to consult upon my flight.

When evening came, Mr. Wadholm led me back

through the rear of the hotel, taking me to a house in the nearby Five Points neighborhood.

Tuesday, March 8 (morning)

There I stayed until March 5, on which day I traveled hidden with Charles and Catherine to Philadelphia.

I have booked passage from Philadelphia for Java in the Dutch Indies, for I feel Europe to be too close.

Today, my ship departs!

I have not yet heard how go Mr. Wadholm's inquiries into the health or fate of Madame Burgundy. I must depart without knowing, but I hope she remains unharmed.

It was here, in Philadelphia, while waiting for my ship, that I completed this record and copied it over, entrusting the copy to my friend, Mr. Charles Dickens, that he may have it printed, in Dutch and English, for private distribution so that friends and family might know what events befell me in the City of New York in 1842.

May the whirligig of time carry me to peaceful lands.
Philip Schuyler, Philadelphia

A Postscript

Having spent the last several months traveling America, I am back in New York for a short time. Soon, Catherine and I will take ship for home. All these months, I have carried Philip Schuyler's journal, troubled by its weight. I wondered what had become of Philip's Madame Burgundy. Had she survived this plot only to succumb to another?

As I would only be stopping one night in the city

before taking ship, I posted a letter from Montreal to Mr. David Wadholm, a man described by Philip in these pages, asking that he update me upon my return to New York. My hope was that he had been successful in delving into the identity of Madame Burgundy.

When I arrived at the hotel a message from him awaited, which I reproduce here.

My Dear Charles,

As you know, I have not been long in the city of New York, having recently decided to devote (some might say squander!) my family fortune to the cause of abolition. New York is the cross-roads. Here are the networks for hiding escapees and for aiding in the buying of broken families that they may be reunited.

Much work is to be done here as well. The legal system is rampant with corruption. Did you know that a Negro may be taken from the street, from his home even, and brought before a magistrate? And if witnesses should claim that the Black Man is an escaped slave, whether true or not, he will be taken to the South in bondage!

I count on you to spread this news in England, that World opinion may help sway that of America.

In conducting my business, I have met many people, of circumstances high and low, of all races and nationalities. It is to these I turned in search of the identity and circumstances of the woman your friend described.

Having the street number made the first part quite simple. It is the home of a wealthy American family of Dutch extraction. I have also discovered that there is a very old and very powerful group of wealthy New Yorkers (both of the city and other parts of the state) who claim their lineage from the original Dutch inhabitants of then New Amsterdam. The Dutch were absorbed into the English population after the colony changed hands, losing their language but not their identity. The group goes under the name Stuyvesant Preservationist Society and comprises some of the wealthiest families in the region. Because of this, I have had to take care, as some of these people are also contributors to my cause.

The basic scenario is thus. A man by the name of Horace Nooteboom, eldest of a family of merchants and shipbuilders, met, in the course of his business, a woman from the island of St. Grillet, a lady of both French and African ancestry. They married, and he brought her to his new home in a most fashionable block.

You can guess the consternation this caused. The mixing of races is not unknown here, but it is generally confined to the lower classes, and although she is not one hundred percent African in her heritage, her coloring is dark enough to cause notice.

In other parts of the nation, in the Western territories, where men and women alike toil in the fields of their farmsteads, I doubt her appearance would have attracted attention. But in New York the complexion of pale cream is the emblem of elegant society.

So you see that even if they had been given peace, the couple would have encountered myriad difficulties. This Society, however, determined that one of their own should not embarrass them in such a manner, and it was they who contrived the scheme which embroiled your friend.

As might be expected, the husband is on the side of our cause, and has, through his business (which takes him often to the South, especially New Orleans), actively participated in aiding the flight of slaves, hiding them on his ships and bringing them to New York.

I have spoken to him, and I am happy to say that Madame Burgundy did survive the attempt! She did indeed destroy the painting. And whether or not you believe that some harm could befall her from this odd series of paintings depicting a garrotter approaching from behind, it was enough for them to know that such had been intended.

They left the city, up the Hudson River, on a steamboat. I believe their final destination was to be Canada.

These boats, as you know, are not the safest form of travel.

On the second day, at an early hour of the morning, perhaps before any passengers had awakened, an accident occurred. The starboard boiler exploded and the boat burst into flame! Few survived, and I am sorry to say Nooteboom and his wife were not among them.

I am afraid we shall never know whether this was truly an accident, or another assault by these persons, whose prey now included the husband, for he knew of their treachery. It is well that your friend the painter chose to separate himself by the gulf of oceans.

I toast your safe and speedy return journey.

Best wishes, as always,
David Wadholm

I handed the letter to Catherine that she might read it too. I wish I could contact Philip to give him the sad news as well, but I expect I will hear from him when he is settled. For the moment, as Mr. Wadholm has said, it is well that he is far away.

Charles Dickens,
Aboard ship bound for Liverpool
Friday, June 10, 1842

6

LEAVING THE CITY
BY UNKNOWN PATHS

Tonight, the streets refashioned themselves. Chanting buildings waltzed along intricate new configurations: walls flowed into halls, right angles and curves separating from the generic stuff of tired masonry. A few desisted, mainly those owning more concrete than brick. Cast-iron façades stretched to form spiderweb twists, each delicate strand a tracery of shadow in the night sky. Unrestrained brick whispered into the darkness, listened, and whispered again. From beneath the streets, ghosts of forgotten buildings sent crisp filaments out to test the air. But elsewhere, hidden in the depths of the darkened city, invisible factories spewed pestilent trinkets, the wares of velvet enslavement: co-op apartments, electronic toys, stock market speculation, while in their darkened offices, the wizards of finance smiled, harvesting crops laid by their ancestors. For who can resist the sweetness, the promises of everlasting comfort?

In a world without divine or diabolical intervention, there is no one to blame for the inhumanity of commercial enterprise but humanity itself, succumbing to the desire for power and conquest, bloody subjugation of the weak, of those unable or unwilling to accept the system presented as their only option.

For the sculptor Jacob Lerner, sitting in the courtyard of secret water, darkness overtook the sky, covering Schuyler's words. The voice of the brook expanded, keening, banished to its life beneath triumphant streets and buildings. Alone . . . alone . . . alone said the water as it tumbled back underground, cascading notes of an infinite composition, taking shape with the passing millennia. And who can say when the final note will be laid?

"Stuyvesant Preservationist Society," said the caretaker of books and hidden water, having returned on silent feet to stand near Lerner's bench. "They brought Schuyler to New York."

Lerner rested the journal on his lap and listened. The man's voice was like his spring, ever-flowing but heard by few.

"The Stuyvesants weren't like Tammany Hall or other societies. Tammany Hall could be brutal, but they were up front about it. The Stuyvesants operated from the crevices. They weren't interested in politics except where it served the needs of wealth. Always there, always listened to. And they're still here. Not like before, not as many of them, but they're still wealthy, and wealth holds more importance than a large membership, in this city more than anywhere."

Shock of recognition, Lerner's form, his face described in pages written long ago, written in blood, a blood that reached forward through the years, a long slim finger tapping.

"Schuyler saw me! I'm in there. Part of his 'other city.'"

He turned to the caretaker for explanation, but the caretaker had gone, talking Schuyler's journal with him. Lerner continued to sit, listening to the brook but hearing something else. Stars emerged, one, two, three, constellations of them, unafraid to show themselves in this shielded zone far from the overwhelming city-lights. The marquee moon cast its glow over the oasis. Schuyler's view would have been similar, before stone, brick, and concrete overtook the island. Lerner smiled at the stars. Ursa Minor, Little Bear, Little Dipper immersed itself in the pond, shook its tail to quench the unquenchable thirst of Polaris. A light rain fell silky sweet, pin-pricking the pond. The brook followed itself back underground, back to the other city, the old havens beneath the streets where the faeries mark their territory in sheep's blood and formulate their marvels.

The painting of Madame Burgundy, its graceful shapes muted by the starlight, filled the surrounding spaces; superimposed on the walls it radiated a sickening glow that drained and debilitated. Lerner ached to see the first, the original portrait—not Freed's cancerous copy.

Ages of bronze, ages of oil and pigment, conquered, replaced by petroleum products, acrylic paint, foam sculpture. Was he too much of a purist? A relic? Not all innovation is wrong. But clay and metal carried the strength of the earth. Petroleum comes from the earth too, but processing and refining casts out all earthly elements, leaving lifeless plastic.

Lerner hadn't slept much last night. Thoughts propelled his mind forward, whirling and singing . . . five guttered candles, five paintings with only one remaining. Five into one. And their successor, Lerner's temple, his *Homage to the Fallen Deities of Commerce*. Would it be wise to place his sculpture on the former altar? He wanted his offering to heal, to erase the rift between himself and Schuyler, to seal the leaking pustules caused by the gigantic formation of pain directed at another human.

Catherine Vanadis would be arriving soon to see the sculpture he had described to her. She had called yesterday while he had been. . . . He was having trouble absorbing the previous afternoon. Had he truly read Schuyler's journal? A fog clung to the experience, hiding the pages, the spring, and he longed for his memory to coalesce into the finality of metal. Silly perhaps, but he believed that if he returned to Quality Brothers Restaurant Supply, he would be unable to find the basement library.

Hungry, Lerner boiled water for rice noodles. While the noodles soaked, he opened a jar of preserved radish and washed some lettuce. When the noodles were ready, he tossed them with leftover roast duck and the other ingredients. He ate with the library book of Schuyler's paintings open on the table, searching for a clue that pointed to the artist's fate. All of the paintings in the book were dated prior to 1842. Nothing existed after that, unless under a new identity and originating in Java, or elsewhere in the former Dutch colonies of Indonesia.

Eating, waiting for Catherine, he idly considered making the journey to Indonesia to search for the rest of Schuyler's life. But he had work to do here. He needed to see the face of Madame Burgundy. He thought he could sketch her from memory, but working direct from Schuyler's creation would be better. He would shape a bust, preserve her face in the permanence of metal.

His buzzer droned, and he let Catherine in.

"So this is where it happens, the creation," she said. "Great light, great space."

"It's home," he said. "Not the quietest part of town, but I work well here. Sometimes I think about keeping it as the studio and moving someplace else, but I don't know how I'd like that. I need to live with my work."

"I smell duck."

She invaded his kitchen.

"There's so much great food down here," she said. "I lived at Grand and Mulberry for a while, but it got to be too much. I needed a neighborhood that wasn't a circus, all those fucking tourists all the time, pretending they were walk-ons in some dreary mafia movie, capped off every autumn by the infernal Feast of San Gennaro. I had to kick people in the shins to make them move—they'd sit on my stoop, blocking the door, eyes slack, faces exploding with sausage. Horrible. Now I rent my aunt's old place in the West Village. It's so peaceful over there, but I miss being close to all those Asian treats. Not that I even have time anymore. And now two restaurants. I must be out of my mind."

"I wouldn't know. We just met."

She laughed and touched his hand. He herded her back into his studio and showed her the temple.

"I see what you mean. And you made this before you saw the

positions of the burned-out candles? It's uncanny. I want it. I like your idea, putting it on the sideboard."

The buzzer droned again. Gary Freed this time, obviously back in the city. Catherine browsed recent sculptures while Lerner waited at the door for Freed.

"I know I know, I never sent the key." Freed pushed past him into the apartment.

"Hi Gary," Catherine said.

"Don't you have air-conditioning?" Freed asked. "I'm sopping." He crossed the room to turn on the window unit and lingered in the path of the flowing air, standing with his eyes closed. "I should've stayed in Vermont. Who ever heard of it being this hot in May?" Freed turned around, letting the airflow caress the back of his neck.

Lerner brought him a glass of water with ice. "Here. Don't want you getting heatstroke, doctor."

Catherine moved to the sofa, and Freed joined her, sighing dramatically as he flopped onto the cushion. He held the glass to his forehead. "That's better, Jacob. Always the valiant host."

Lerner told them about the journal.

"I don't want to see the painting again, not with what I know, but I need to, at least one more time, so I can sculpt her. Madame Burgundy. And after I finish my sketches you should destroy the thing."

"I don't have it anymore. Dora and Denise Kreunen bought it. That's why I came back early. They called, offered twenty percent more than what I paid. Of course I suspect something—they don't *give* their money away. I figure they know someone who'll pay a lot more for it. But that's okay. They've done pretty well for me over the years."

Sold . . . whisked off, no chance to bid farewell. Dark forces closing, arrayed against him, against Schuyler, with all the weapons of their arsenal: wealth, property, control.

"Is Kreunen a Dutch name?" Lerner asked. "Those sisters have to be connected to the Stuyvesants. Maybe they'll let me see the painting. But they went to the appraiser. All the records destroyed. There's no buyer but them. They're tidying up. Surprised they didn't buy it first, but they probably didn't hear about it. They don't give a shit about art. Just chance that they saw it at your party, Gary."

"I don't believe in Dutch secret societies," Catherine said.

"You didn't read the journal," Lerner said. "They're still around, these Stuyvesants. Old money like that lasts forever. Especially here, right? This is the place money comes from."

"So they went to the appraiser to see what it's worth," Freed said. "So they had him purge the records? I never said they weren't a bit ruthless. Making money has its own etiquette. I wouldn't expect Jacob the Artist to get that."

More fog, razor vapor, talons raping his flesh, suffocating him. . . .

"God Jacob, you should see your face," Freed said. "You always did get yourself over-excited. You want to see the painting, call them." He dug their card out of his wallet and held it out for Lerner. "Call about the painting, call about investments. Whatever."

They talked on without resolution. No explanation could serve as replacement for what Lerner had seen and experienced, Schuyler's face in the window. Lerner's face in Schuyler's journal.

Catherine had to leave for work. She said she wanted to fix them a special dinner; Lerner agreed to join Freed at Gingerleaf at seven. After they left, he pulled a block of wax from a bin and began shaping it, sloughing off the layers to see if he could uncover Madame Burgundy's face buried within.

Later, much later, he stopped, unsatisfied with what he found. The next time, he would use clay; wax was too unsubtle for his needs.

He showered and dressed to go out, but dawdled, in no hurry to return uptown so soon after his last visit, though the prospect of sampling Catherine's food intrigued him. Looking up the address, he discovered the restaurant was around the corner from the apartment of Hannah Rezinsky, owner of his former gallery. He hadn't seen her since last May, at the wake for Claus Von Sem. So many of her older artists had died, and the few younger ones had, like Lerner, fled for more vibrant representation.

The Kreunens' card lay on his table. His phone receiver lay on his table. Together, conspiring. He stared down at the card, fingers scant inches from its edge; he lifted his phone and punched in the number.

" . . . you have reached the office of Kreunen Investment Services . . . "

"This is Jacob Lerner, a friend of Gary Freed's, he's one of your clients . . . he had a painting . . . I need to see it . . . he told me about selling—"

And a click that Lerner thought meant that the connection had broken. He was about to hang up when a toneless, echoey voice spoke: "The painting is ours."

"Who are you to inquire about it?"

"Who is he, Dora? Do you know?"

Not one echoey voice, but two speaking together. Their talk, more statement than question, presented no room for response, leaving Lerner mute.

"Someone who knows about the painting, Denise.

"You mustn't ask about the painting.

"It is ours now.

"It has always been ours.

"We don't allow visitors.

"We don't allow questions."

The line clicked again. Lerner held the phone to his ear a moment longer, suddenly fearful that by his calling them, they had somehow invaded him, slithered out of his phone and into his apartment, and once here they could never be eradicated.

Now, he *wanted* to go out, convinced that staying made him vulnerable to an attack. Outside, he waited at the light to cross

Canal Street for the uptown number six train. Diesel trucks coughed past him, the constant flow of goods and materials in and out of the city. A few times he had seen this street quieted, after massive snowfall brought stillness to everything, a blinding whiteness soon corrupted by the filth of the city. But for a day, a weird and marvelous calm overtook Manhattan. Few people left their apartments. Few businesses opened. Lerner strode down the middle of Canal Street as though alone in an arctic waste.

The walk sign flashed green; the masses parted on entering the crosswalk, veering into the intersection. When Lerner reached the spot he saw a man sprawled on the corner, face overgrown with beard, clothes dark and stained; he stared out at the street, shouting in a voice like a barking dog. Beside him, propped against a lamp post, was a figurine swathed in a dirty blanket so that the only exposed part was its head of reddish glass. Lerner tried to work his way closer, curious about the finely formed glass head, but the pedestrian wave pushed him ever forward.

On reaching the opposite shore, he broke free and turned around, searching back toward where he had been, but saw only the usual cars, delivery vans, and the multitudes weaving their infinite dance.

With nothing to keep him above ground, he entered the subway stairs. Partway down there came the push of an approaching train, subtle first, then a mounting pulse of hot breath. Someone clattered past him. Lerner never rushed to make a train, considering it an unsavory attribute of the wage-slaves, demeaning to his artistic nature. He would be the anti-frantic one. At times, he purposely impeded these frenetic wagers, taking more space on the stairs so no one could pass without pushing (many did), being slow and meticulous with his insertion of token or fare card. But most of the time, he stood aside, allowing all inclined to speed to their destinations.

This tube was the perfect symbol of the city's contrasts; the broken people, the rushing people, enjoined here, encased in metal lozenges hurtling down a black throat. If the city had a god, it would possess the deepest, darkest maw imaginable, swallowing everything and spitting out shiny bits to keep the worshippers preoccupied.

Perhaps it would have been better to have lived in Schuyler's time, when the chaos was contained within a few blocks, though the onrushing sprawl could never have been stopped. New York had always served as the nation's model. The rules of commerce: build up tear down crush nature—a triumph of engineering over geography. The grid, imposed on the landscape, which had to conform or be banished, given the small freehold of Central Park, though that was, of course, merely artificial nature. What if, instead of leveling hills and covering streams, New York had grown at its landscape's dictate, following contours and inconsistencies? What then for the rest of the nation? Perhaps commerce would have been replaced by coexistence and harmony, cooperation instead of endless divisiveness.

The train slowed and shuddered its way into the 59th Street station, and Lerner (again being contrary) remained in his seat until movement ceased. Pushing through the entering mob, he alighted on the landing and moved toward the exit. He soon found himself alone, one of those rare moments between the city's heartbeats, when one could imagine oneself the sole inhabitant of an abandoned street, or subway stop, an experience of such minimal duration that it might transpire unnoticed.

The slap of Lerner's footsteps echoed in the empty corridor. Posters decorated the walls: for jewelry, for clothing, for Hollywood movies. The floor sloped gently downward and the passage narrowed, concrete surface becoming pitted, uneven, turning into rock, dirt, and mud. A fissure ran along the floor, and in it, water flowed, a swift ribbon.

An arm of sunlight bounded in from the entrance, and Lerner looked out from a cleft above a creek. The ribbon of water tumbled over the lip and into the creek, a shower bejeweled in the setting sun.

How beautiful it all was! Just as Schuyler had entered the shadow-city—Manhattan of Schuyler's future—Lerner had left *his* city by unknown paths and entered the uptown of Schuyler's time, when farm, field, and wood still reigned. Or . . . perhaps this was an extension of the book caretaker's downtown oasis.

Lerner skimmed down the bank to the water's edge and stepped across, using groupings of scattered stones for a bridge. The ground on the opposite side was lower, and once past a line of trees with ridged, shaggy bark, he found himself on a narrow cart-track. Shaggy-bark trees flanked both sides, their branches meeting overhead. The wind blew in warm gusts, but beneath the interlocking branches, the air was still and cool, so much cooler than the stale city-air, and heady, a brilliant tonic of oxygen for lungs he hadn't realized were starved.

The track opened into a broad meadow, where cows grazed, a dun-colored variety with short, thick horns; one looked up at his passing, ceased its chewing, and stared, eyes dark, unfathomable; Lerner stopped, caught by the dark eyes, finding in them a minute map of the city, of the city that might have been, ribbons of grass and fern replacing concrete, hills populated by tree-towers that dominated the island . . . then the cow moved toward him, and he took a reflexive step back, startled. He resumed his walk, wary of the lack of fence separating him from the herd. Did cows charge pedestrians? He didn't think so, but cows were well outside his normal range of experience.

Farther on stood a square house, pale stone two stories high, with a thatch roof. He expected he would soon reach it, but a peculiar enfolding of the terrain had made the house appear closer than it apparently was. He walked faster, uneasy in this solitary world after so long on mobbed city streets.

Aside from the cows, he saw no apparent signs of activity, no smoke roiled from the chimney, nothing moved past the windows. The scene had the static quality of a painting, or a diorama.

The front door came into view, a solid slab of wood painted dark terra-cotta. A stone path led toward it. He thought he might knock on the door and see where he was. But what would he say? What *could* he say?

From behind, a growl erupted, the sound of a gigantic, grotesque beast, terrible to behold, loaded with viciousness and fury, fueled by mistreatment, neglect, and torture. Lerner whirled around to face the creature . . . fanged and razor horned, a snout of flaring nostrils . . . he turned, tried to run, but was toppled by an onrushing force.

Sensations followed: a shriek tore up from his lungs and into his ears; a thump as his body struck the ground, cutting off the shriek; a gray haze filled his eyes, as though he was submerged in the Hudson's murk; breath stopped, then pushed outward with renewed force; pressure grew on his chest, a wriggling weight; points emerged from the pressure zone, pinching his torso; and a clamp of thorns enveloped his wrist. The individual sensations merged and separated, waves repeating, carrying him into a lighted chamber, and in this chamber, the gray drained from his eyes and the pressure solidified into a brown shape of dog puncturing his wrist with its teeth.

Which came first—his sight of dog and wrist enjoined, or the pain of that unexpected combination? And the shriek, the old shriek back again, with increased vigor, boiling out of his throat.

At some point, a part of him, remote yet observing, noted the freedom of his right arm, and with it he pushed at the dog mass. His legs took part also—he used them to turn his body, dumping the dog from his chest, but it maintained its grip on his wrist and bit harder. His wrist muffled the sound of its growl.

7

GOOD DOG

"Petrus . . . PETRUS . . . DOWN Petrus!"

These words—from whose lips did they emigrate? Formed by tongue and breath, throat and lip, they hung, cloud-like in the dank air, but they were soon carried off by taxi, by delivery van, by the onrushing traffic of Lexington Avenue.

"Good dog . . . never done this before . . . never."

The words dissipated, uttered but lacking substance, as if their maker failed to coat them with validity.

"Keep his arm up. Don't move him. I'm a doctor." Another voice, then a sharp intake of breath—"It's Jacob!"

This new voice, a tone of concern, of youth's dusty days, of softball, hikes in the woods, marijuana smoke inhaled.

"He's not rabid. He's had all his shots."

Something happened to Lerner's wrist, a kind of sucking feeling as the pressure eased, then a warm tickling slid down toward his elbow. The rip of fabric and a new pressure to Lerner's wrist, tightening, tightening, pinching skin and hair. . . . He opened his eyes, unsurprised to discover Freed bending over him. "I was just thinking about summer camp," Lerner said. He sat up. Standing at the corner, as if unsure whether to go or stay, a woman bundled a dog close, the leash wrapped around her wrist and reddening hand. When she caught Lerner's gaze striking her, she turned and entered the crosswalk. Once on the opposite side of the street, she glanced back at him, then continued.

Freed started after her, but stopped, returned to Lerner. "That bitch. Her fucking dog jumped you for no reason." Agitated, he seemed unable to stand still, bouncing-swaying his weight from one foot to the other. "I should go after her but I don't want to leave you."

"It's okay," Lerner said. He examined his wrist, wrapped in fabric torn from the sleeve of Freed's stylish shirt. "Am I bleeding? It throbs."

"I was on the other side of the street, going the opposite way, and that fucking dog got loose, came right at you from behind and knocked you flat. I didn't even realize it was you till I got over here."

"He was only keeping me from getting too close to the house."

Freed helped Lerner stand, and Lerner took a cautious step toward the curb. His back ached, his wrist too. Freed stayed close to him.

"You're in shock," he said. "Can you walk okay? Let's go to my office. Walking will be faster than a cab this time of day. Probably couldn't even *get* a cab."

"This was all farms once," Lerner said. "You can see them if you try. And before the farms, woods, streams, hills. Gone. All of it gone, even the hills."

The light turned green and they crossed among the throng, the passing bodies awash with evening's colors.

"I think you'll be okay. You weren't even going the right way, did you know that? Maybe the dog was trying to turn you around so you wouldn't miss dinner."

At Freed's office, Lerner lay on an examination table while Freed cleaned the puncture wound in his wrist and wrapped it with a bandage. He closed his eyes, listening to the murmur of Freed's voice on the phone, calling a hospital to have rabies medication sent over, calling Catherine Vanadis to tell her they wouldn't make dinner, and it seemed that as soon as he got off the phone, Catherine was there. She put a hand on Lerner's shoulder as Freed described the dog attack, relating the details with a combination of unease and awe.

Freed explained rabies treatment, telling Lerner he would need multiple vaccinations at specific intervals over the next 28 days. "It's probably not necessary, but we can't take any chances with that crazy-ass dog."

After a time, their voices lapsed, sinking too fast and too deep for Lerner to follow; he swayed on the fragile lip of a volcanic crater, and far below, smoke . . . steam . . . fumes . . . sulfur jetted from arterial cracks stretching to the earth's core, where, should one dare venture, uncountable riches await, a subterranean plain littered with nuggets of gold, diamonds, pearls stacked in pyramidal cairns, assembled by generations of dragons, a race long-extinct, long-forgotten, and in their places, their vacated thrones of antiquity, nothing but shadows — sparks once flew from the dragons' nostrils, twirled upward into the night air, and extinguished.

Unable to rise from bed. *Unwilling?* The covering, a cotton sheet, thin for the warmer months — it lay upon Lerner like a band of iron. An endless sheet, extending in one sweet wave to the horizon, beyond hunger, beyond pain, beyond despair. Lifting it would dent the smooth lines, destroy its mesmerizing comfort. Mornings possessed a magic lost to other parts of the day, and mornings beneath a cotton sheet, old and worn to an exquisite softness, those were by far the most magical. Against his bare feet the floor would be gritty. The trauma of rising could damage an entire day. Entire civilizations rose and fell before such sheets were perfected, before colonizing conquerors discovered cotton fabric, and as the inheritor of their largesse, Lerner wished to do them honor, prostrate himself beneath the cotton banner. Each day, each morning came the need to isolate the exact spot from which to transform sleep into waking. There — the reef of balance loomed; passing over it would risk imbuing the day with lethargy, the dire enemy of art and thought.

Ready to begin the transition to activity, Lerner reached for the remote control to his stereo.

One of his few concessions to the mania for electronic toys, his compact disk changer with remote, pair of speakers in the bedroom and another pair in his studio. He loved, mornings, turning it on without rising from bed. An allowed laziness. A prescribed indulgence that strengthened his otherwise spare life-style and commitment to art. And the morning music was how he always began the day's work, lying in bed under the guidance of word and melody.

A guitar emerged, spare notes, a long, entwining sound that brought ideas bubbling into consciousness. Lerner allowed the notes to re-smooth the morning sheets, adding their own layer of magic, a caress of sound that activated his creative impulse.

... survivors of war—his installation piece—not buildings under construction or demolished for urban renewal.

... victims, casualties, buildings destroyed by conquest and battle, former inhabitants dead, maimed, homeless.

He closed his eyes, bidding layers of bronze arise in his head, casting fantastical shapes of slithering bronze notes.

... war: the only export worthy of a great nation—its benefits could never be denied. But as a nation falters it must take care to prevent a trade deficit, importing what once it exported with such ferocity. Which corporation would reconstruct Lerner's bombed-out structures?

... structures?

... yes. A different scale. Not one large installation. A city of ruins, an area matching the shape of the original Dutch settle-ment, each structure the size of his current pieces, but a mass of them, a diorama—the tip of Manhattan to the old Dutch wall of Wall Street—containing a landscape of tumbled skyscrapers.

... and a partial covering of soil, plants growing, a bonsai tree perhaps—the triumph of nature over architecture.

Lerner hadn't planned to work today. Last night he had fallen into bed soon after returning to his apartment, brought to his door by taxi and a still-concerned Freed. Dinner had restored him, a coconut-milk noodle soup that Catherine had brought to Freed's office, for medicinal purposes she said, but this morning, in addition to his normal hesitation at breaking the spell of sleep, he was apprehensive about the consequences of the dog's assault; moving, rising, would show the compass of bruising and soreness, which he was in no hurry to find. But the Requirements of Art always Defeat their Obstacles.

Freed had said that the wrist puncture didn't need stitches, but he should avoid lifting things with his left arm for a couple of days. No sculpting then. He curled and uncurled his stiff fingers. Freed had given him pain medication, but he wanted to wait till afternoon before taking more. He could sketch—that was the only way to begin a piece like this anyway, map out lower Manhattan, the shoreline and streets. Soon after arriving for art school, Lerner had bought a book of New York history to send to his parents. Looking at the old maps and street grids had fascinated him, laying his experience of the city atop the old: Collect Pond, the Dutch wall, the expansion of the island's girth as land was claimed from water.

Lerner wished he had made it to Catherine's restaurant, which likely stood on the exact spot of the long-departed farmhouse. The farmhouse was connected to Schuyler, or to that group of Stuyvesants; Catherine Vanadis had chosen the site of Schuyler's captivity for her second restaurant, and had found the painting there. No Stuyvesant—her actions liberated the past, where theirs were meant to bury it. Unwitting catalyst, she set all in motion . . . and he stared out toward his apartment's front windows, seeing bricks, the wall of the opposite building; on its surface, shadows of clouds. Yesterday's trauma inhabited a corner cabinet in his mind, a lonely but secure place filled with other incidents, both ordinary and fantastic.

Life in Manhattan inured the psyche to all but the most voracious traumas; confusion dripped from the skies here, desperation paved the sidewalks, and between them the residents carried out the business of the day, rape and wealth, art and love, friendship and alienation, all coexisting as always, sometimes communicating, sometimes not. At least that was what he had been taught soon after arriving from Texas, not at college orientation but in a smoke-filled studio inhabited by his first painting teacher, the one-armed Henri Camelminder (later a fellow client of the notorious Hannah Rezinsky).

Little painting was done in those sessions. Technique could be learned at any time, Camelminder said. This was before Lerner turned to sculpture, when art *was* painting and nothing else would suit, when gods still walked the streets and inhabited the cafés. The less you know, the more familiar it feels, Camelminder often said, and Lerner took that as his mantra, avoiding the intellectualism then sweeping the art world. The same avoidance of intellectualism kept him from speculating on his cross-time joining with Schuyler, their shared glimpses of each other and of their respective Manhattans. For Lerner, it was enough that Schuyler's painting moved him. They connected through art. The reason was unimportant.

Lerner sat at his table cutting melon into a bowl to mix with yogurt for breakfast. Showering had been interesting. Freed told him to keep his injured wrist dry for a couple of days, so Lerner had cut the bottom from a plastic produce bag and slipped it over his wrist, with rubber bands to keep the ends mostly watertight.

He was lucky to have a doctor friend. Though he did have health insurance, it was limited to the catastrophic, covering only what was dire enough to send him to a hospital. Each year, when the policy came up for renewal (along with its inevitable price hike) he considered canceling, but each year he found the money. Others were not as able as he, or were more willing to risk not having it. Buddy Drake had lived without health coverage for nearly ten years and hadn't needed it. Another friend had been bankrupted by surgery to repair her detached retina.

With the world having intruded on Lerner's morning mood, he looked at the calendar hanging on the wall by the table, days and dates a meaningless jumble. The past days had blurred, and as he stared, the squares separated, extending into their seven-day rows, each defined by the number in its upper left corner, and today . . . Friday? Sculpture seminar! He needed to be in New Jersey *that afternoon* for his final session with his students before the release of summer, and for the thesis plays that evening.

He and Tansy had planned to meet at a dinner party before the thesis plays, and he would likely spend the night at her apartment in Hoboken. One of the three plays was set in a landscape of towering boulders and spires, which his class had been responsible for crafting. Tansy's advanced fabrics class had designed the costumes.

After breakfast, he packed clothes into an overnight bag, including his sketchbook and the slim library book of Schuyler's paintings. He called Ventricle Savage and left a rushed message describing his latest idea, saying that he would like to feature it in the group show that autumn, which gave him the summer to complete the work.

Today the air tasted fresher, more spring than summer, a comfort after the humidity of the past week. Along Broadway first, past fabric stores, remnants of a commercial past soon to be overtaken by encroaching national chain stores, an incoming tide leaking from SoHo, a reclamation actually, as these blocks had once been a shopping area for the elite: here, a parking lot at Grand and Broadway, which on weekends hosted a flea market, was once a grand Lord and Taylor. Sharing the sidewalk with tourists, shoppers, visitors to the remaining galleries, he was the walker from the past, accompanied by the spirits of deceased artists, an excited chorus, twirl of song and color. Ryder! Piambo! Henri! de Kooning! Warhol! With pride they

wore their mantles, exquisite drapery reflecting their oeuvre—
in death, artist became art.

But not all sang, not all danced, feeling, as they did, the
onrushing footfalls. Mr. Artist Sculptor Jacob Lerner among
them, was he truly a fit heir? Alone, always alone in creation,
alone on the street of millions. "Not Alone," the chorus cried,
and cried again, until. . . .

He wasn't there yet, had yet to reach the until, and perhaps he
feared the prospect.

Clarity descended, the biting clarity, separate from the
body, and with it, he smiled, a self-satisfied smile as he crossed
Broadway at Prince, striking west, thinking to enter the subway
at West Fourth rather than Broadway/Lafayette. This was
the block where he once saw his then-wife Beth embracing
her lover, a man Lerner had known but not befriended, had
known but obviously not as well as Beth, and seeing them,
seeing them . . . he had attacked, an onslaught of rage and pain,
smacking the man's head into the building. Buddy Drake had
been with him, had stopped him before he caused much damage,
and shuffled him off.

Clarity receded, drifting over the surrounding rooftops, and
he thought back to other walks in the neighborhood, his first
visits, memories more pleasant—art student ogling the galleries,
seeing artists in every passing face. Licked by these memories,
he yearned for clarity, for a sign that he was still that person, still
awed by simplicity, by movement, by curvature and structure,
shapes bathed in golden light or purple dark. With time comes
age, and with age the exhaustion of the soul (whatever soul is),
but that wasn't him either. Not impressioned youth or jaded
flop. He hadn't changed. Older, having gained in experience and
knowledge, and the ability to use what he gained to shape him
further—the accumulations of existence form a mosaic, movement piece by piece toward the whole. He preserved his youth
by accepting his age.

Schuyler? His face, his tattered gray coat, how he had wrapped himself in it for warmth as the southward-bound clipper ship passed Cape Horn and ploughed from Atlantic to Pacific, then east, east, ever east, through a continent made from ocean, past islands scattered like the crumbs of a god's lunch. At which did his ship call? A new land. A safe land. Beaches, reefs, rainforest, gods of stone and earth. Distant. Past. Gone.

8

THE ACROBATS OF DESIRE

And here? Washington Square Park. The blocks, where had they taken themselves? Receded with the years. Brought to this spot, then abandoned. Lerner sat on a shaded bench, filled with a sudden exhaustion. A dog passed, a poodle, leading a dark-haired woman. On the next bench, a man and woman, young—college students?—sat eating ice cream bars. The doughy richness of spring turning to summer surrounded them all.

Beth again? Uncalled for, this phantom former wife and lover. Not welcome amongst the dancing singing ghosts of artists past. He knew he had never fully dealt with the refuse of that fiasco. They had met here in the park for the last time to discuss their divorce. She had moved back into her old apartment, having sublet (in this city, no one willingly gives up an apartment), and really, once she had removed herself, shoes and all, few artifacts remained besides memory. Lerner's place returned to being his alone, as it had been when he first claimed it, as it still was. She had married the man soon after. Perhaps they had stayed together. Feeling merciful, Lerner granted them happiness. A change in the weather could do that, open one to magnanimous gestures.

In the center of the park, a performance was being readied. The stage, a table-sized area with a backdrop painted to look like Manhattan row houses, street and sidewalks dotted with trees, horse-drawn carriages, and pedestrians . . . but something was off . . . and the realization made Lerner laugh: The scene was an adaptation of Magritte's painting, *The Dominion of Light*, which showed a dark street overhung by a daytime sky.

A banner draped from the front of the stage read: THE ACRO-BATS OF DESIRE.

Drawn by the Manhattan street scene, Lerner moved to a closer bench and sat, affixed, thoughts of trains and classes shunted, consigned to a distant hum, a whisper that he thought to heed but then ignored, and once ignored it receded, withered, soon emitting nothing but an occasional scent of remembrance.

Cymbals clanged, the backdrop split in the middle, and through the gap appeared a marionette fashioned from rosy glass, a dapper man-puppet about three feet tall with a gray felt bowler on its translucent head and silk tie hanging down its chest. Arms wide, the marionette welcomed the crowd of passersby and observers, and soon the numbers billowed, thousands crowded the park, cheering the escapades of the glass marionette, which roamed the stage, peering between unseen rocks and into the branches of imaginary trees. A hidden saxophone player accompanied, expelling a sustained a frenetic screech . . . until . . . both marionette and music stopped. The dapper marionette stood, viewing the crowd, with a hand held flat over the eyes as if shielding them from the sun. Searching for someone.

The bottom of the backdrop rumbled, then pulled apart on one side, and a nude, puppet-sized woman appeared, holding what Lerner thought was a large, dark snake, but as she released it, causing it to swing back behind her, he saw it was her hair, a braid hanging past her thighs. Lean and muscular, she stood at least half a foot taller than the dapper marionette, which at first seemed thrown off by her arrival, this unexpected Amazon. The saxophone shrieked, and the marionette backed to the edge of the stage, stopping with its heels overhanging the air. The nude woman remained near the backdrop, and after a moment's pause, the marionette took one step toward her, then another.

She reached out, holding her hands palm up. Apparently recovered from its initial hesitation, the dapper marionette moved closer and grasped her waiting hands. They stood for a moment, facing each other, arms outstretched, fingers entwined. The music resumed. Matching their movements to the music, the marionette leaned back and the puppet-woman put one foot, then the other, on its thighs. They began a slow ballet of balances, the marionette anchoring or lifting the woman. Despite the difficulty of the act, she managed to keep from entangling herself in its strings.

Lerner pulled out his sketchbook and drew her, resting the book on his legs and sore wrist. With his pencil shaping her figure, an erection pushed the fabric of his underwear and jeans, which surprised and embarrassed him—why now?—he had been drawing nudes for fifteen or more years, first in college, then periodically at Minerva's studio on Spring Street.

The dapper marionette lay on the stage with one arm raised to form a pedestal, and the woman, muscles etched by the needs of her profession, held herself in perfect balance, legs outstretched, arms straight, both hands holding its pedestal hand. She froze there, a time-worn statue against the backdrop of Schuyler's New York. Lerner sketched, entwining her body with the buildings behind her. Doors opened, a group of men in top hats gathered in the sitting room to plot their next acquisitions. The puppet-woman watched, unseen behind the veil of a century, until the men dissolved into dust.

The puppet-woman lowered her legs to the stage, and the marionette rose to stand beside her. They bowed and the audience applauded. She smiled, and the smile gratified Lerner; her face had previously been so immobile that he had worried she, however lifelike, was a puppet too. A waltzing bass line joined the saxophone. The woman wrapped her braid around the dapper marionette's arm, and they danced, holding each other close, the marionette's face pressed between her small breasts.

Lerner sketched, putting himself in place of the dapper marionette, cheek to breast, cheek to chest; heat from her body filtered into his face and traveled down his neck.

The music's tempo increased; notes accelerated, collided, casting splinters into the air, showering the crowd with their translucent forms. Facing each other, hands linked, the marionette and woman spun. Her long braid unwound from the dapper marionette's arm and swung outward with the momentum, tracing designs in the air. Twirling ever faster, her feet lifted from the stage, her body splayed out in line with her braid. Woman and marionette merged into one rotating creature with feet on two ends (one set airborne, the other rooted) and two heads in the middle. But with a final screech of saxophone, they separated, a quick cutting movement. Accompanied by silence, the woman flew up and up, arcing out over rooftops and water towers.

Alone on the stage, the dapper marionette stopped spinning. Alone in the park, Lerner sat on his bench, torn by the abrupt and inescapable exit of the woman. The dapper marionette looked at Lerner and spoke.

"Did you know that Washington Square used to be a graveyard? For the poor, for slaves, yellow fever victims." The dapper marionette's voice was smooth like its rosy body, clear like a glass flute. "There were over 20,000, most of them still here. To make the park they scraped out the top few layers and dumped the bodies elsewhere, dead black people obviously having the same rights as living ones. Then they leveled it off, planted trees, grass, and said *c'est fini*. Seems like a crappy thing to do, but what do I know. I'm just a fucking puppet."

Milky fog crept down from cloudy heights, pale film populated by scattered shimmerings, like a shroud of fireflies, distant at first but drawing closer, enveloping Lerner with a subtle flicker, a cold, tactile glow; he shivered, huddling into himself for warmth, but the chill crawled inside, claiming ponderous and painful custody. Freezing teeth clanking jackhammers shattering into ten thousand ivory fragments flying straight out into starlit ocean depths. Fog withdrew, and the stage vanished, replaced by a stump, remnant of an immense tree; a boulder took the place of Lerner's bench, and a glade of trees circling their seats replaced the park. Amongst the trees, all signs of the city receded as if *they* were the dream. Warmth replaced the cold, transforming the cold into memory of past cold, easily banished.

"I like this spot," the dapper marionette said. "Sometimes I just have to get out of the city."

The dapper marionette, now untethered by strings, threw itself forward, cartwheeling from rock to ground, stopping in front of Lerner; it pulled off its hat and bowed. Bushy red hair covered the top of its head. It ran a glassy hand through its curls and replaced the hat.

A fine hand had been responsible for the work, the subtle curve of chin, lips curled into a hint of smile, and the rest: facial structure, arms, torso, and below the waist . . . but on the stage, it hadn't looked like *that*, not this . . . appendage . . . erect, exaggerated size, a darker hue than the rest of its rosy body, detailed map displaying veins, uncircumcised tip, the whole thing pointed outward like that of a fetish statue.

"Fuck man, what do you expect?" the dapper marionette said. "You saw her. All that rippling flesh. Good god it takes concentration not to let my thing hang out while we're on stage. Don't want us to be cited for public indecency."

The dapper marionette flopped to the ground. The penis disappeared, re-absorbed, perhaps, into glassy thighs.

"Have you ever . . . ?" Overcome by a sense of the absurdity of talking to a marionette about sex, Lerner let his voice fade without finishing.

This beautifully crafted, animate glass figure—he had seen it carried by Chinese children, sitting with the howling man on the street, even Catherine Vanadis had mentioned a marionette show—the dapper marionette had been appearing to him since he first saw Schuyler's painting.

"She'd like you, I'm sure. Not that I can speak for her. She's got her own mind, you know. Just because the act calls for nudity doesn't make her easy."

"My . . . class . . . I'm going to be late."

"Fuck's wrong with you? Sit here, let it fly, man."

Lerner's sketchbook lay open to the drawing of himself dancing with the woman. With a quick thrust of an arm and nimble fingers, the dapper marionette grasped the pad and pulled it closer.

"Not bad. Interesting transference." The dapper marionette flipped back a few pages, grunting at each drawing of the woman. The next page showed a sketch Lerner had made from memory of Madame Burgundy. The dapper marionette glanced at the sketch, then shut the book and gave it back to Lerner.

"In Java, Schuyler started making Wayang puppets. For a while, they all had the face of Madame Burgundy."

"I want to sculpt her. So she'll be preserved in something besides that . . . painting."

Again, the milky fog draped them. Their surroundings shifted, to the entrance of a room at the Metropolitan Museum . . . but, it wasn't. Lerner's vision, muddled by the fog, began to clear. Not the Met . . . a gallery, a private gallery, that of the Kreunens, a floor of their 65th Street home. A hallway lined with paintings: each one he saw he hoped would be . . . but here a farm, then a city street. The hall ended in a larger room, filled by a platform, twenty, twenty-five feet square, over which hung a gaudy canopy painted with streets and buildings. And on the platform, a model of a city. A poster, encased in glass, illustrated by a woodcut of New York Harbor, proclaimed: "The Miniature City . . . in Carved Wood . . . perfect *fac-simile* of New-York, representing every street, lane, building, shed, park, fence, tree, and every other object . . . 1846." Not long after Schuyler then. These buildings represented the New York that Schuyler knew, the New York of Madame Burgundy.

Where did they find this magnificent, impossible object?

Something so brilliant, so marvelous shouldn't be hidden . . . he crept closer . . . face hovering over rooftops, and there, Colonnade Row fully restored. He sent his gaze flowing along miniature streets, replicating Schuyler's route, but the light fled in one long, tearing rasp, leaving him blind, gasping—light, sweet light, desert me not in times of peril!—and unseen arms, long and dank, reached out, wrapping him. He lunged away from the city model, finding himself back in the hallway, dazzle of light restored.

"Next room," the dapper marionette said.

Down the hall then, past a leather armchair, blue with gold trim, that likely cost more than the yearly rent of his apartment; a door opened into another room, and inside, the painting of the garrotter and the woman, Madame Burgundy.

The face of Madame Burgundy, once calm and proud, now bore the expression of one resigned to loss, sadness, tragedy, as though aware of and accepting the doom promised by the man behind her.

And the garrotter had moved several steps closer.

What happened, after the five become one? Did the painting's outward appearance fluctuate, frame-by-frame like an animated film? Lerner had once watched the animator, Lazlo Strahan, in his studio as he worked on *Penguin Politico*, the last brilliant creation before his stroke. Few people bothered to master the craft anymore. Madame Burgundy's portrait was an early animation, though not aimed at entertainment. Its buried layers served a darker purpose.

Lerner glanced toward the dapper marionette, which lay propped against the wall, a block of lifeless glass. When he turned back to the painting, the garrotter had resumed his position in the doorway.

"I need something," Lerner said. Looking around but not finding anything appropriate, he unbuttoned his shirt and hung it over the end of the painting, shrouding the garrotter's twisted face. Lerner smiled, calmed by his action. "I should paint the bastard out of it." He turned to his companion, the dapper marionette, but the dapper marionette was gone.

Lerner dragged the leather armchair into the room and took a tin box of colored pencils from his satchel. He drew Madame Burgundy, filling pages with details of different features, an overall view of her posture, her face, eyes, hair, committing her to paper and engraving her into his memory.

In his drawings, he glimpsed a different world, fountains glittering on sunlit plazas, fewer cars, more pedestrians. More life, but not the frantic life of *his* Manhattan—everyone in constant flutter of movement, unable to stop out of fear that in doing so, something vital would be lost, taken forever and unable to be regained by credit card purchase. In the city, stopping meant death. Economic law stated that growth and profit must always increase at an acceptable rate. Earnings up? Yes, that excited the market forces. Frenzied shopping for The New protected the public from the decay of urban ghettos, where life bore the value of rotten meat. War zones don't have to be overseas as long as the victims have dark skin.

"Time's up," the dapper marionette said, having re-appeared at some point in Lerner's flurry, to perch on the chair's padded arm. It reached down and flipped back a few pages. "Not so bad. Don't forget your shirt."

Class . . . not possible now. He would make excuses, something, the dog attack—after such a trauma, no one would criticize him for taking the day off. "I have to take the painting. They can't be allowed to keep it. Not theirs." He slipped his shirt back on and reached to lift the painting from the wall.

Madame Burgundy's face—he would fill the city with sculptures of it, Freed's apartment, Catherine Vanadis's restaurants, each would have its version. Shapeless, everything shapeless but her face. Though what does shapeless mean? *Everything* is a shape. Mud is a shape. Shape is abstract. Shape is representational. In his studio, cold, damp clay formed successions of shapes, each imbued with a part of him, electrons, quarks, soul—the definitions were unimportant. An artist scatters his work with minute keyholes into hidden lands.

He longed for the damp dustiness of his clay, but found himself instead deposited onto the New Brunswick train.

Outside the windows, the world passed. His watch displayed a later than usual time: not his regular train then, but the one after. He might not even be late to class. Today, this moment, felt beyond him, as if he needed to catch up to the future, having lived, experienced, half a day or more in the last hour. The dapper marionette had taken him through a window, several windows, then returned him, but without the painting. His satchel lay on his lap; he took out his sketchbook . . . his drawings from the painting of Madame Burgundy were still there! He ran a finger along the line of her jaw and closed his eyes.

After his class, Lerner went for an early dinner at the home of a member of the drama faculty, a woman who had once attempted, without success, to charm him into constructing an elaborate set for a small production of one of her plays.

"Bernard is cooking," the woman said. She gave him a perfunctory embrace. Bernard was a friend of hers, a chef with problems retaining restaurant jobs, and when he was out of work the woman would hire him for dinner parties. His creations were undeniably flavorful, though veering too far in the classical direction for Lerner's taste.

The woman placed him across the table from Tansy, who had arrived a few minutes earlier and sat, head turned, listening to her neighbor, the gray-haired impresario of the drama department. Lerner admired the tilt of her chin and sweep of red hair along her shoulders. She wore one of her designs, a creamy-black sheaf of fabric that fastened over a shoulder, leaving the other bare.

"Your poor wrist," she said, disengaging from the impresario. She reached past their plates and glasses for his hand, touching the edge of the bandage with a fingertip.

The stage: bare save for the boulders made by Lerner's class. Lighting: dim and tinted blue. From the sides, one person entered, then another, and more, dressed in gray robes with stiff, high collars. As they moved, a fluid waltz among the boulders, each spoke a line, so that the words sounded from all parts of the stage.

— A beast born long ago in a cauldron of ice.
— Its porcelain underbelly shone with herbal heat
— A rash of light oozed from its carapace
— All rancid buttery red, glowing before a backdrop of cloudy night sky.
— Stars banished behind the virulent blackening veil.
— The beast swam.
— The beast flew.
— Both simple passages through disparate elements.
— Luminescent swaths it cut, purposeless wanderer or questing for elementals?
— Only it knew.
— Then as well as now it yearned for a way to approach the universal, to transform gas into solid, sorrow into joy, or joy into sorrow.
— For to it, all were the same.
— We call it beast, but by that we mean no insult, for we are all of us beasts.
— This beast flew
— And the land parted to allow its passage.
— On one of its journeyings, it came upon a woman weeping beside a broken statue of her father.
— In a clearing outside her ancestral village.

— Asking, why are you weeping? would not have resulted in answer, for if the beast revealed its presence she would have fled.

— Hiding itself in the air, the beast waited.

— As the woman knelt, in a clearing outside her ancestral village, a traveler happened by, who though man was more beast, beast in its way of taking what it found as prey, and it took her, tearing her clothes to paw the ripe flesh beneath.

— Before the man could complete his rape, the beast revealed itself.

— The man died of fright.

— The woman, struck blind by joy.

In bed with Tansy that night, no one else existed, not Madame Burgundy, the acrobat woman, or any hybrid. They made love with tenderness and desperation, saying little, careful with his injured wrist, then both drifted into slumber.

Lerner woke in the gloom and shadow of deep, early morning night and lay on his back, needing to piss but not wanting to leave warmth-comfort-bed, Tansy's body beside his, breathing the easy breath of untroubled sleep. He knew the only way to return to sleep would be to rise, walk into the bathroom, yet . . . the prospect seemed daunting . . . trek of miles across a floor littered with remnants of degraded civilizations, each built upon the carcass of its predecessor, compacted lumps of frightened ghosts longing for release . . . he slipped out from under the sheet. Afterwards, not yet ready to return to bed, he sat on the sofa in Tansy's living room. Through a curtain gap, a streetlight illumined a shoe in its path, a comfortable sandal of cork and leather that Tansy had worn that day. What is real? Tansy. Reality clung to her like an unconsumed force. He had lived a day in unreality, lost among the murk of ageless wandering. In the Kreunens' gallery, did Madame Burgundy's portrait experience the night as restlessly as Lerner? He had seen it . . . sketched her—the dapper marionette should have allowed him to take the painting. He could have painted out the garrotter. Or destroyed the thing, burned it. Yes, that's what he would have done. He needed to find the dapper marionette again; this time *insist* he be allowed to do the necessary.

"Would you want more out of our relationship?" Lerner asked later, as they drank coffee in Tansy's kitchen, all nighttime rumination banished by sunlight.

"I'd like to go away soon, now that classes are finished. My aunt says I can use her home in the Poconos. Before I go to Massachusetts to work on the Shakespeare festival."

Lerner watched a cat walk along the top of the fence separating Tansy's building from the neighboring one. "I can't go anywhere for at least a month," he said. The cat stopped, arching its back at something beyond Lerner's sight. His question answered, they continued to sip their coffee, and later, he cut up strawberries and bananas while Tansy made pancakes.

REAL ESTATE HISTORY

Oscar Kreunen arrived in New York City in 1786 after selling the family estate near Albany. With his wife and three young children, he relocated to lower Broadway. Once in Manhattan, Oscar set himself up as a merchant dealing in metal household objects; he also bought land that included would eventually become 5th Avenue and 33rd through 41st Streets. A family never interested in displaying its wealth, the Kreunens nevertheless inhabited a variety of fashionable addresses, from time to time relocating farther uptown ahead of the waves of urban expansion: Lower Broadway, Washington Square, 40th Street. In 1880, Archibald Kreunen built their current home, on 65th Street between Lexington and 3rd Avenue. Though appearing to be a group of three separate brownstones, inside its walls is a single residence for the extended family.

Willem Kreunen, great-grandfather of Dora and Denise, wrote in his diary soon after the family relocated to 65th Street:

> Papa moved us to a new house. My old room was nice but my new room has a castle in it. That's where I sleep. It's mine and no one else is allowed inside.

The Kreunens assembled wealth much like others of the time, but unlike most of the New York moneyed class, they rarely engaged with New York society, held no costume balls or ten-course dinners. They conducted business in a small building on

Pearl Street. Unlike investors such as the incomparable John Jacob Astor, who continuously bought and sold property, reinvesting the profits, which grew to seeming infinity, the Kreunens increased their holdings through reinvestment of proceeds from other businesses; property once obtained was rarely sold.

Their most profitable investment over the past twenty years was a string of parking garages scattered throughout most of Manhattan, which provided a constant flow of income. Many of the investments recommended to clients of the sisters included shares in such ventures. Gary Freed owned one percent of a garage on 12th Street.

After the death of Dora and Denise's parents in a car wreck when they were in sixth grade, the girls were raised by their childless, unmarried Uncle Nelson. Having exhausted their summers since age fourteen learning the family trade, they required only two years at the Wharton Business School to complete bachelor's degrees and another for their Master's, after which they became full members of the firm.

In accordance with family tradition, they shunned publicity, re-investing their money and serving a limited clientele brought to them through referrals. No doubt there were others like them, willing servants in the multiplication of assets, but it is doubtful that any would ever surpass them (though compared to that of their ancestors, the sisters' capacity for gathering wealth was greatly diminished, and the necessity of selling several properties to give them an influx of capital was likely).

Would the family line end with the childless and unloved Dora and Denise? For the past ten years, the firm had offered two scholarships for graduate study in business, given only to applicants who excelled in a rigorous series of tests. The recipients' progression through the world of business was monitored, and in 1999, one was chosen to combine sperm with eggs provided by each sister. Embryos were implanted in surrogates. Two Kreunen boys were born the following year to claim the new century.

9

WORK

Lerner left Tansy around noon and took the PATH train back to Manhattan, getting off at Sixth Avenue and Ninth Street; from there he returned to Washington Square Park. He strolled along all the walkways, then bought a cup of coffee and sat on the bench from which he had watched yesterday's puppet show, waiting, looking at everyone who passed, hoping for some indication that the dapper marionette would reappear.

Later, back at his apartment, the pollution of dust and clutter depressed him; he embarked on a frenzy of cleaning: scrubbing the bathroom surfaces, mopping the floor around his stove and kitchen sink. The phone rang while he was vacuuming.

"Fabulous idea." Ventricle Savage said. "Bold and sweeping. Grand and ambitious. Truly."

At first Lerner thought he was talking about the Madame Burgundy statues he wanted to make, although he didn't remember having told anyone.

"Tomorrow," Lerner said, responding to Savage's question about starting. "I'll show you some sketches middle of next week." He told Savage about the dog attack, and they hung up. The answering machine indicated several messages, which he hadn't checked earlier. The first two were Freed and Catherine, asking about his wrist; Freed reminded Lerner to stop by his apartment so he could examine the wound and give Lerner his next shot. Freed had said 4 p.m., which gave Lerner enough time to finish cleaning.

Naked from the shower, Lerner unpacked his overnight bag. He carried his sketchbook to the kitchen table and flipped to the drawings of Madame Burgundy; he tore one out and tacked it to the wall in his studio. Turning back a page, he saw himself marionette-sized, dancing with the dapper marionette's acrobatic partner. Recalling his arousal during their performance, he touched the tip of his penis.

"I'm going to see the Kreunens Monday," Freed said. He snipped through Lerner's bandage and peeled it off. "End of the day, after the market closes—that's when they see people—so it wouldn't get in the way of *your* work either. You should come with me."

Twilight crashed asthmatic and cold, splashing into the sprawl of congestion buried within individuals, the hapless rushing individuals, who spread over the city in complex formations, mean and vicious like the beast-man who tried to rape the weeping woman in the play. Hiding from them, hiding and fearful—with what threats had they menaced the appraiser? And now, soon, him.

They sat at a wide desk, wide enough for their two-person seat, their bodies separated by an armrest, and on their wall, a mural, portrait of Peter Stuyvesant standing tall upon the battlements.

The morass of their colorless voices merged, individual speaker unimportant, words rising from either, or both simultaneous. After a time, he was unsure whether they still spoke aloud; their thoughts, a dull, acidic concoction, pushed directly into his brain.

"You, the artist. No connections. Family?"

"What if your grandfather fell ill?"

"What if something were to happen to him next month, when he goes to Israel to visit his cousin Gershon on the kibbutz?"

"Your parents are in Oklahoma now?"

"Visiting your aunt."

"Anything could happen to them."

At repose in a leather armchair, Freed nodded, as though the Kreunens merely spoke of bond packages, portfolios mired in non-performance, needing only their magical touch to flourish. They sat, now silent, having said enough: no specific threat uttered, no need for it. Lerner could scream, he could flee, but they would always block him. The sky darkened. Nausea roiled his stomach. He shouldn't have come here, into their realm, deep in the land of commerce, where no help could reach him. His strength lay in tree root and soil, in moving, singing water. Rain drummed the windows. Lerner smiled, triumphant. He rose and walked to the door, but it had vanished, replaced by the garrotter, leering, gigantic.

Lerner woke, and laughed. He *hoped* that would be how their meeting passed, in stale melodrama. He didn't even have an aunt in Oklahoma.

Forms, shapes, ideas in three dimensions — what drew Lerner to sculpture, to tactile rearrangements? He worked on the plans for his installation, deciding to separate it into two sections, four-foot by six-foot plywood panels (allowing easy passage through his door). For the initial sketches, he tacked sheets of graph paper to the boards, assigning a scale to a map of Dutch lower Manhattan. When the map was finished, he would trim the boards to its shape.

Alongside his work on the installation, he sculpted a few small clay Madame Burgundy heads. He also cut her face from one of the drawings in his sketchbook and slipped it into his wallet, wanting to keep a piece of her with him always.

Having declined Freed's invitation to visit the Kreunens, work descended again, wiping out distraction. Days passed. Lerner's wrist flexed supple again. At the library he found a copy of the

1660 Castello Plan of Dutch Manhattan, which showed early streets and neighborhoods. He tore the graph paper from the board—too precise, instead tacked several sheets of paper to the wall and drew the island's shape free-hand. Outline only, or streets as well? But he wasn't trying to recreate the old city, merely use it as one layer, substrate subtext subliminal organ for transforming his subconscious to the physical . . . intonation of the grand scheme (grand schemer!) . . . the artist in his haven, weaving magic shapes, free of expectation, loose redundancies cast aside for pure thought, but no, not thought, sub-thought, free-flow of creative essence, for there is nothing else so grand, and so frightening as that . . . the blade, the sharp dance, each stroke, each shape seen as he reached it. Faith? Trust, more like. The will to expend energy and the expectation that the answer will come, each answer leading to another question, another answer, interlocking chains and strands. But the cost? Outside, the passing world, its energies of relationship, fraternity—while here, in the artist's studio prison where solitude holds court, smiling jailer and vicious taskmaster. His own will trapped him, kept him inside, insulated, phone ignored. But his mind flowed free, in and out of random shapes, girders, his miniature city of ruins—the life it once contained held such promise, before the scimitar of greed rent its arteries and severed its spinal cord.

Sawdust gathered on Lerner's floor, jigsaw blade shearing unneeded elements, leaving the shape of his dreams. And the surface? Plaster, tinted gray, the gray of concrete. To make a broken building, must he make a whole one first? And how many? Answers arrived as needed, and new questions followed. The focus of the end is the next beginning. Pauses came, exhaustion of impulse, dissatisfaction with present movement; fortification then, the everyday world of food and companionship, the denial of which is not recommended.

Lerner stood back, examining his creations, indexing his ideas. The city of fallen temples, its worshippers scattered and broken. Though not forever. From each collapse a new civilization arises.

The English replaced the Dutch, but the Stuyvesants triumphed, casting their influence over the new city, the new nation-to-be. But not theirs entirely: free enterprise and free will, twins in conflict eternal. Perhaps neither can exist independent of the other. What use has oligarchy for art, save the art of propaganda? And far too many so-called artists answer the call. Bodies litter the artistic and intellectual battlefields as well as the military ones. Soldiers are not the only heroes who fight for freedom.

Keeping the populace occupied, sated, distracted with an infinite array of golden shiny baubles in the form of electronic toys and sugary snacks.

Slack-jawed supplicants, whose moral outrage big-voice bravado (the more vocal force you expel, the larger you seem), polices the landscape, covering nipples lest some breast-fed child's psyche fragment into irretrievable chaos while cheering the home team to victory. And football rhetoric replaces discourse, when the nation shows only two colors, true diversity banished and ignored. What then what then? Walled enclaves of true patriots, free to shop, free to decorate their homes and bodies with the blood of those not fortunate enough to be born into the correct national family.

But he would not fall. Not to the Kreunens, nor to the current rightist government, though their shadowy machinations spread throughout the land. If the Kreunens represented the incarnation of commerce, then Lerner was the purity of artistic creation. Who would succumb in this confrontation?

The phone rang. For a moment he feared answering, thinking that the Kreunens would be returning the challenge, but he had not yet confronted them. Instead, Buddy Drake's Mississippi drawl greeted and comforted him, a gentle wash of drawn-out syllables and familiarity. Buddy Drake said he would be leaving the next day for his tour with that band. They agreed to meet at Geraty's, the day having passed into evening despite Lerner's watchfulness.

The world of the surface pushed itself back into his awareness.

The thrum of life continued, passing beneath his windows as usual. Lerner tidied his studio, readying it for tomorrow, another day, another joust.

Darkening sky skimmed the tops of the buildings, shrouding the city with stiffening air and the musky odor of molten concrete. From a nearby window leaked the bay of a hound, a muscular tone that reverberated from the neighboring brick and glass. Whispers uttered by structures on both sides of Grand Street carried omens. On Wooster Street, a man, unshaven, hair limp and greasy, wrapped in a gray overcoat despite the heat, sat on a stoop, staring into the street and emitting a dirge, his voice low and rasping. The building, now offices, furniture stores, and expensive lofts, had once been a warehouse, erected by the Kreunen family in 1872—but how did he know that? The journal, the dapper marionette, appeared to have invaded his consciousness, his subconsciousness, laying a foundation of knowledge and insight that percolated, hidden until called into existence by circumstance.

By the time Lerner reached Geraty's, the onerous sky had dulled his mood, casting a shadow of inertia along street and sidewalk. Having arrived before Buddy Drake, he took a seat in a back corner booth and watched the other patrons. He would like to see Warsaw Lorca again, perhaps speak to him, but in this city of millions, seeing a person once was a likely occurrence, twice a rarity.

He listened to the talk at a nearby table: buying and owning, using and selling. Faceless robots purchasing trinkets, here, in the place where trading one's life for trinkets took its start.

Could he be the only remaining idealist?

Seeing Schuyler's Madame Burgundy painting at Freed's had banished the prior simplicity of his life. The dapper marionette, by taking Lerner to the Kreunens' museum, had given him a sign, a warning, an unspoken explanation of the need for resistance to the encroaching spasm.

Allies, he needed allies, but he didn't have the words to describe the increasing density of commercial malaise surrounding them, radiating from New York and enveloping the world. Too few in control, without compassion to balance greed. A mania for money convulsed the land, from the big-business presidential pretender to the unemployed auto-worker convinced that his job's migration to the Third World would somehow bring him freedom, though if questioned he likely would be unable to explain why, other than offering radio talk shows as his spiritual guide. Monopoly was born in New York, when J. P. Morgan tried to bring the railroads together to halt "ruinous competition."

Buddy Drake arrived, followed, over the next half hour, by several other friends. Lerner said nothing about the war, not knowing where to start, not wanting his friends to think he had cracked. Perhaps he had cracked. All his work, and obsession. He should go with Tansy. A relaxing week in the country, walks in the woods, sex—that would set him right.

Someone was telling Buddy Drake to buy a new car, something with four-wheel-drive. "You can totally afford it. Get rid of that crapped-out wagon."

Lerner was unsure who was speaking. All voices had begun to take on the faceless aspect of the Kreunens. "Has anyone noticed there's some sort of über-capitalism out there?" he asked. "Everyone's buying. You want Buddy Drake to buy. These days everything has to be new."

"That's what money's for," someone said.

"There's a force here—everywhere actually, but strongest here. It's a necessary force, yet. . . . " Lerner allowed his words to fade, unable, for the moment, to maintain the fight.

On returning home, he called Tansy. She was leaving in two days and was pleased that Lerner wanted to join her.

10

AWAY

While Tansy drove the welter of New Jersey highways, Lerner described his first moments of seeing the painting. He told her about Schuyler's journal and the Stuyvesants, the Kreunens. Bringing his memories back to the beginning (such a short time ago!) had a settling effect. Stupid of him not to have involved Tansy from the start. She was one of the few able to understand. He should have told Buddy Drake more as well. Cutting oneself off from friends is a dangerous practice.

But was that annoyance on her face? And what did annoyance look like—curl of lip combined with slight furrow over one eye? He had already told her everything about Schuyler, he knew that, and now: repetition, the tired drone of the self-centered boor, filling all space with talk, empty bulldoze words that suck life from everyone around them. He closed his eyes, but he had already seen Tansy's expression, her irritation. That wasn't him! Not a boor. Obsessed with Schuyler, yes, no denying, but not the rest, not a spewer of empty words, talking *at* people, no regard for whether others wanted to hear. He knew people like that, and hated being stuck in their numbing word-flow, a torrent that drowned his own words, slapped them down so deep that they dared not emerge again until the word-spewer had gone.

"I'd like to see it," Tansy said. She touched a hand to his leg. "But I don't see why you can't just ask those sisters to show it to you."

Hadn't she been listening? The Kreunens were part of everything! Of course they wouldn't let him, or anyone, see their secret gallery. And he *had* asked them . . . but he hadn't told Tansy about *that*, or about the dapper marionette. He had *his* secrets too. He shouldn't criticize Tansy when he hadn't supplied the whole story.

Sunlit trees, streams, hills, breezes: these are the tonics for obsession, for despair. Yes, he could have stayed in the city and progressed on his installation, but when he returned to his studio, rejuvenated from time away, the resulting labor would be so much finer. They held hands, he and Tansy, they hiked the trails near her aunt's house, and at night they cooked, drank wine, built fires to celebrate the chill evenings. They read books. They talked. They ranted about politics. One afternoon, they drove to a nearby town to browse the antique shops and other tourist attractions. A flea market had been set up in the parking lot of an abandoned chain-store giant (a concept that gave Lerner a thrill of victory until it occurred to him that the giganti-store had likely replicated itself with an even larger version nearby).

Tansy shut off the engine. Lerner thought, by the shape of her lips and tilt of her head in his direction, that she was preparing herself to say something; instead, she turned, smiling, a smile that said many conflicting things, and opened her door.

Rain had fallen earlier in the morning, and scattered puddles remained in the weathered parking area, but the air sparkled and dissipating clouds revealed patches of blue welcome. They picked their way among the vendors, taking pleasure in the weather, in the wares spread before them: brass, plastic, wood, and items beyond understanding. Lerner considered seeking a bookcase to eliminate his over-population problem, but the logistics of transport into the city was always an issue. While Tansy dipped into a bookseller's stall, Lerner wandered piles of architectural salvage, wrought-iron railings, filigree—the scattered bones of long-dead houses, their voices stilled by age and decrepitude, by the leveler of progress. This town was perhaps a two-hour drive from the city. He could return next weekend with Buddy Drake (and his station wagon) to collect some of these fragments, for which he would find new lives, incorporating them into his work. But Buddy Drake had gone to Europe. Lerner should have arranged for use of the car while Buddy Drake was out of town.

He bought several squares of ceiling tin with the shape of a sailing ship embossed.

Excited by his purchase, he crossed into the bookstall to see Tansy, finding her in the rear, at a display of children's books from the nineteenth century. A thin book with a plain brown spine arrested his attention.

The book's dimensions . . . its age-darkened leather—familiarity slammed into him, the stench of despair leavened by hints of cinnamon and cloves. He reached toward the thin book, but his hand passed into a realm of disquiet, clash and decay flowing outward with sickening force that could only be comprehended by short-quick-sideways glances, lest one be swept beyond hope of return, and even *if* returned, what would that return bring?— the world transformed in absentia, crystalline and fragile, dripping with memories taking the form of scorched pleas for solace, and buried somewhere, melancholy remnants layered one atop another, so lost that future generations might pause on discovering, as if a loose chill swept upon them unawares, but nothing more than that.

Lerner found himself on the pavement, sitting, hugging his knees. Had he cried out? Tansy turned and looked down at him. "Could you . . . that book. . . . " He pointed to the plain leather spine. "Pull it . . . show. Show me the front—I need to see, need to know."

Tansy reached for the book and extracted it from the shelf. Her mouth was set in a firm line, not smiling, not frowning . . . a line that Lerner wanted to understand, but understanding would have to wait—Schuyler's journal had thrust itself up from the detritus of history, and Lerner welcomed it.

All the way back to the house, Lerner sat with the journal in his lap unopened. The blank leather cover, stained and worn by time, by neglect, stared up at him. Numbness spread from the tips of his fingers, crawling along the territory of his palms, a glacial creep into once-thriving lands. A call sounded from treetop to treetop. Welcome? Warning? Symphonic currents surged, infinite directions, but underneath, a faint emission of hope, an attempt to postpone the inevitable crush. Warm colors spread, tints of orange, earth tones, rust, and the scent of bark mulch, masses of it, piled into mountains, and he lay beneath, its home-like weight a comfort, transforming him into sediment, into one layer in a many-chaptered history.

A removal, an extraction, release by his fingers, which mourned their loss, though unable to ascertain its definition. Another hand—not his?—entered, a strong newcomer that gripped with assurance.

Tansy built up the fire as Lerner hugged a wool blanket around himself.

When he was in high school, Lerner had taken a course in scuba diving, and one of their diving trips was to a spring-fed pool and cave in the Texas Hill Country (a cave later closed to diving because of several deaths). The spring emptied into a creek that flowed downstream to his and Freed's former summer camp. This trip took place on a February weekend during which the temperature dropped to the high teens (cold for central Texas), and although the water in the spring maintained a constant temperature of 67 degrees, changing after the dive, from wetsuit to dry clothes, eliminated all warmth from their bodies. Cold enveloped them, pushed the ten-minute van ride back to their rented lodge into eternity. The dive leader fumbled a fire to life, and they crowded around the fireplace until feeling returned.

Shivering depths. Blue on the fingers, blue on the lips. Why is blue the color of cold? Winter had no part in today's chill.

A damp log hissed with released steam. The journal? Had Tansy cast it to oblivion? Perhaps she had thought to help him, protect him from the journal's harmful effects, its memories of suffering. The suddenness of his tears startled him. The lives maimed and ended by greed and intolerance, innocence warped, art corrupted . . . but the memory must be preserved. That was why Schuyler entrusted the journal to Dickens. And from Dickens to Lerner, who gladly accepted the responsibility.

"What's the matter?"

Tansy's voice floated out over the gulf of time. Strong hands took his shoulders. He looked into her gray eyes and smiled. The fire had faded to a jumbled glow, but the warmth had renewed him.

"I was reading some of that journal," she said. "In the bedroom. I had planned to look at the first entry only, but then I couldn't stop." She slid her hands down from his shoulders to his hands, wrapping her fingers around his. She kissed his forehead. "I need to make supper now," she said. "Soup. I think soup would be good for you."

Feeling better after dinner, Lerner stood at the sink washing the dishes while Tansy showered. Their dinner conversation had avoided the journal and Lerner's resulting infirmity. Two nights remained of his sojourn with Tansy. Worried that if he picked up the journal, he would submerge into its depths, he planned to avoid it until he returned to his apartment. He would ask Tansy to bundle it in a paper sack so he wouldn't have to touch it until he was ready.

Having his own copy of Schuyler's journal . . . knowing the

Kreunens . . . his position as artist: the concatenations swelled far beyond coincidence.

"A pattern emerges from *seeming* chaos only with inspiration and insight." (Wisdom bequeathed to him years ago by the one-armed Henri Camelminder.)

Lerner would wait for the emergence.

Hearing the creak of Tansy's return passage down the stairs, Lerner looked in that direction, but she had yet to emerge from the dining room. He returned to the task of cleaning. A few minutes later, he sensed her behind him, then her lips touched the back of his neck.

"I thought you'd be finished," she said.

"I didn't want to use all your hot water."

She continued kissing his neck, pressing her body close to his. When one of her hands slid under the elastic waistband of his sweatpants, he turned off the water.

In bed, they reversed their positions; she lay on her side, her back to him. Detachment colored his desires tonight—the influence of the journal—and he was glad not to be looking into her eyes when his thoughts strayed from her. Long ago, she had told him of a strong disconnection that she had always experienced during sex, distance from the intimacy, but with Lerner she said she felt closer. She said it was because they had been friends first and lovers later. Now he was the distant one. He kissed the back of her neck at the hairline, pushing his face under the wave of her shoulder-length hair, still damp from the shower. Lately, he had been keeping his hair trimmed close to the scalp, and he liked breathing the scent of her pear shampoo and feeling the heavy tickle of her hair flopping onto his head.

He reached around, pressing fingers to her small breasts, taking a nipple between thumb and forefinger, kissing the base of her neck and progressing down her spine, a slow journey to the roundness of her bottom. The muscles of her back tightened, quivered. His penis hardened against her, and she reached around to hold his erection. He moved his hand from her breasts, sliding it over her belly, pausing on her cushion of hair, then lower, stroking; her hands pressed his, guiding his fingers. She breathed short, sharp waves, easing him inside her from behind, and he gasped, detachment banished.

After breakfast, they walked their usual path. A dirt lane led to a small lake, intersecting with a road that ran alongside the lake to a lakeside park. Past the park, another road took them into a neighborhood of bungalows and on to the main road through town. Since their arrival earlier in the week, they had made the circuit several times, occasionally pausing at the lake to sit for a while, other times continuing.

"I've been thinking about us," Tansy said. They hiked along the dirt lane, holding hands. A turkey vulture flew toward the lake. "You know confrontations make me nervous, but Carl"— her therapist—"says 'just say it' so that's what I'm doing."

He waited for her words, but as they walked on for a few more feet without her next statement, he wondered whether she expected him to ask her what it was she was going to say. Mud, remnants of yesterday's rain, made it necessary to walk with care. They dropped hands to avoid a puddle, taking opposite sides in search of dry footing.

When they reached the end of the puddle, she glanced at his face, her eyes meeting his for a moment. Rather than take his hand again, she pumped her arms out in time with the rhythm of her stride.

"We've known each other a long time," Lerner said, hoping to prompt her. "You can say whatever you want."

"We've always said we weren't able to commit to living together, to being more of a real couple. Not just you. Me too. I think I've always been afraid of that kind of commitment. We're good friends. We like having sex together. It's what I've been going over in my therapy, so I wanted us to talk about it."

"You know I think you're great. I don't want to become so

mired in my routine that I can't change anything. Stuck personal life turns into being stuck artistically. I think I would have to live outside my studio, so that the studio remains my separate world. That's been my thinking lately anyway."

He glanced at her, then at his feet, and moved behind her to avoid a muddy stretch. They turned onto the paved road running alongside the lake, which was narrow here, full of reeds and other aquatic plants. "We've been friends long enough that we don't have to hide what we want," he said.

"The other thing, for me, is having a child. Something else Carl has been guiding me through. This isn't some approaching late-thirties thing. I've always wanted to be a mother. Not now, but in a few years. Which means being open to meeting someone else, someone who shares that."

Leaving the road, they walked along a path to a picnic table and sat on opposite sides. The quarter-moon of beach was empty, the water still too cold for swimming. Toward the far side of the lake, two boys piloted a rowboat.

"I'm glad we can discuss these things," she said. "It wasn't as hard as I thought it would be."

No trash, no abandoned cans or fast-food wrappers polluted the park or lakeshore. Perhaps later in the season that would change, but for now, the uncontaminated area provided welcome contrast to the dirt and refuse of the city.

"Being out here in the green makes me think about leaving the city, going someplace nicer," he said. "Temporarily anyway, a visiting professorship somewhere. Or maybe I could somehow make the city green. If I had super powers that's what I'd do." He laughed. A breeze rippled the water. The kids in the rowboat had taken out fishing poles; their boat drifted. "I never fished growing up."

"Isn't that supposed to be a boyhood requirement?" Tansy said.

"There was a drainage ditch near the house—we called it 'the bayou' but really it was just a ditch, though it did empty into a real bayou a few blocks further on. The bayou had been tamed, dredged out, sides lined with concrete, but my ditch was all over-grown and natural. I'd catch turtles and tadpoles and take them home, keep them in a bucket. I got a leech stuck on a finger once. So I did do *some* boy things."

For supper they ate leftover soup, having spent the afternoon cleaning the house in preparation for their morning departure; after washing the soup pot and bowls, they flopped onto the sofa to watch a video, that comedy from the fifties where Cary Grant fights sponge-like aliens, which mesmerize hapless humans with the spiraling dark shapes that ooze from the backs of their heads. Lerner and Tansy sat close as they had many other times, bare legs touching at the knee, here and there commenting on some-thing or laughing at the campiness. An hour or so into the movie, Lerner reached over to weave fingers through her hair, and she arched her neck and back, catlike.

Wanting to kiss her, he leaned toward her. She smiled, kissed him. But when he eased a hand beneath the fabric of her tee-shirt, she pulled her lips from his.

"Since we're going to be thinking about meeting other people, I think it would be better if we take time off from the sex."

Had they decided? He thought she had presented that as something they should consider, not as a fact.

"And last night I started having that disconnection again. I want to pay attention to that."

"Okay." He turned back to face the television.

"I like the way you hold me in bed though." She pushed closer to him.

The movie ended, and she went into the bathroom to prepare for bed. "I'm going to watch TV a bit longer," he said. He flipped through the channels, remaining on sports to look at baseball scores. He didn't want to be petulant, but something about the way she rejected sex but wanted to be held bothered him. He felt rejected. But he didn't need to take that attitude. They had years of friendship guiding them. Or did sex ruin that? Perhaps they wouldn't be able to transition back to a simple friendship. She would be leaving soon for the rest of the summer. The time apart would help. Likely in the autumn they would return to their former, pre-sex, relationship.

Flipping channels again, he stopped on one of the classic movie stations, which showed a silent film. A clown on a stage, accompanied by piano and saxophone, pulled and pulled an endless rope of scarves from the front pocket of his baggy trousers. Scarves piled beside him; when the mound reached hip-level, he stopped and, looking at the audience, raised his hands and shrugged, as if saying "what the fuck?" Then he pulled a pair of shears from his other pocket and cut the scarf-rope. From stage right, someone tossed three balls, one after the other, and he juggled them. A few minutes into this act, a lampshade appeared above him, being lowered on fishing line. It settled over the clown's head, but the clown kept juggling. A spotlight caught the descent of something else, something that sparkled in the light, making it difficult to discern.

The spotlight died, revealing a glass marionette wearing a tie and bowler hat.

A broomstick descended, handle toward the dapper marionette. Taking the broom handle, the dapper marionette swung (highlighted by the honking of the saxophone), slapping the balls from the clown's blindly juggling hands, which continued to mime the act of juggling as if nothing had happened. The piano rolled on, mimicking the clown's motions. The dapper marionette again swung the broom, this time knocking the lampshade from the clown's head. Seeing his tormentor for the first time, the clown's mouth opened, a giant "O," and he tore the broom from the hands of the dapper marionette. Their positions reversed, the clown swung the broom and the dapper marionette fled the stage. The film ended.

11 | JOURNALS

Lerner paced the length of his apartment, booted feet clumping their rhythm on the wood floors. He didn't recall the start of this pacing, shifting from some remote, other activity to this endless back and forth. He didn't recall returning to his apartment either, or what events might have preceded his return. And if he couldn't recall something so concrete as returning to his apartment, how could he be expected to remember when he started pacing? Perhaps he *had* no other history. This was his life, this lone activity. No food. No drink. No sleep. Like some desperate rodent in constant motion on its exercise wheel, pacing directed his days and nights.

When he was in fifth grade, he had a pair of gerbils named Hazel and Dierker. After putting away whatever book he was reading and turning off the light, the song of their exercise wheel accompanied his sleep.

There. That was a *memory*. Something that had occurred before pacing. But the in-between years—he had long since passed the age of eleven. On reaching the far side of his apartment he stopped, turned, and recrossed the floor.

Darkness dominated his windows, a band of ash descending, eating at the city until nothing remained. Sinewy darkness prodded him, catalyst of pacing, and inside his pacing, inside the broad movement flowed micro-movements, ever-pacing cells and molecules. Dark within the body, everything singing through moonless vascular tunnels, audible only at the rarest moments, time-crystals that coalesce and shatter, coalesce and shatter in infinite waves.

Something slammed into his back, knocking him to the floor. Light steps shuffled toward him, glassy feet stopped near his face.

Lerner pushed himself into a sitting position, face level with the dapper marionette. He touched his chest, which throbbed from its impact with the floor.

"We have work to do," the dapper marionette said. "And here you are, pining over your girlfriend."

Was that the source of Lerner's pacing? Tansy and he had driven back to Hoboken where she dropped him at the PATH station. Today? He couldn't have been pacing longer than the crying moon's long journey outward, into the colliding stars and impenetrable dark. He rose to his feet and resumed a course toward the rear of his apartment.

The dapper marionette followed.

"Sorry I knocked you over. I do shit like that. I was in vaudeville, man. Part of my training. Can't help it."

At the far wall, Lerner turned to repeat the journey. The dapper marionette blocked him.

"Stop it. Stop it. Stop it. Stand still. What was it? The fucking journal?"

Lerner sank to the floor and sat, remembering. . . .

. . . . earlier: home once again, unpacking—a corner of the paper-wrapped journal poked from under a shirt.

He tore off the wrapping.

Touching the stained leather, his connection to Schuyler deepened. Fellow artist, fellow warrior—what would Schuyler think of the modern world and Lerner's art? He opened the journal and read. But after Schuyler's final words, at the point where Dickens's postscript should begin, additional pages appeared, further narrative by Philip Schuyler.

Batavia—August 12, 1848

This entry marks the end of my stay in the Dutch East Indies, following upon those written in the City of New York, 1842.

While packing for my return to Europe, I unearthed my New York travel journal and decided to expand upon its pages.

The retrieval of this artifact brought forth a series of feelings and images: the maddening byways of New York, the beauty of Madame Burgundy (how I hope she escaped and lives in contentment somewhere with her loyal husband!). Also my captors, the deceitfully amiable Mr. Lilley, Bookman/Beekman, and the garrotter, that detestable man with whom I was forced to collaborate.

The intervening years—endless sea voyage east around Africa to this tropical land and my new life here—constitute a shadowy realm, as if my departure from New York, instead of giving me freedom, served to ensnare me in dream-life. I know this is not truly the case. The cause of my feeling is the contrast: the slow, heat-steeped pace of existence here compared to the intensity of my time in New York. And, despite the distance, the ever-widening gap of time, I am unable to purge the feeling that I have not truly escaped. Despair is never far. It clings, like the smell of offal, to everything I do here.

For a time, thoughts of Madame Burgundy overshadowed much of my art. I painted her face upon a multitude of Wayang puppets (having become enraptured with the Indonesian art of puppetry).

Of my intersection with the shadow city of motor carriages and broad pavements, there have been no recurrences, no disturbing glimmers of some other Indonesia.

I have spent much of the past year in company with

one Franz Wilhelm Junghuhn, a naturalist of prodigious energy. I have provided numerous illustrations for the books he will complete after his return to Europe.

Both of us have suffered greatly from the unrelenting tropical atmosphere of this place.

I long for snow, for the fair seasons of Northern Europe! (And, in looking back through the pages of my journal, I smile, for I said much the same as my work on Madame Burgundy's painting neared what I thought would be its end.) The tropics have been a necessary haven, and life here has changed me, but the unrelenting heat, the damp, and the lack of familiar places and things have been a trial.

Therefore, I have decided to accompany Franz Wilhelm, to return to the land of my birth.

Franz Wilhelm proposed the idea of traveling to Europe overland, rather than by sea, and I found this amenable, for it will give me the opportunity to see many nations before settling in Holland.

Despite my feelings of despair, my rational mind tells me that enough time has passed since my experiences in New York, and that even if some representative of the group which imprisoned me still searches, my time in the tropics has transformed my appearance enough to throw off detection. I have not used my true name since bidding farewell to Charles and Catherine Dickens, re-christening myself Cornelis Steenkamp. Occasional letters from my parents have arrived addressed to their "cousin" Cornelis. It is possible that these attempts at subterfuge were unnecessary. It is also possible that they have fooled no one.

I will never know what my fate would have been, had I remained captive. Likely, they would have eventually released me with a generous payment to ensure silence. With the passing years, my former suspicions of ill-intent, of bizarre rituals, seem farfetched. Yet, unease lingers, staining my days.

In less than a week we sail, making our way toward the Red Sea and Egypt, overland to Alexandria and from there across the Mediterranean to Europe and home.

A port of call, Southeast Asia, September 6, 1848

Overlooking the darkness which the sea becomes after the banishment of day in lands without artificial illumination, I stood, aware of nothing but my own beating heart.

Everything stone, old stone laid long ago, and against the stone the sea slapped and chortled, unseen but not unheard, wet cracklings as though alive, or at least partway so. Before sun gave way to night, I had sketched the stone, lost in the joy that art brings, the last moment of joy I was to experience for some time.

This ancient city was to be but a way station on our long voyage.

Our ship, the bark *Flying Princess*, captained by Mr. Howard Phillips, had set off from Batavia sandwiched between a sensational blue of sky and sea (the brilliance of which no painter could ever hope to capture), but two days out, heavy seas and foul weather descended.

Below deck, Franz Wilhelm, myself, and the several other passengers passed the time with increasing discomfort. We Europeans had all made at least one voyage, that which brought us to the Indies, but to those not accustomed by constant exposure to the sea's fickle nature, such proved difficult to endure. Above deck, general havoc ensued (or so it appeared to my untrained eye on the storm's second day when I attempted a turn on deck). As a youth, I had spent much time in boats, but had never witnessed such ferocity, as if both sea and sky conspired to propel us to our doom.

After another day, the winds abated. Captain Phillips informed us that we would need to make an unscheduled stop for repair, and for water and other provisions—the ship's stores had shifted due to improper stowage, and several barrels were broken, scattering their contents throughout the hold.

"We are quite lucky to have survived at all," the captain said, expressing himself in the jocular way of those accustomed to danger.

Having been blown several leagues off course, this place was our nearest port of call. Access to its harbor proved difficult, as we had to ease through a cleft in the reef. Captain Phillips sent a ship's boat ahead to take soundings. Had the sea been less calm, I doubt he would have chanced the dangerous passage. On clearing the jagged teeth, one of the sailors, an older hand called Helmut, brought some charm to his lips and kissed it, then muttered a brief prayer.

I asked him what he knew of this port, and he shuddered.

"You may think we sailors a superstitious lot, but those of us who have survived many voyages have learned to trust the stories we hear." He turned and lowered himself along the companionway ladder. When his head was level with my knees, he stopped and looked up at my face, staring hard at me for a long moment. "I won't be walking on these shores, and neither should you if you want to keep your health." With that, he resumed his descent, soon passing from sight.

How I wish I had taken heed!

The town was comprised of a multitude of low stone buildings arrayed along a horseshoe bay and extending back to the surrounding peaks, the stark sides of which formed a natural barrier, separating the port from the interior.

At the foot of the bay, the buildings receded, allowing space for an open-air market, similar to those in Batavia and elsewhere.

Because we would be a few days refitting damaged spars and rigging, and arranging the cargo in a more secure position, Franz Wilhelm proposed a trip into the dark hills beyond the town. An English-speaking Chinaman who ran a maritime business at the harbor had described a path through a saddle of rock, the which would be the goal. Franz Wilhelm soon set off with two other passengers.

Perhaps due to the old sailor's words, I found myself reluctant to accompany them. I remained near the ship, sketching the harbor stones as described, later returning to my cabin to sleep.

But the following morning, as bright and pleasing a day as anyone could desire, I threw off the old sailor's warning and resolved to walk the streets of this curious town.

The people here are of small stature, with dark hair and features similar to those of the Malay. Most of the buildings are nondescript, though a cluster at the base of the cliff on a direct line from the harbor is of greater size and ornamentation (these I studied with Captain Phillips's glass—an instrument of astounding precision fashioned by Alderlieste).

From the harbor, it looked as if a broad avenue led directly to these structures, but after setting off, the avenue branched into innumerable winding strands. I soon became disoriented amongst streets seemingly laid out by a madman: nothing but odd twists and blind alleys. If a pattern existed, I would not be able to decipher it without assistance!

At street level, it was impossible to view anything far-off—though the majority of the buildings were but two stories high, with the tallest having only three, they bowed outward, broad eaves overhanging and casting gloom upon the narrow streets. Having expected a rather simple trek to the larger buildings, this snaking jumble quickly became a frustration.

Throughout my walk, I passed many inhabitants, performing whatever duties and recreations a population does. I saw no open areas other than the market in the harbor, but various buildings served the purposes of trade: kitchen goods, butchery, building supplies, and similar. Many fruit and vegetable stands carved out territories between street and building. Few horses or wheeled vehicles impeded the pedestrian traffic. Nothing and no one had given reason to support the old sailor's fears.

After a time, I reached the hills that enclosed the town, here a steep upthrust of sickly colored granite—indeed the foulest-looking stone I had ever seen, resembling petrified flesh, or moldy pudding studded with stale bread crumbs. A three-story house, the last on the street, bordered the rock.

I thought I would try scrambling up a lumpy outcropping to reach the roof and use it as a platform for observation. Not without some disgust, I laid my hands on the flesh-like stone (which fortunately held the solidity inherent in its attractive cousins of other locales), and made my way upward. On achieving the roof, I raised Captain Phillips's glass (his secondary piece, actually, for he would not part with his finer instrument!); with its aid I surveyed my surroundings. I was pleased to have attained a spot on a direct line of sight with the tallest of the structures I had studied from the harbor.

From my vantage I observed that the first two floors of

the larger structure (which I will, from this point onward, refer to as the temple, for I believe such to be its purpose), were drab like the rest of the town. Beginning with the third floor, elaborate designs of an abstract nature decorated the walls. The complex patterns elicited an odd and unwelcome sense of revulsion, and I could not stare long at any particular section.

The temple's shape was an inverted pyramid. Its third floor and those above possessed the same outward bow as the rest of the town, though in the temple's case, because of its greater size and higher reach, it cast a pall over much of its surroundings. Viewed from the side, the temple bore a striking resemblance to a ship. The roof was flat, save for a small round structure in the center, which had a door on the wall facing my position, and from that door flowed a procession of figures cloaked in hooded robes of a bronze color.

What I saw on that rooftop plaza arrested my attention for quite some time.

The sun inundated the city from directly overhead. Though I have nothing on which to base my assumption, I believe I was observing a daily ritual, held when the sun strikes the noon position.

As the last figure exited, the first in line turned right, the second left, the third right, alternating. Marching along the periphery, they made a circuit of the roof, meeting and passing each other on the opposite side. They returned to the side from which they had emerged and formed a double line, leaving between them a corridor that bracketed the doorway.

A glint from another rooftop drew my attention. It appeared I was not alone in my observations.

Training my glass toward the glint, I searched for its source among the anonymous rooftops. If not for a lucky gap between shifting clouds that sent a shaft of light at the perfect angle, I doubt I would have located the object of my search. What I discovered, I found difficult to accept.

I shifted my gaze back to the rooftop plaza. A section of its floor had risen to form a ramp that pointed down between the columns of bronze-robes. A dark line ran from the ramp to the edge of the roof. I determined it to be a shallow trough that ended at the roof's edge, where a pipe ran down the side, out of my range of vision.

Then, back to the other observer: this individual held a telescope, but that instrument is not what reflected the sunlight. The figure holding the telescope, aside from a beaver hat and an ascot around its neck, was naked, and its body appeared to be formed from rosy glass! I stared hard at the apparition, examining its construction, the well-shaped joints that reminded me of a marionette. And as I stared, this dapper marionette turned, pointing its telescope straight at me!

Though feeling a certain sense of absurdity at the action, I raised a hand in greeting, and the dapper marionette did the same. Then we both returned our gazes to the temple.

As I have said, during my early days in Batavia I became enraptured with the Indonesian art of puppetry. Besides those with Madame Burgundy's face, I made others in a more traditional style. But after a strange and foreboding experience at a performance, I shied from that art, instead transferring my energies to botanical illustration. I had been abed with malarial fever for several days and, thinking it had abated enough to allow me some recreation, I attended a puppet show. As the evening advanced, my fever must have returned, and with it a strange impression ... I began to see a separation, the puppet-shadows acting independently of their masters, roaming the stage, grappling in conflict. The visions disturbed me, and I fled back to my sickbed, shaken by these strange hallucinations. And now, on seeing this dapper marionette, I sensed a dismaying return of my infirmity.

But the activity on the rooftop temporarily banished such thoughts.

During my observation of the dapper marionette, a body had been secured to the ramp. A naked man lay with head pointing toward the lower end, feet high, arms and legs splayed, with fist-sized crystals placed along each hand and foot. A larger crystal stood at the crown of the man's head, making five in total. The long-forgotten phrase "five into one" asserted itself in my consciousness.

The man's occasional quivers told me that he was alive.

The cloud, which earlier had pointed my attention toward the dapper marionette, had dissipated, and the sun caught the crystals, bringing them to dazzling display.

From the head of each column of bronze-robes, a priest (for that must be their function) detached and moved into the doorway of the structure. They soon returned, carrying between them a wide, shallow bowl of highly polished metal with long handles on either side. Keeping the bowl between them, they stood on opposite sides of the prisoner. The shining bowl caught the eruption of light from the crystals and reflected it back down upon the man's neck.

Fire is often used to cauterize a wound, staunching the flow of blood, and persons injured by flame do not usually bleed. But this flame of light showed different properties. The bowl gathered the five shafts into one brilliant blade that slashed downward, obliterating the man's head. Blood flowed into the narrow trough, then down between the columns of priests to the edge of the roof plaza and beyond, to what purpose I cannot ponder.

Blood, five into one, reminders of New York and Madame Burgundy haunted me. Perhaps I should have remained in my Indonesian haven, where, despite my unease, I had at least happened upon no grisly rituals. Was the world teeming with dark forces hitherto unknown to me?

The priests restored the bowl to the building and took their places at the head of the columns. I remained, appalled yet unable to force my gaze elsewhere. The priests appeared to be chanting (truly, all I could see was the nod of their cowled heads, but I interpreted the activity thusly). At some perhaps predetermined point, both lines of priests turned and repeated, in reverse, their procession around the roof.

Alchemists and philosophers say that if one gazes at another person, the observed will eventually become aware of the observer. Perhaps this is doubly true for practitioners of obscure religious cults, whose preternatural senses enable them to hold sway over their followers. Alas, I focused too long upon these priests. Though their hoods obscured their eyes, when the leaders of each line, in unison, swung their heads in my direction, I knew I had been detected.

Dropping flat upon the roof, I made myself as small as I could.

Our pasts—the accumulations of a lifetime—reside within each of us, some parts remaining submerged forever, others surfacing from time to time, and with these accumulations come, if we are lucky, insight, which connects past, present, and future. When those hooded priests sensed my presence, I knew with immediate certainty that clouds of despair and darkness had overtaken me. New York had not released its hold, and now it saw me through the eyes of these priests.

This knowledge threatened to immobilize me, but I forced myself to crawl to the edge and make my way down the rock, the stability of which I found comforting despite its loathsome appearance.

My goal was to regain the ship with all speed. I knew from my rooftop observations that the street pointed in a harbor-ward manner, but keeping to this direction in all the windings and turnings would be difficult. Haste was needed, but not so much that I would become lost.

A right turn here, then a left, concentrating on the business of flight.

The avenue ended in a curve like the head of a question mark, forcing me to retrace my steps to the last intersection. But, which way from there? I turned onto an even narrower lane, dark beneath the leaning buildings. I passed no residents, no other wanderers on the maddening street. The clatter of hooves on cobblestones reached me, an indication of a broader lane somewhere.

Coming upon the ruins of several fire-damaged houses, I glimpsed open spaces beyond them and slipped through the wreckage to a wider street, which in turn opened onto the edge of the harbor market.

A dark coach lumbered in my direction, scattering passersby. I stepped under the eaves of a building to wait until the vehicle passed.

It stopped abreast of my position.

Its door swung open. I was confronted by a dark, cowled shape and a coldness, a numbing serpent that encircled my chest.

On Board Flying Princess *Again*

The muscular sea stroking and pushing the hull of a ship—my ship!—awakened me. I lay in my cabin aboard *Flying Princess*, and stiff roots of an unhappy dream relaxed their hold. I had been alone, cast upon a blackened shore, surrounded by pulpy creatures, octopi without arms, which did not speak, but emanated. Red, black, and gray eddied around their head-bodies, forming clouds, distorted masses that could have been anything, or nothing.

I felt as if I had been saved, but only temporarily. A partial reprieve. The cold red clouds would discover me! Now, despite my relief at finding myself here, the tiny cabin stifled; I rose and made my way to the deck.

Captain Phillips, Franz, and the open ocean greeted me.

"For many leagues you slept," the captain said.

"I and my companions found you amongst a scene of great distress," Franz Wilhelm said. "Rearing, screaming horses, an overturned carriage. And you, lying senseless on the pavement. We gathered you up and brought you aboard."

"The tide being with us, I put off immediately," Captain Phillips said. "What refitting remained could be done at sea."

The ship mounted a swell and I stumbled. Franz Wilhelm gripped my arm. "Come, let us get you below and put some food into you." Franz Wilhelm preceded me down the ladder and waited at the bottom. "We witnessed the strangest sight," he said when I reached the deck below. "As we entered the market we saw a small boy, shiny like some reddish glass, lashing the horses, but when we reached the scene he was nowhere. Run off into the crowd and lost."

I sat down to a meal of fresh bread with butter, and cold fish, while Franz Wilhelm told me of his group's experiences among the sickly stone peaks surrounding the town.

"We never did find a way through. It was effort enough making our way *to* the mountains, along the mystifying avenues. I have seen much geology, but never anything like that forlorn rock."

"It certainly isolates the city," I said.

"Perhaps I will return someday to study the area, though I care for the expanses of nature much more than architectural stylings."

"I will never willingly return," I said, and shuddered, feeling that some residue of cold lingered deep.

And that evening a chill pursued us from the east, a wind that numbed our bodies without filling the sails. Had our ship been powered by steam, such a wind would have mattered little.

"There is wind, and there is something *other*," Captain Phillips said. "More a ghost of a wind than a physical one. The body feels it, but the ship does not."

The sails hung limp despite the captain's attempts at various seaman's tricks. The true wind eluded us. We were becalmed on a mirrored sea.

Becalmed! What a strange word, for I experienced nothing calm in our situation. We were trapped, bound helpless while some unseen doom advanced. Franz Wilhelm laughed at my fears, but he had not witnessed the sacrifice on the rooftop platform nor felt the icy emanations of the limbless octopi.

"We haven't the numbers to carry it out," Captain Phillips said when I suggested using the ship's boats to tow the vessel.

"I, and I'm sure the other passengers, would be willing to take our turn at the oars," I said.

Captain Phillips shook his head. "The procedure has little effect. In truth, it has been used more to boost morale and distract a crew than to make actual progress. Periods of calm always last a much shorter time than appears." He pulled out his watch and held it up for me to see. "Why, I'll wager that we will be moving again by late afternoon, evening at the latest."

But nightfall overtook us without the situation changing.

After dinner I retired to my bunk, declining an offer of a glass of Madeira in the captain's cabin, for only solitude could guard against the chilling calm. Hoping the activity would soothe my nerves, I documented my experiences. On finishing, I flipped back through the pages of my New York entries to view the various sketches of Madame Burgundy that I had interspersed throughout, finding comfort in her serene face. Then, slipping the journal into the pocket of my coat, which I wore as armor against the creeping cold, I closed my eyes.

Lost!

When I opened my eyes, awakened by one of the usual shipboard sounds, a purplish glow seeped through the gaps between the jamb and my closed door. I dozed, and later, strange light filled my cabin, purple like a bruise, and thick, a tactile mist that reached into me with chill fingers. Clouds enveloped me, shapes of dogs and demons. Gaining sustenance from the air became difficult; I opened my mouth wide, trying to draw in as much as possible.

Realms of darkness sundered by deeper darkness, wallowing figures shaped by pitch, by foul airless muck. No breath here, no thoughts, nothing. Coal dust filling lungs, coating flesh, reforming bodies into flowing shapes of molten coal, viscous oily blackness.

"No Phillip, you've ruined my drawing!" his father cried as the upturned bottle of India ink sent its contents

161

over the paper, blotting hours spent designing a fine country estate for a wealthy client.

And his own work? Nighttime scenes punctuated by the glow of a candle, and outside the candle's reach: dark snakes writhed, hidden, waiting for the hapless traveler.

From the depths of a pit far from sunlight he gazed up and wept. He? Detached. Lost.

Not he—I.

I brushed my hands on the borders of my prison, and from this touch recognized the sickly granite that surrounded the town from which I had thought myself escaped.

My father had punished me for defacing his plans, banished me to my room, where I sat amidst my toys. But that was long ago—was it not? This darkness which now oppressed me lived far from my boyhood home.

A scraping issued from a distant corridor, a wet and horrible noise, like that of the flayed carcass of some beast being dragged over pavement.

In the midst of my despair, I remembered the dapper marionette of rosy glass. I hoped that it had not fallen to the same oppressors who had pursued me and cast me into this place. The darkness battered my senses. I saw it as a series of interlocking shards of blackness joined by black mortar. Such complete darkness, layers of it—velvet veils caressed my skin, scraping their way inside, turning my tender flesh into pulp. Even the air here smelled black, an absence of scent so profound it left me stunned and unable to take more than shallow half-breaths.

I must have screamed.

Time passed. I believe I slept. At some point I opened my eyes. Slivers of light had appeared, bursting in through narrow clefts, giving shape to my surroundings. I lay on a pad of rough fabric stuffed with clumps of dried grass, points of which speared the weave. A room the size of two prone men, with a ceiling so vague I could not be sure of its existence. The walls were a combination of natural rock and mortared brick. I could find no door.

My coat still shielded my body. I slipped it off and smoothed it over the pallet as buffer from the grass shards, then extracted my journal and a pencil, writing while the light allowed.

The wall at the foot of my bed swung upward. I forced myself to stand and confront my visitor. A woman stood before me, small like the people of the town, hair gray. She carried a metal tray on which sat an earthenware pot. Kneeling, she lowered the tray to the floor. Without waiting for thought, I swept past her.

And stopped.

Darkness filled the outer hall, a shape devoid of definition, containing only the color of dark and the dark of despair.

I staggered back into my cell, landing on the floor beside the tray. The woman touched my hand, her face expressionless yet somehow communicating concern and sympathy. She removed the lid from the pot and made scooping motions with her hand, then she left. The door lowered after her.

I marked my time according to bowls of rice gruel. Rice gruel with bits of fish and vegetable sustained me. Why was I so hounded and oppressed? Had Vanderkemp's group been responsible for my imprisonment? I thought it unlikely, but the echoes persisted, blood, five into one, violent rituals serving obscure purpose.

Waking another time, I found the dapper marionette sitting on the floor beside my head!

It, or he—because such a being, though perhaps not alive as we know life, was more than an object—wore the same hat and ascot I had seen previously, again with no other covering on his glass body. If the door had opened, the sound had not disturbed my slumber, yet there was no other way the thing could have been placed here. Viewing the marionette-like figure so closely cast doubt on my prior sighting above the maze of roofs, him animated, independent of strings or paddle. Again, I recalled the shadow puppets, and wondered if this figure before me had somehow emerged from the workings of my own brain.

When I sat up, his eyelids flipped open, revealing twin globes the color of purest cochineal carmine.

The dapper marionette spoke: "You're in a fine and desperate state."

My voice ached from lack of use, the air of this rocky prison sapped my capacity to articulate, and, in truth, I knew not how to reply to a talking glass marionette, which continued speaking without waiting for my response.

"Mariners shun this place. Chinese, Malay, Indians, even the land itself abhors the town, heaving up a range of rock to contain the disease."

The dapper marionette hopped to his feet and stood at the doorway, head tilted as if to listen.

I could hear nothing, but after a moment of standing with an ear pointed toward the hallway, the dapper marionette turned and leapt toward the high slits that admitted sunlight.

A moment later my door swung upward to reveal the small woman with my tray.

The next time the door opened was not to admit sustenance. Darkness rolled into my cell, the same darkness that had pulsed in the hall when the door first opened; this time, the shapeless dark entered me, slicing into ears, eyes, mouth, a writhing pain that filled my head. I fell to the floor.

Among the Clouds

"I might be able to free you," the dapper marionette said.

I sat up, and nausea overwhelmed me. The dapper marionette reached out to give me support. "They know about New York," I said, my voice so low and hoarse I wasn't sure I spoke audibly. "The limbless octopi drew things from my head. Maybe they intend to sell me to Vanderkemp's group."

"Tell me about Vanderkemp," the dapper marionette said, and I related my experiences in New York, for emphasis showing him journal entries, sketches of Madame Burgundy and others.

"They recoil from art here," the dapper marionette said. "Art is responsible for the barrier of surrounding mountains. Prison walls made by art, imaginative outpouring transformed into physical manifestation.

"The ones you call Stuyvesants—I doubt they know these cowled priests, not directly, but they obviously worship the same creatures. I've encountered them elsewhere ... Bokhara ... Moldavia. I'll have to go to New York sometime and see. I don't like these limbless octopi, I don't like the way they interfere with the natural order."

The dapper marionette hopped up and began to pace my room, the impact of his feet ringing on the stone floor. I leaned against a wall for support.

"I hadn't meant to come here either," the dapper marionette said. "Flying in from the north, the twisting currents brought my airship too close to the peaks and I ran aground. I had to climb down here to look for materials to repair it. What I need is in this complex, and the best time is during their mid-day ritual. I've been piecing together a floor plan so I can get in and out fast. I can make it so they can't see me, but I can't do it alone.

"My second day here I witnessed one of their rituals. They knew something had seen them, but they can't sense me fully. I'm sure they think you were the one, so I feel responsible."

The dapper marionette stopped before me and stood, glassy red hands on glassy red hips, staring into my eyes, and I thought of Madame Burgundy's dress and her blood that I spread into the canvas.

What craftsman wrought this fine form?

"I have a drug," the dapper marionette said. "We have to hurry. The ritual will be starting soon. If you take it, they can't get inside you, but you will need me to control you."

I swore I would do anything he asked of me in exchange for my freedom. The dapper marionette drew a parchment-wrapped bundle from somewhere and opened it, exposing an oily, lumpy substance that reminded me of the tamarind pulp for sale in the markets of Batavia.

The fetid aroma of the stuff filled the room.

"I have to smear it on the inside of your mouth, especially under the tongue."

I gagged and backed away, my eyes tearing, but the he leaped to my shoulders and forced open my jaws. A numbness pierced me the moment the substance touched the inside of my mouth, then nothingness.

My mouth burned. I gasped and writhed, but a firm grip held my torso rigid. I opened my eyes. Below stretched a desert plain, rock and sand devoid of all but the sparsest vegetation. The seat upon which I rested swayed with a gentle motion, and a warm wind flowed around me.

I had been bound to a wicker seat. Before me stood the dapper marionette, holding out a canteen. In all the world, water is unequaled; nothing else soothes and sustains with such ability. I sucked restoration into my throat and swallowed.

Then, memories, sharp and bitter, flowed into my exhausted mind and I cried out: "Blackest arms ripping and shaking—away away!"

Their emanations, sickly black strands waving, buoyed by subtle air currents, burned where they had touched my skin. I saw it all, I saw it all. Slick and greedy they sought me in the rocky dark. Startled perhaps when their touch failed to win me to their control. Or perhaps these were but a mindless net, its job to hold intruders until the masters chose to pull them in for harvest.

Safe from the stinging strands, I entered a world of crystal, cobblestones of quartz, structures of garnet and aquamarine, populated by bald-headed, translucent beings, their dark skeletons showing beneath shimmery flesh.

A woman stopped. She stood a head taller then me, and wore a short skirt with nothing covering her upper body. Her nipples, a darker hue, floated on translucent breasts, with various organs visible beneath skin and muscle and bone. Her voice, crystalline as well, floated from a nightmare mask of bone and tooth. So clear were her words that I could only understand them as strands of colorless glass.

She held my hand and guided me past fine structures built from crystal lace displaying many shades of orange, enflamed by the setting sun. Her skin on mine, soft despite the visible bones, soothed my fever. The sun also caught the spiderweb of her words, bringing forth a rainbow of hidden colors. What meaning did these hues signify?

A crowd gathered near the seashore, stirring the sand with their bare feet. The woman presented me to several others, each sharing her clarity of skin and tissue, blackness of bone. These people with their glassy yet supple flesh made me think of the dapper marionette—perhaps this was the land of his origin, and in traveling from his realm to mine, his body hardened and compressed, shrinking him to his current size.

Some time passed; several frighteningly beautiful specimens of male and female (each clothed in short skirts like my companion) examined me—tugging at my fingers and the flesh of my arms, pinching my cheeks. They spoke to each other in those clear sounds which tickled my ears and projected indecipherable ribbons of glass into the air. Close by where the waves lapped the bright sands, I sensed a stirring, and soon the crowd separated, leaving an expanse of sand between them as a dark bulk pulled itself from the ocean, a beast turtle-like in its shape and movements but lacking a shell.

Perhaps Franz Wilhelm would be able to identify the creature, but I had never seen its like.

The beast crawled inland, each forward heave propelling it several yards, and my hypothesis was confirmed when it scratched out a trench and began laying eggs.

The clear-skinned folk watched from a safe distance, and when the creature finished, covered the nest, and lumbered back into the waves, I expected them to descend on the cache as their rightful banquet. (In one of his accounts Franz Wilhelm describes the raiding of a nest of sea-turtle eggs.) Instead, five of the folk, two men and three women, took positions around the low mound left by the creature, facing outward as if to deter predation. A woman clad in a skirt of some gold material presented to each of the guards a staff of pale wood carved with a web of fine lines, and the crowd dispersed.

My guide brought me to the gold-clad woman, whose height exceeded that of my guide by another head. This translucent giantess placed her hands on the top of my head and rubbed my forehead with her thumbs as though attempting to erase the color of my skin. The other, still holding my hand, did the same, and after a few moments my pale bones became visible.

This erasure apparently pleased the women, and the strands of their conversation intertwined, a three-dimensional display of unintelligible beauty.

My weight seemingly not more than a child's to her, my guide lifted me and followed the gold-clad giantess back into the town. We entered a low, square building, constructed from blocks of saffron quartz, which proved to be a bath house. They removed my clothing and seated me. They clipped my hair short, lathered what remained, and shaved my scalp clean. Then they lowered me into a warm and fragrant pool.

I lay in the shallow water unresisting, as if drugged, as if observing myself from great distance, bemused and unperturbed by my lack of volition, by my transformation into puppet.

The women removed their skirts and joined me in the pool. Taking sponges, they scrubbed at my flesh until it took on a rosy hue and I could view my bones shimmering beneath the surface.

The sight of my bones shocked me from my stupor. I screamed, a wordless shriek of cascading sound. The women drew back, and as my shriek continued, their distance from me increased, shocked, I suppose, by the volume, by the solid vocalizing, so different from their lacy speech.

Alone, I closed my eyes to my own body and submerged, sinking into the fragrant pool until my face scraped the bottom and I knew no more.

And the warm breeze held me, a grip comforting and strong.

"We're well distanced from that place," the dapper marionette said. "I hope that no other memories plague you, for it was not a pretty thing we did, crawling through corridors of solid scum, all the time fighting off the black tendrils. But here we are. Does the sight not fill you with joy?" The dapper marionette spread arms to encompass the sky.

"Release me," I said.

"You need to remain tethered to the gondola until you are sure of your footing, but I can untie you from the chair."

Free from the confining straps, I leaned over the side of the gondola and vomited. And still weak, I collapsed again into the chair's comforting hold.

Blasts of air, baked by the sun and imbued with the tastes of cloud and aether, tickled my newly shaven scalp. In the distance, the lip of ocean painted the horizon, meeting the blue of sky.

Now I walk the sun-graced deck of a ship that travels along currents of air, far from the care-worn lands I once knew.

12 | BUSY DOING

Pacing over, Lerner stopped near his sofa and sank into the cushion. He closed his eyes. Spirals of interconnected consonants and vowels transformed into lines of names, lines of dates, lines dividing the winners from the starving wretches who inhabit the shadowy worlds beneath everyone's vision, drunken, drugged, broken former humans scuttling for scraps of light, morsels of air, ribbons of purpose, sparkling towers with banners of gold and a blue so crisp it carries taste and scent, a spiciness that jets upward in complex geometries. And out past the horizon, a dark finger-shape that moves at angles to the wind, tacking like a sailboat, a slow progression across the sea of sky. Did the winds ever carry Schuyler home, or was he doomed to sail the skies onward to stranger and stranger lands?

The clicking of glass feet sounded on the floor, crisp on the wood, muffled on the rug. Had the dapper marionette taken up Lerner's abandoned pacing?

Lerner opened his eyes but avoided looking at the part of the room containing the dapper marionette. "You really should have made an appointment," he said. "I just got home, don't you know. And I'm a bit . . . dazed? Events. Events and occurrences accumulate, and I need time to digest. Waiting for the pattern to emerge. Not expecting much." He laughed, a sharp, self-conscious "ha!" and succumbed to the dapper marionette's demand for attention.

"We need to be busy doing," the dapper marionette said. It

pointed a finger at Lerner. "We need a tidal wave of nature to offset the un-nature. Trees, Mountains, Rivers—all flowing downtown to reclaim what was lost. You know what this island was like before the city came? That fucking grid plan—as if nature had no consequence—all straight lines and flat streets, water paved over. As if they were embarrassed by the natural opulence. Can you imagine what the Mayans could have done with a paradise like this? They didn't even have any fucking water and look at the civilization they built. We can make it like it should have been— *you* can! Your legacy! Make it like this cesspit city never existed."

"I like the city," Lerner said.

The dapper marionette's words flowed through him like sugar, leaving him both energized and spent. Blackness returned to the windows, blotting everything. "That second journal . . . you . . . Schuyler—is he here too?"

Glassy hands on glassy hips, the dapper marionette faced Lerner. "Those Kreunens—they'll be coming for you, you know? To co-opt you, or scare you, or both. They don't know why, or what, but they know secrecy; they know that Schuyler's painting showing up again means something. So they cover it up, buy people off. Talk to Freed. See what he says now that he's met with them again. I bet he'll pretend to have forgotten all about the painting. The crap those guys did with Schuyler, that was nothing. Remember the city model?"

If only the black of his windows would change to a pleasing green, and the dapper marionette would leave him to his pacing . . . but that time was past, he had no more need for pacing, not with so much to accomplish, and time, the air, everything, compressing . . . how could he continue his work?

"Well? The city model? Why do you think they had that thing made?"

Lerner lay back on the sofa, staring at the lines in his ceiling. He spoke with a voice exhausted by Schuyler's years of exile in the tropical East. "I can't believe after all Schuyler went through in New York he had to face something so much worse in Indonesia, or wherever that city was. I don't suppose it's on a map. What happened to him later? Did he go back to Europe? No record of him in the art world. I'll have to look for a painter named Steenkamp. I'd be able to tell if it was Schuyler. If he kept painting . . . but let him rest."

"The city, the fucking city, I'm asking you about the city model!"

Lerner turned his head toward the dapper marionette, wondering what internal device modulated its speaking volume. The sound of the voice held nothing to betray its glass origin. It—no, he (like Schuyler, Lerner could not define the dapper marionette as lifeless object), he was a wondrous being.

"The city model was like Schuyler's painting. The Stuyvesants commissioned it, but not just for some petty racism. They wanted to reshape New York to fit their needs. Now we can use *your* art to change it back."

"I had this stupid dream about them," Lerner said. "The Kreunens. They were trying to intimidate me. But that's crap. They're not—"

The tin ceiling-squares that Lerner had bought lay on the coffee table. The dapper marionette lifted them and slammed them to the floor. "You know nothing!" the dapper marionette said, voice blaring over the clang of tin.

Perverse, concrete-trapped heat generated fangs and claws, adamant in its desire to colonize the city. Great mewling things, things not quite dead that had never quite been alive, things indifferent and things of great malevolence. Brick buildings groaned in the night air, the temperature too much a reminder of their fiery birth. Haze clung to walls, a nebulous skin, fumes and particles caged by humidity, bound in the bubble of smog. The buildings yearned for fresh breath to carry off their oppressors. But there was none. Onward . . . onward . . . blank expressions, crossing streets paved with trampled souls, upward-staring silent screamers desperate and desolate, their presence comprehended only by the senile or insane. No glass of chardonnay for these weary laborers, no soothing spa night in a shiny bistro; for them only the thick rot stench of the subways. Offshore accounts fill with gold, the fruit of the toiling class, who receive little fruit of their own, and what does trickle in their direction takes the form of spun-sugar artificial flavor artificial color mockery.

Lost in the maze of heat, maze of days since his departure for the countryside, walking, always walking, the sculptor, the seer, Mr. Artist—but he should be home, working in his studio, not wandering the petrified air of the hopeless. Working—for the idle accomplish nothing—but the dank city night drew him forward, into the wandering joy that fuels imagination. These streets were his laboratory, his sketchbook; inspiration and ideas lay everywhere, scattered jewels for those able to see them. A conflicting vision arose, each detail pristine, complete: the companion to his installation, companion to his destruction city—the rest of the island clothed in the sheltering green of its pre-European state, forest, hill, and stream unimpeded by human intrusion. Yes! Opposite of sprawl, opposition to it all, to every brick, every car, the smothering stifling pavement prison. A chorus of excited yes! accompanied him, an aria of the banished and extinct.

On Hester Street he passed the door of his laundromat, still open despite the late hour; a calendar hung in the window, its back to Lerner, showing scenes of cheerful beaches—the other side drew him, digging into the heavy air of washer and dryer, which churned and spat the heat that now enveloped the entire city. Squares of days and weeks defied him, a meaningless jumble. He had taught his last class, gone to the play, returned from Tansy's apartment, worked-worked-worked, then away. . . . For how long?

The proprietor, a small Chinese woman with a huge laugh, sat at the counter, head drooping, eyes dull; even *her* irrepressible spirit enslaved and beaten.

"Today?" he said, tilting his head toward the jumble of numbered squares.

"Sa-tur-day," she said, slowly. She placed a finger on the date. So now it was June.

Craving neither solitude nor companionship, Lerner turned east and uptown, letting randomness dictate his direction, but each step through the humid muck that masqueraded as nighttime filled him with dread, while around him lonely buildings crumbled, awaiting their turn for dismemberment and revitalization. Were these structures so awful, these tenements and warehouses? Not all that was urban, constructed, should be condemned. Their voices called to him, their song lightening his mood.

Blocks later, he came to Freed's street. Freed owned a unit in a tenement building that had been remodeled and converted to condominiums. The original six apartments per floor had been combined into three, with some original features retained, others demolished, to provide space for those who could afford it. But at least its brick exoskeleton remained, even if it was a sham, an idiot strip kept to preserve the atmosphere of the neighborhood. And not only was Freed home—he was hosting a party. He greeted Lerner, offering a mojito. Was this the *same* party? Did the first sighting of Madame Burgundy await?

Lerner pushed past Freed, moving toward the hall, but no Schuyler hung there. Instead, a bland woodblock print of the city's 1940s skyline.

"I see you've already found a replacement for your Schuyler," he said. Was that an affectation of bewilderment from Freed? "You can't act like it never existed, Gary. I don't care how much money those sisters have."

Freed moved away from him, stopped, waved a hand dismissively. "Sometimes you have to accept the reality of the material world. We're not still at summer camp playing at being grown-ups. Everything has its cost, every transaction has rules. You want a world run by artists? Who would maintain the infrastructure?" The buzzer sounded and Freed started toward the door, stopped, and looked back at Lerner. "Idealism is dead, Jacob. The revolution never happened."

Alone among the faceless guests, Lerner sat in Freed's living room, near his immature sculpture, which, despite his dissatisfaction with its flaws, gave him small comfort. How could something be dead if it hadn't happened yet?

His front pocket bulged; reaching in, fingers detected the dusty-hardness of air-dried clay, and he pulled out one of his Madame Burgundy heads, the last he had made before leaving for the Poconos. Had he put it there during his pacing? He set it in the middle of his bronze cage. More green arose, sprouting from fragments of brick and stone. The fetid city of Schuyler's journal, ruined now, reclaimed by nature. In its crumbling vine-draped towers the mad gods call out at moonrise. With no one to sacrifice, no priests to offer bloody worship, the mad gods wither, dry skin hanging over leather muscle and flaking bone. The dust of their passing flutters on the breeze. But such couldn't be reproduced with Lerner's style of sculpture. Green and rot needed paint and canvas; he hadn't the skill. Dioramas of bronze and clay with canvas backdrop. He would have to study Schuyler's style and attempt to create something worthy.

The dapper marionette, he had known Schuyler, had saved Schuyler . . . would save Lerner from the Kreunens, heirs of the Stuyvesants, acolytes of the limbless octopi. And what of this new Freed, cruel and practical, conjoined now with the Kreunens' world?

Someone, a caterer, passed with a tray of grilled shrimp pierced by toothpicks, and Lerner took one. Holding the shrimp close, savoring the spicy-sweet aroma, he couldn't recall his last meal. Surely, he had eaten something after returning to the city? Journal, pacing . . . dapper marionette . . . the succession of events had swallowed everything. Hunger carried him into the kitchen, a narrow rectangle divided by a counter with three bar stools; across the counter from the bar stools, sink, stove, refrigerator. He half-expected to find Buddy Drake and that writer he had introduced Lerner to, re-enacting the last party. Instead, a man wearing a white apron arrayed food on Freed's chrome, 1950s table, beckoning morsels tastefully displayed on rosy glass trays. Lerner chose a plate, assembled his own collection, and sat at the counter to eat. He missed Buddy Drake, his lack of guile, his ability to laugh, and to listen. When all of this . . . whatever it was . . . started, Lerner had refrained from telling him much; now, he needed Buddy Drake's presence, needed to confide.

"You always find the cool people in the kitchen."

A woman with short, dyed-blond hair stood beside him, smiling as though they were friends. She emanated a bitter, smoky odor.

"The building next door to the restaurant caught fire. No damage to Gingerleaf, but we had to close, what with all the smoke and sirens. So here I am!"—she leaned forward and embraced him—"and I'm starving. I never eat till after we close."

Lerner finally recognized Catherine Vanadis, long dark hair changed. "I've been gone," he said. "Got back in town this morning." Should he mention Schuyler's painting and gauge her reaction? He couldn't. He didn't want to find out that she too had been . . . corrupted.

"You need to cook for me soon," he said. "Last time didn't count. Though that soup *was* the perfect antidote to crazy dog bite."

She touched his hand, turning it flat to see the fading splotches that marked his wound. "Good thing you're friends with a plastic surgeon," she said, tracing the zone with a fingertip.

Closer, her smoky residue seemed more mellow, a perfume suitable for a chef. Her contact, the airy sensation of her fingers atop his skin, reminded him of his thoughts on first meeting her, a flashback to his former time of parties, his addiction to the thrill of new people, new sexual partners. In bed, she would be lavender and cumin, the heat of chilies.

She assembled a plate of food and set it near his. "I'll be back in a bit—I need to go use the toilet," she said, and moved off.

"Cath! I heard about poor Gingerleaf."

Lerner turned; a bearded, gray-haired man had stopped Catherine Vanadis. The mundane, Lerner thought, the mundane expanding, bulging into new areas, displacing beauty, crushing creativity. This city of millions was a beast in slumber, sometimes stirring, but rarely fully awake. In what form would its waking state manifest? Lerner's creations: dichotomies of concrete and earth, tower and tree, street and river.

The bearded, gray-haired man pushed aside Catherine's plate with his own and sat next to Lerner. "That Gary Freed sure knows how to put together a spread. Even the chefs agree." The man lifted something from his plate, half of a small fowl, skinless, pink, charred in places from a grill. "I mean look at this tandoori quail. How many parties would you find this at?"

"Are you a chef then?" Lerner asked.

"See that woman over there?" The man pointed to a man and woman talking by the sink. "She's an excellent therapist, sharp, insightful. Me, I don't practice anymore. Figured I'd do myself and everyone else a favor."

Lerner recalled a snatch of gossip given once by Freed, about a therapist in the office across the hall from his, whose license had been revoked for having sex with a patient.

"So you and the noodle chef, you together?"

"Friends," Lerner said. "Just met her."

"You'd like to be though. She's a nice looking lady. Good hands. Strong. I guess they'd have to be, with all that chopping. Just think how they'd feel on you."

Lerner considered mentioning what he knew of the man's past.

"Name's Charles Rouge, by the way."

Lerner introduced himself.

"The artist, yes? Freed must have told me something about

you. An artist with a chef? Not a match I would recommend. The narcissism alone would be enough to wreck any chance of success."

Lerner caught the edge of a conversation, flat, airless voices: "...if you must sell, wait until interest rates go down in November...." The party din swallowed the rest. He turned around, but whoever had been speaking had left the door.

Rouge leaned close to him. "Maybe you're thinking: 'why does this asshole keep bugging me about sex?' Maybe you're getting annoyed. But maybe I just don't give a fuck, okay?"

The therapist woman and her companion passed on their way out of the kitchen. " ... definitely paranoia," she said.

Was Lerner paranoid? Those Kreunens—he should challenge them, demand an explanation for their forcing Freed to sell them the Schuyler, or ... ingratiate himself, consult with them on investments, feign ignorance of their true nature. Surely they gave parties for friends, investors. Freed could help him get an invitation, and once in their apartment....

"Man, I bet that Cath knows a few things about the erotic uses of chilies. Like that Peruvian tribe where the men put a dried pepper over their cock."

Why was Catherine taking so long? He resented having to deal with Rouge on his own. Fucking asshole. And what do you say to someone so proud of his own asshole-ness?

"I actually haven't had sex since my freshman year of college," Lerner said. "It's ... "

He paused, looking down at his plate, pretending to be too embarrassed to meet the probe of Rouge's gaze.

"It's very personal of course, but I feel like I can talk to you ... it's about my art. You know the story of Samson and Delilah—that's how it is for me. He can't cut his hair, and I believe that if I have sex I'll never be able to paint again."

Rouge shook his head as Lerner spoke, holding his temples in both hands, as if afraid his brains would spill out. He muttered something, but Lerner kept talking.

"Some say I idealize women too much, that my paintings are anachronisms, like Bouguereau's hyper-real maidens—"

"Look, buddy, stop it. I'm sure you're a good painter and all, but nobody's art is *that* important. I've treated heroin-addicted musicians who thought they'd never be able to write songs once they got off the junk, but this is fucking crazy." Rouge grabbed Lerner's uninjured wrist and shook it. "You listen to me: You need to get laid!"

The air contracted, and Lerner became aware of rustlings, faint, and hidden, but when he turned to identify them, there was nothing. The sounds reminded him of the feeling prior to the dog attack, the regression of uptown Manhattan. As if inflamed by proximity to the same phenomena, his healed wound throbbed. Though Rouge remained on the periphery of Lerner's awareness, darkness and contracting air hid detail.

Lerner tried to shut out the rustlings, concentrating on simple elements: his plate, his hands, until the room steadied and the darkness receded. Then, without saying anything to Rouge, he got up and left the kitchen. On his way to the front door, a glance toward the living room showed those sisters, the Kreunens, their backs to him, engaged in conversation with Catherine Vanadis, a few feet from the Madame Burgundy head.

13

THE ABILITY TO SEE

Blinds open to welcome Sunday morning light, Lerner reclined, his back propped with pillows against the headboard, reading his mail from the past week, which he had only just retrieved from the box downstairs. The first item he opened now played on his stereo, a baroque piece for flute and harpsichord, a gift from the flautist, Bolotowsky, whose father, now deceased, had been one of Hannah Rezinsky's most acclaimed clients. Bills; art supply catalog; financial statement (and check!) from Ventricle Savage; letter from a friend in Pittsburgh; music magazine; and . . . from the director of the Menil Collection in Houston, a letter saying that they would like to curate a retrospective of his work for the following autumn. Lerner was to be paired with another native Houstonian, a painter.

He could feel a silly, gaping smile stretching his cheeks—he had been smiling since opening the letter, smiling and talking to himself. This wouldn't be his first museum show, there had been others, in smaller towns, smaller venues, but this . . . in a museum housing an incredible collection of surrealist masterpieces . . . in the city where he grew up, the city to which he never cared to return (his parents having moved to the Pacific Northwest years ago, the place had little to draw him), but return he would, for this.

He read the letter again, savoring it . . . recognition, success, returning in triumph. There would be the usual preparations: selection of works both new and those scattered about in private or museum collections; interviews for the catalog; money—they planned to purchase for the museum two or more of his newer works. The need for money was impossible to avoid, for living, for art supplies. His art was a starving beast, eating everything but giving him so much.

Today, then, would be a day to savor . . . brunch . . . then maybe to the East Village to browse used records. Perhaps Catherine would be free for dinner. Not clear how long her restaurant would remain closed, but . . . when he left Freed's party she had been talking to the Kreunens. Their inevitable presence, and now recollection of them infested his special day. No—he wouldn't allow them that power. *This day was his.*

Dressed, he was soon on his way to Margaret's Calf, a place on Avenue A where he, Buddy Drake, and others met for occasional Sunday brunches. Buddy Drake was gone of course, but someone Lerner knew would likely be there; if not, he would take pleasure in the morning regardless.

Another swirling day. Thick air and misshapen odors surrounded him, city summer taking hold: dull, implacable, and merciless. Summer was bovine: chewing-chewing-chewing. Not like the fangs of winter—those you could shield yourself from, add protective layers: thermals, coat, gloves, but this flat chewing sucked everything out. He labored on, step after step, prison of air dulling his mind. Pale shades surrounded him, passing on all sides—no need to interact, like Schuyler, with a shadow-New York, for New York was *all* shadow, each rushing form self-contained and oblivious to whatever surrounded it, pain *or* joy. But he didn't really believe that, not today anyway—he wouldn't let the oppressive weather dictate his mood.

The restaurant's air conditioning blasted him a greeting. From the doorway he surveyed the crowd. His damp shirt clung to his back and sweat dripped down his cheek. The restaurant was a narrow, red-walled box, with booths, a few tables, and at the counter a line of stools. Seeing no one he knew, he claimed an empty stool and ordered coffee, then went into the restroom to wipe his face with a damp paper towel.

"Jacob."

Lerner looked up, pleased to find Simon Hoff beside him, having emerged from the nearby toilet stall. Hoff was tall, muscled from a rigorous workout schedule, looking more like a retired basketball player than a librarian. Lerner hadn't spoken to him since the day Hoff called to direct him to Schuyler's journal.

They returned to the dining room. The stool next to Lerner's had been vacated and Hoff took it.

"Hash browns," Lerner said. "This is one of the few places that knows how to crisp the outside while maintaining a creamy-textured middle. It's not that I dream of them, but I do crave them sometimes. I do wish more places had the knack."

"I'm not disagreeing with you," Hoff said. "But for me, it's the pancakes. Flour, buckwheat flour, and cornmeal. I'm in a rut but I can't help it."

"Where's Dr. Randolph—off digging up ant hills again?" Hoff's partner, Randy Turner, was an entomologist specializing in tropical ant colonies.

"He's coming back next week. Then we can take a real vacation at our place in Springdale."

They talked on, the amiable conversation of long-term familiarity. Hoff invited him to spend some time in Massachusetts—they could attend a performance at the Shakespeare festival where Tansy was working, but Lerner didn't think he could leave again so soon.

Their food came, and while Lerner ate, he thought about the dapper marionette's agitation over the city model. At the Kreunens' gallery, Lerner had been so intent on the Madame Burgundy painting, he had forgotten about the miniature city and its nightmarish pulsations. What other commissioned works of the Stuyvesants did the Kreunens hide? He resented their invasion into the realm of art, his realm.

"Simon, have you ever heard of a scale model of Manhattan, from the 1840s—"

"E. Porter Belden's miniature city? Wow—I haven't thought about *that* in years. I came across the reference in Kouwenhoven's book—he said that the only record we have of it is woodblock prints from ads in Belden's *own* book. I got intrigued and did some research. Not only is there no record of what happened to it, there's no speculation about it at all. It was put on display, then nothing, no reports of whether it was destroyed or how it disappeared, or even *that* it disappeared. Like it was withdrawn from common memory somehow."

Lerner's told Hoff about finding the journal—a different version of the journal. Hoff wanted to see it; after breakfast they took a taxi down the flowing Broadway river toward Lerner's apartment. Broadway had begun perhaps as a watering trail for deer, eventually co-opted by local tribes, the Dutch, the English, newly independent colonists—the downtown flow of traffic made little sense, considering its origin as the main path up the island, dirt to cobblestone to modern pavement. Early on, traffic had flowed in both directions, changing at some point, victim of urban planners proud of their lack of aesthetic understanding.

Faces, sidewalk faces flashing past. Lerner recalled Schuyler's dream-vision of a cab ride. Had they merged consciousness then, Schuyler entering his mind at some freakish moment of attunement? He wanted to believe that his actions in *his* New York somehow helped to free Schuyler from the Stuyvesants in the past.

The taxi turned left onto Grand to drop them at the corner of Crosby. The driver cursed—an accident blocked the intersection. Ahead, another taxi waited. The cars would be stuck until traffic cleared. Hoff paid the fare, and Lerner added an extra tip.

Throbbing tone-scream sirens filled the street. A mangled bicycle lay on the sidewalk, and past it, an ambulance, a police car, and a dark limousine. The ambulance started off, turning onto Lafayette and uptown. The siren faded with distance. At the limousine, a policeman leaned into a half-open passenger window; fragments of atonal words drifted from the car. As Lerner and Hoff walked past, Lerner could make out two figures in the rear, seated close.

"Sorry to keep you," the policeman said, but the window hissed upward before he finished. The limousine detached from the curb.

Lerner left Hoff to browse the various sculptures in the studio while he searched for the journal. Finished reading ... pacing, the endless pacing ... dapper marionette ... convoluted confusions pressing down on all sides. Not many places to hide. Here, night stand. Bookshelf. He opened his closet, finding the journal atop a stack of books, and carried it into the living room.

"Overdue," Hoff said, waving the book of Schuyler paintings. "I'll fix it for you."

"Never underestimate the value of a friend at the library," Lerner said. He gave Hoff the journal and went to check his blinking answering machine. Hoff settled on the sofa to read.

A message from Catherine: "Sorry I didn't get to say good night. Was no doubt off talking to someone. Come to dinner at seven? Ring me if you can't make it."

Did his entire future rest on this single decision? Dinner: yes/no. The act of going could unleash innumerable consequences. Every decision took on more weight, paths once chosen couldn't be avoided, and he was far, far from the spot where he had first viewed Schuyler's painting. What lay beyond, he couldn't predict, and in fact he had no desire to do so. Retreats were possible: he didn't always complete each piece of art he began. Some needed to be abandoned, due to mistakes, missteps, misconceptions, but this current path he chose to follow to its destination, wherever it lay, and not simply follow, for his actions, his investigations, helped to create the path. The web had a pattern: Schuyler, Catherine Vanadis, Kreunens, Freed, his own art . . . but he was no detective. Dinner with Catherine simply meant *that*, a quiet dinner with a recent acquaintance.

Leaving Hoff undisturbed with the journal, Lerner moved to his work table and opened a large sketchbook. Yes, dinner would be agreeable . . . surely he had conjured her invitation out of his own desires — declining would be impolite. And today invulnerability cloaked him, a layer of armor fueled by his excellent news.

Flipping to a clean page of his sketchbook, Lerner considered his new installation, his Manhattan. Despite the city's present appearance, despite the general air of *as it is now, so it always was*, the island of Manhattan indeed had been a wilderness, a landscape of ponds, streams, hills, and forest. In 1821 the grid was created, a flat grid on flat paper, covering the entire island at a time when only a small part had actually been urbanized. Rather than fitting the city to the existing terrain, the grid makers leveled to match the flatness of the paper. And where Manhattan set the tone, the rest of the nation followed. If the city had acted in concert with the land, bridging streams rather than covering them, building on the sides of hills instead of obliterating them . . . how would that have affected development in the U.S.? Not only physical topography, but social as well.

Manhattan Green/Manhattan Greed — one letter of difference, a million miles of change. Two separate works, with the overall title he had earlier devised: *The Reflection of the Beginning is the End.*

For this cityscape-landscape, he would take Dutch engravings of the Manhattan countryside and recreate them in three dimensions. But he didn't want to make every rock and tree himself. Such things would be available in catalogs, though expensive; he would scale down the size, and combine it with a smaller version of his lower Manhattan destruction. Still . . . so much detail. Like museum displays, he would have to abut three-dimensional elements with a painted backdrop. On a childhood trip with his family to New York, he had wandered the exhibit halls of the American Museum of Natural History, fascinated by the combination of display case and painted background; he would stand at an exhibit, staring, trying to discern the exact spot where setting ended and background began. His last visit to the museum had been at least a year ago, if not longer. Perhaps he would go uptown tomorrow. Seeing some of the exhibits would help form his vision. *Manhattan Green*— an essence of the city owing nothing to commerce or public relations, appended to *Manhattan Greed* and its destructive consequences, the painting and the city, the paint of Schuyler, the clay and metal of Lerner.

"I wish I'd been able to see that painting," Hoff said. Still holding the journal, he stood and walked over to a window and looked out. Lerner joined him. Hoff opened the journal and pointed to a page—"The sketches he made—a taxi!—this could all be a clever forgery, but the paper, the printing and binding, it all says mid-nineteenth century. He was either more prescient than Jules Verne, or . . . he really saw this stuff.

"Aside from the visions or whatever, the 1842 Manhattan part feels right. In the later part, the description of the glass marionette sounds a lot like the one Gabriel Mesa is supposed to have created for King Philip II of Spain to spy on the Dutch. Schuyler likely knew of Mesa's journals. Art and alchemy used to be a lot more closely linked. And Lost World stories—those were popular . . . so . . . he could have made up the stuff to pass the time on the long voyage home . . . but the taxis! Jacob—I don't know what to say about that."

Shapes of questions slithered into Lerner's vision, green and molten, filled with elements too diffuse to analyze. The presence, the real presence of the dapper marionette in his life . . . everything else in the journal was real too, the bloody city, Schuyler's non-human captors. . . . He made his way to the sofa and sat, staring at the haze that seeped through the gaps between floorboards and window frames, a haze that bound him to this spot, this time and place. With so much he wanted to tell Hoff—his Schuyler sighting that linked with Schuyler's description of the man on the street . . . the dapper marionette—Lerner felt suddenly mute. Words attempted to form, but dissolved on reaching his lips.

Hoff set the journal on the coffee table and stood facing Lerner. Outside the window, a flash of red, glinting sunlight rosy aura. The encircling threat of the Kreunens and their allies, the bloody priests . . . would telling Hoff about them place his friend in danger? But if the dapper marionette wanted Lerner's help, he would need assistance, his own allies to combat those of the Kreunens.

"That was me Schuyler saw from the window, Simon. I saw him too, looking out, making a desperate plea for rescue . . . and . . . I've seen the city model. The sisters, the Kreunens—they have it. They have a lot of things. I think the city model was created like the Madame Burgundy painting, to enact something. Where the painting was small, petty but vicious, the city model must have been used to transform Manhattan. The grid had already been in place, but . . . and what's the grid anyway if not a drawing? Who knows what went into the making of *that*? Five into one or whatever.

"I don't think they're still doing that kind of thing—I doubt they know how anymore. But they're still mean greedy fucks."

"Jacob, do you still have that Williamson 16-year-old that Freed gave you for your birthday?" Hoff went to rummage in Lerner's cabinets, returning with two glasses of Scotch. "Here, drink." He picked up the journal from the coffee table and sat in its place, opposite Lerner, with the journal in his lap.

"I can't say any of this surprises me, Jacob. Librarians, some of us, are responsible for a lot more information than what's in the public card catalog. Remember the caretaker of books I sent you to . . . he thought it would be safe for you to see the journal.

Beyond that . . . the second journal . . . that *is* a surprise. And the rest—I've been in New York a long time. We have to co-exist with so many different things, different kinds of people with different agendas, some odious, some not. Most people relish their happy oblivion to all this. But you're an artist, a real one. You've always had the ability to see. Now that you've seen more, you have to learn to live with it."

Hoff leaned his long body forward, reaching for Lerner's shoulders. "And Jacob—nothing rash, okay? I'm not saying you can't change things. Your art is all about change—keep that—but don't take on some vendetta for Schuyler's sake, okay?"

And later, in another taxi, foil-wrapped half of a roast duck warm in his lap, Lerner made his way to the West Village apartment of Catherine Vanadis. She lived in a row house on a street buffered from much of the city's tumult. There were times (many times) when Lerner craved such a place. He didn't think he ever really slept well. Outside sounds were muffled but never absent, and even when he could hear nothing, he could never wholly shut out the constant flow of humanity, which coated everything with dust-like microscopic tatters. But his body adapted. And his art—where would it be without the energy generated by the passing throngs?

On impulse, Lerner had placed another Madame Burgundy head in his pocket. Though he hadn't decided whether he would leave it at Catherine's, after seeing her with the Kreunens at Freed's . . . its weight in his pocket was a comfort, and combined with the Madame Burgundy sketch in his wallet, he was well-fortified for whatever lay ahead. Talking to Hoff had also been a comfort, lifting some of the tension that had been compounded by finding (and reading!) the second journal. Hoff hadn't questioned *how* Lerner knew that the Kreunens hoarded the city model, and he couldn't tell from Hoff's expression whether Hoff thought Lerner had omitted anything. Maybe he should have told Hoff about the visits from the dapper marionette. Vendetta . . . why else would the dapper marionette have recruited him?

Deciding he wanted to walk the rest of the way, Lerner had the driver let him out a few blocks short of Catherine's place. Ahead, past the intersection of Hudson and Charles, people massed on the sidewalk, a buildup of bodies drawn by chance, by the universe of infinite possibility. He moved into the crowd. Murmurings surrounded him, voices of his fellow-New Yorkers, talk of fashion, of television, of money. Then he saw the source of the sidewalk blockage.

From the alley between two buildings issued a river of iguanas, scaly bodies quivering in evening light that flashed on colors as brilliantly varied as a cross-section of granite. The river bridged Hudson and continued down the opposite sidewalk. Not everyone stopped. A woman talking on a mobile phone entered the street at a diagonal with the saurian flow. Nearing them, her body contorted. Her legs became smoke, and she uttered a sharp grunt, looking around as though startled; her torso dissolved, more smoke, a greenish smoke that shot upward like fine dust. Minutes later, the same thing happened to a bicyclist, the dusty smoke including his bicycle as well as his body. Perhaps before Lerner's arrival several cars had experienced something similar; now a line of cabs and other cars stretched, horns blasting.

The iguanas varied in size, some about the length of his hand, others impossibly large, with ribbon tongues flapping in and out. Though all moved in the same direction, their progress wasn't uniform, or orderly: large ones stepped on their smaller cousins, some swatted at those around them, claiming position in some inexplicable order. And perched on the back of a massive beast, blue-gray with a flowing crest—the dapper marionette.

As the iguana passed Lerner, the dapper marionette saluted him.

The flow continued, fewer now, a mix of smaller ones with duller coloring and short, spiny tails, and several larger ones, stocky with horn-like snouts. The last ones crossed, a grouping of five, turquoise-colored, each about the size of a dachshund. For a moment the street remained empty. Then, spell broken, automobile traffic resumed. Lerner made his way to the other side of the street, hoping to follow the iguanas, but couldn't find them.

The universe dips and twirls, heaving from the reality of concrete to fragmentary glimpses of worlds superimposed on this one, worlds made from feathers, and from iron ore, worlds of solidified argon that splits to allow passage of miniscule nematodes with the power to reshape mountains, and worlds much like his own, with subtle differences that become apparent at unexpected intervals. Lerner walked along a hidden path, sometimes stepping off, sometimes not. And sometimes the divergence overtook others as well—what happened to the woman who contorted and turned to smoke? Lerner's fellow pedestrians had resumed their lives, unwilling, perhaps, to admit what they had witnessed. But Lerner, as Hoff had said, carried the ability to *see*. He hoped he was worthy of whatever this vision signified.

14

A QUIET DINNER

Catherine Vanadis opened her front door, and Lerner, having stood at the corner for several minutes, attempting to calm his incoherent thoughts after seeing... after the passage of the iguanas back into whatever realm they had erupted from... presented his package.

"Oh... I thought that smell was your aftershave," she said, then laughed. She leaned in to embrace him. "Thanks Jacob! Roast duck is *always* welcome in this household."

He entered a narrow hallway and stopped, confronted by a downward spiraling pit that emitted reds, purples, and a moist cold that coated everything with icy pearls, and upwards... a wooden ladder stretched into blue distance, its rungs rotten, splintering... walls stripped....

"The kitchen is in the back," Catherine said. "Let's put the duck on the counter; then I can give you the tour."

Walls returned, painted in warm colors, deep and orangey reds; the pit and ladder became staircases pointing up to the next floor and down to the basement. He followed Catherine through the dining room—table with *four* place settings?—and into the kitchen.

"It's my aunt's house and a lot of the things are hers. She's always threatening to sell, but she doesn't really need the money."

A bed of wide rice noodles filled a glass bowl. Catherine set the package of duck beside them. On the stove, cloves, ginger, coconut milk simmered in a wok.

"My workspace is too small, but you're not allowed to make structural changes in these old row houses. Who needs a big formal dining room anyway? I could move the wall between here and the kitchen. The place has already been modified. Years ago someone made the basement into a separate apartment." They ascended to the second floor. "Up here's my bedroom and my office. My aunt keeps a bedroom on the third floor for when she visits."

For whom were the other two place settings? And what did he know about Catherine Vanadis, really? Her house formed a story he was unable to read. Neat, clean, tasteful, but what did the assortment of objects signify? Her country-kitsch bedroom décor surprised him—knobby tree-trunk-and-branch fashioned into bed, into night stand with moon and three stars inlaid on its polished slab-of-wood top. And hiding beneath all surfaces, another layer, one with no shape or color, that existed only at the edges of his vision.

But on a wall of the office, a familiar sight: Buddy Drake's series of Chinatown outdoor market photos, taken about five years previously. "There's my hands," Lerner said, pointing to the second photo. "Buying that purple spinach stuff, whatever it's called. Obviously you can't tell the color in a black and white photo."

"Neat! I didn't know he was a friend of yours. An ex of mine gave me the photos for my birthday one year. I'd love to meet him sometime."

"You should get him to shoot some of your food, and put the photos on the walls at your new place."

"That's a fabulous idea, Jacob."

"Who else is coming to dinner?" he asked, but she had started down the stairs and didn't hear him. The ring of door chimes rose, catching them on their way down. For the first time since this Schuyler business began, Lerner felt a tug of something approaching fear, coils of apprehension like an infinite, snaking rope.

"There they are," Catherine said. "Could you let them in? I need to get back to the kitchen. I'll meet you in the living room."

Even before Lerner opened the door, time had ceased to flow in its accustomed manner. Moments grew lumpish and corpulent, stretching out, an extended time in which beginning and end, past and present, became irrelevant. Time churned, taking on new shapes and colors, fourteen-sided tangerine crystals, oblong clumps of purple smoke, but no matter what the shape, color, or density, a white line, sometimes plain, often a mere blur, bisected each—a safe path should one need it. Part of him churned also, but part remained, held to the white line.

The front door appeared. He grasped the warm porcelain knob and turned it.

Against a hazy background stood the Kreunens, distorted, arms and legs elongated and indistinct, as if sections were engulfed by the surrounding mist. His first impulse was to push, watch them tumble the ten or more steps to the sidewalk. He waited, they waited, but time contracted, the moment for action passed, unheeded.

"Catherine is in the kitchen," he said, and stepped aside to allow them entry.

Riding a beam of rosy light, he led the Kreunens into the living room, where he sat facing them; on the wall behind them hung a particularly repellent example of Are No's sludge-art (foam, now hardened, that had been sprayed onto a plywood rectangle in two broad curves, one painted gray, the other a lime green; where they intersected, the green covered the gray).

Catherine brought in a platter and placed it on the coffee table. An assortment of appetizers: puff pastry rounds with a shrimp embedded on the top, tofu skin wrapped around asparagus spears, fried pork dumplings.

Lerner detached, a detachment that allowed him to sit, appearing calm despite the churning. He sampled the items. As did the Kreunens. And surely they spoke? Lerner concentrated on the white line, willing the disorienting swirls to dissipate, leaving only a fine, rust-colored film over the evening.

"The artist benefits," one of them said. Accompanying their words, a fringe of black particles emanated from the crowns of their heads; the particles rose, collecting around the crystal chandelier, muffling its light.

"No reliable system for rating creative output. Not like refrigerators, for one. Fashion dictates: why this car and not the other? Risky. Best to avoid. Some things remain true. Land. Resources. But still, tax-exempt foundations are not required to show a profit. If an art is funded, the artist's income will eventually lead to new investment opportunities.

"From this all follows."

The particles collected, darkening the room. At some point Catherine Vanadis called them to the table. She seated Lerner beside her, with the Kreunens opposite. She lit candles, and in their wavering light, the Kreunens' faces appeared inhuman, their true selves showing through their protective masks.

"We have a coconut milk curry with lotus root, sweet potato, and monkfish; cold rice noodles with pickled vegetables and roast duck—courtesy of Jacob; and stir-fried Shanghai cabbage."

Normally these items would have thrilled Lerner. The smells signaled that exquisite tastes would soon follow, but he couldn't discharge his apprehension. Catherine served him; he lifted chopsticks, but his esophagus contracted: no food would it allow to pass. Chilled, creeping chill, toes, fingers, waves of it. And on their side of the table, the Kreunens smiled. Their cold attacked him, like those creatures from Schuyler's journal; here they were, before him, somehow compressed into person-shapes but unable to hide their nature. A dark outline of gelatinous cold surrounded them, giving them monstrous strength far beyond what their human forms signified.

Lerner glanced toward Catherine, fearing that she, too, radiated gelatinous cold, but from her came the wholesomeness of chilies, ginger, garlic, coriander. He tried to speak, not knowing what to say, knowing that words were his only weapon, but the same constriction of throat that prevented eating cut off his speech as well. And yet, he had the impression of events occurring on other planes; that his body, seated beside Catherine, made an outward show of normality, eating, drinking, speaking, while the rest of him conducted itself elsewhere.

"Dora and Denise are helping me with the construction permits so I can expand the kitchen here," Catherine said. "They know how to get around the regulations."

He concentrated, glimpsing himself through the rust-colored air, inside of which he spoke to Catherine Vanadis, to the Kreunens, simple, easy words, expounding his views on art, description of the bands in which he had played during college and just after, giving up music to focus solely on art, for art could only be made through long, dedicated attention, casting aside distraction. He relished the Kreunens' dismay, their inability to comprehend why someone would devote so much time, energy, money, to something that gave such a negligible monetary return.

"I live in a former sweatshop," he said. "And sometimes, at night, I can hear the ghosts of sewing machines." But as he spoke, he felt parts of him decay, crumble, made brittle by the Kreunens' creeping cold. His hands! Looking down at his right, gripping chopsticks, the skin stretched and faded, becoming translucent; his metacarpals shone through, gray-outlined and distinct, like the glassy women of Schuyler's journal. On the table, flakes of skin and muscle lay scattered in reddish mounds. Could no one else see what was happening? The Kreunens ate, Catherine Vanadis talked, filling the air with a variety of cheerful syllables.

Lerner pulled himself to his feet, muttering something about the restroom, and Catherine Vanadis pointed him to the second floor.

The dapper marionette had taken Schuyler aloft in his balloon, soaring far above earthly enemies, and here, Lerner soared as well, looking down at the dining room scene. But somewhere, the avatars of the Kreunens waited, fangs and tentacles poised to strike. Fog shrouded them, fog engulfed the city, though taller buildings pierced the fog, and from their windows the city appeared as a limitless, gray landscape.

What creatures flourished here, among the fog-dunes? Lerner trudged up the slope of one, its surface spongy, resistant to his steps.

Shrill winds tugged and pushed, making passage even more difficult, and the air had turned cold, all summer heat gone. Bullets of cold pierced his diminishing skin, dislodging jagged sheets of precious insulation. Ahead, the top of a building jutted a few feet from the fog, but how to reach it? . . . the fog sucked his feet—lift one, tear it free, step farther, higher. On hands and knees now, crawling, never stopping, never giving in to the cold cold sweep of gray. Stopping, he knew, was impossible. Forward motion was the only thing that kept him from sinking into the viscous cloud dune. Somewhere in its sunless depths the Kreunens lurked, waiting for him to falter. Determined, obstinate, he pushed on, climbing, but the top of the building came no closer. Unable to bear the sight of his distant salvation, he closed his eyes, shut out the hiss of the wind, felt his way . . . and with a final heave he attained a firm surface. He lay on his back, staring at whorls of jellied sky, lucid stars dissipating, swarms of predatory birds ready for his collapse to become complete, for only then would they descend to tear at his wasted body.

Desperate, he reached into his pocket and grasped the Madame Burgundy head. Breath and warmth seeped back into him, and the sky became Catherine's blue ceiling, the birds a mobile hanging at the top of the stairs. When he felt recovered enough, he returned to the dining room, giving no indication to the others of his trauma. He left the head on a bathroom shelf.

15 | MADAME BURGUNDY

A time of focus ensued. Materials, supplies, his workspace—the universe of the necessary. His installation took shape: plywood sheet cut into the shape of the map, principal streets drawn with pencil. He troweled on a layer of plaster, first the streets, which he painted ochre, then the rest, in gray. The shattered buildings would rise from this surface, but for now they existed only as strips of bronze, thin bars pounded flat.

He pondered *Manhattan Green*, the anti-twin to his city-in-ruins . . . trees and hills a tonic for the frenzied, but lost among edifices of greed and incumbent ruthlessness, whose tall and shiny glass boxes fill with restless minions striving for the ultimate success, unrealizable because corporations dictate mandatory growth—corpulent slavering beasts tear at carcasses, flesh sweet, but when all is eaten, resources "fully utilized," the beasts turn on themselves, rabid in their desire to succeed, even if only to preside over a constituency of bones. But outside his windows life continued, not bones yet, still strong in their pursuit of happiness. He had seen a film once, streets and sidewalks of the city shot from rooftops in various locations, the results accelerated and looped until everything became one arterial flow superimposed on the body of a nude, hairless man, the god of urban landscape, his body imbued with the riotous essence of city life. Twenty stories tall, he gazed down upon his subjects, his expression benign and powerful. With one flick of a fingernail into the stream that traversed his torso he could level entire blocks.

Venturing uptown to the American Museum of Natural History, he studied the dioramas and backdrops. Merging his city-in-ruins with nature backdrop would be too difficult, too time-consuming at the scale he had devised. Therefore . . . a second city-in-ruins took shape in his sketchbook, smaller, the tip of Manhattan, with a pair of skeletal buildings, the Dutch wall of Wall Street, then a hilly, tree-covered landscape joining a painted canvas, all enclosed in a glass-walled box, like the New York model now held captive with Schuyler's painting deep inside the Kreunens' fortress.

He looked up at a dinosaur, expanse of ancient fossilized bone stretching toward massive, duck-billed head, its jaws locked in radioactive decay, eons of limestone, skeletal layers pressing and pressing, handy for the building trade. But not all trust the scientific explanation—some acknowledge nuclear power but not its method for dating the world, believing instead in fantasy, in biblical mythology as literal truth, which they force on others, attempting to return the country to a medieval level of knowledge and belief (though retaining medicine and all the modern toys that wouldn't exist without art and science).

Work continued. The bulk of his time he spent on *Manhattan Greed*, needing it to be ready for the early November opening of his group show (the other piece, though not less important, wasn't part of the show and therefore had no deadline). Studio time, walks, meals, reading, but little social interaction. One Saturday he met friends for dinner, after which they went to hear some bands. Freed had departed for a month in Italy; a few postcards and a letter arrived from various stops. Buddy Drake would be returning soon; Lerner set that as a deadline, after which he would resume a normal, more sociable schedule, for too much isolation can be dangerous.

Then a week of intermittent rain dulled his mood, and he suspended work on his city to shape several small clay figures that he wasn't sure he would use.

With the return of sunshine came a visit from Ventricle Savage, to check his progress and examine recent work. And Catherine Vanadis arrived to pick up his ruined-temple sculpture, *Homage to the Fallen Deities of Commerce*, her new restaurant having neared completion. Aside from a thank-you note he sent after the dinner at her place, he hadn't had any contact with her, had been unsure whether he *wanted* contact. He decided to put her in the same category as Freed: corrupted by the Kreunens but not monstrous, no need to shun—he had to co-exist with the world, in all its variations.

She told him her plans for a party at the new restaurant for the first weekend of August, to celebrate its opening. "Nobody's around then, but debuting in the summer gives the restaurant time to cohere before autumn. I've got a plan to offer a special with the Public Theatre's first show of the season to stir up interest in the neighborhood newcomer."

"That sounds like fun," he said. "I should be ready for a break by then. Busy doing, as usual." He paused, studying her face, narrow chin, green eyes, deciding it harbored no horrors. "Catherine ... those sisters ... I know they're helping you, but you should be careful around them. They live in a different world, they *see* a different world ... money and death—"

"They live in the business world, Jacob; I live in a part of it too—not the same part as them, but it intersects. And what about you? What's Ventricle Savage? There's nothing wrong with making a bit of money. You have to live. You have to buy art supplies. And noodles!"

Restless after her visit, he left his apartment and walked eastward into the sultry day, taking a canvas bag that contained his sketchbook, to which he had recently added his copy of Schuyler's journal—a duo that formed a reassuring weight at his thigh despite the heat.

Along Grand Street the city eventually thinned, lower buildings dispersed like a suburban street, with a few high-rises closer to the river. The traffic of FDR Drive separated city life from the riverside, but a pedestrian overpass a block north made crossing possible. In the great cities of Europe, life began at the water's edge and even when the city moved inward the water remained its locus; New York, however, chose to ignore its coastline, placing highway along waterway, obstructing the river's egress into metropolitan consciousness, save as an obstacle to be crossed over or under when commuting to work.

Stopping, sitting on a bench, meant succumbing to the heat—sweat covered him, thin shirt wet and clinging, but the expanse of river, far-off Brooklyn side joined here by the Williamsburg Bridge, formed a tableau worth the effort. He raised his arms to catch whatever cooling breeze they could, and when he felt somewhat more comforted he reached into his bag, fingers first finding the rough binding of Schuyler's journal, which he pulled out and held for a moment before exchanging it for the sketchbook; opening to a clean page, he aimed his view toward bridge abutments and suspension cables. A fever of ideas guided his pencil, and by the time he closed the sketchbook, fog had pushed in from the Atlantic. He observed the fog's advance with bemusement, playing a game with landmarks: select a building and watch fog devour it, pick another, until the opposite shore dissipated and the bridge extended into nothing. He drew the bridge, recalling a highway under construction in his Houston childhood that seemed locked in an abbreviated form, raised pavement ending in nothing—the diving board, he had called it.

Houston's growth, though starting much later, was perhaps as insane as New York's; unconfined by geography or zoning, the city splayed in all directions, a huge, oily beast wedded to its partner, the automobile, for true commerce can only thrive when the highways run free and clear, with no rivals, no democratizing mass-transit to distract the populace.

The fog cleared, taking the bridge with it, altering the coast-line—pavement along the river dissolved into water and mud, though his bench remained; a pocket of fog anchored it to his New York.

A two-masted sailing ship moved upriver, passing fishing boats and other small craft. Of Schuyler's time or earlier? Dutch Manhattan? Lerner had no way of knowing, not being versed in the evolution of sailing vessels, but he thought the remaining buildings had more of a nineteenth-century appearance. He wanted to move from his bench, set off to find Schuyler . . . here somewhere, either still working with Madame Burgundy or confined to Bookman's house, with the garrotter. And Madame Burgundy—seeing her, if only for a moment. . . . Mist hid his feet, but what of the pavement beneath them, the base of the bench? As though numbed, his feet seemed to float, each a broad balloon, touching nothing, and the lack of contact with a sur-face made him doubt their presence. He lifted a foot; it emerged, solid. He re-tied his shoelaces, then repeated with the other, hoping that such a practical action would precipitate a change, but once returned to the mist the foot resumed its bloated and numbed state.

He pulled both up at once and sat, hugging his knees.

Some moments must have passed, but he was aware of little besides the thought: *keep yourself where you can see yourself to know yourself is there*, repeated endlessly, like a sob, or a hys-terical laugh, though with no sound.

A movement drew his attention. The two-masted ship had docked at a pier extending into the river from what had been the base of the pedestrian overpass. Workmanlike cries and a flurry of activity greeted the ship's arrival; a cart carrying assorted barrels and crates pulled up to the vessel, which appeared to have nothing to off-load. A carriage stopped at the head of the pier, and a figure stepped down.

Lerner had no difficulty recognizing her from her posture, the tilt of her head, though her face was turned from him.

He dropped down into water.

Holding to the back of the bench, he searched with his feet for river bottom, found it, and lowered himself. His feet sank into muck, and the water came chest-high. He pushed his way shoreward, keeping his bag overhead.

Once again on land, he stood on a carpet of reeds, water streaming from his sodden clothing. Chill surrounded him, chill from more than his wet clothes. Grayness covered the sun, not the low, lifeless gray of winter but not an overcast day in late June either. Schuyler's visit had begun in February and ended in early March.

The woman ... Madame Burgundy ... walked toward the ship, and Lerner followed.

In *his* New York, her coloring would likely have attracted no attention, even in society, for society women worshipped the sun more than anyone, rowdy debutantes frequenting beaches in assorted locales. The women roasting in the Hamptons were at least as dark, though their skin might fade in winter and Madame Burgundy's never would. In his world, she could pass as white, if she chose to; here, she was a target. Passing. Lerner had never suffered from anti-Semitism, and even with his painfully Old Testament first name he could pass as, not Christian exactly, but as not-Jewish, which essentially meant Christian in these United States. At various times, when the subject came up, acquaintances, friends even, had said: "I didn't know you were Jewish," as if knowing held some importance, would have changed their view of him, or it meant nothing but the awkwardness people feel when confronted by something unexpected.

How soon before Madame Burgundy and her husband boarded the ill-fated steamship that was to be their doom? He wondered whether Schuyler had ever read the printed version of his journal, with Dickens' postscript detailing Madam Burgundy's fate in the riverboat's explosion. Though why a steamship anyway? Nooteboom, the husband, was owner and captain of ocean-going vessels; surely they would have been safer under his command. And if Stuyvesant spies controlled the South Street docks, Captain Nooteboom could move a ship to some secluded spot where they could embark unobserved. To this place. Today. Lerner jogged after her, calling out, surprising himself with the urgency of his cries.

And she appeared to hear!

She looked in his direction, but did she see him?

"Madame Burgundy, Mrs. Nooteboom," he said, and kept repeating her name, hoping that would somehow link them. Drawing closer, he slowed. He took out the journal, flipped pages to Schuyler's first meeting with her, and read aloud:

> The arrival of the lady of the house caused me some surprise, for her skin, though not of the darkest hue, marked her as at least partially connected to a race not commonly found in the houses of the wealthy, save as servant (or slave, in the southern climes of this free land of America). But she wore clothing typical of the comfortable class: silk taffeta dress with embroidered over-sleeves and a pleated bodice. She appeared to be at her ease here.

A yard or so now separated them; her eyes were a surprising green; he thought she looked tired, strained.

> Mere paint would be unable to capture the loveliness of her skin, which had the quality of coffee blended with a modicum of cream.

He flipped pages, searching, then:

The lady entered, at last, attired in the red dress. On her head she had placed a charming straw bonnet decorated inside the brim with lace and flowers of silk, and over her shoulders was a shawl to cover her flesh where it was bared by the cut of the dress. I bade her place the bonnet and shawl out of sight. As she settled onto the sofa, I decided I would henceforth call her "Madame Burgundy," for the color of her attire and in honor of her French heritage, which elicited, when I informed her (in French), a lovely, unselfconscious sound of delight.

He searched for Wadholm's letter to Dickens, then remembered: it wasn't in his version of the journal! Years of Schuyler's life enclosed here, unknown to her, to anyone. Closer now, he extended a hand toward her, but although the distance between them seemed to decrease, his fingers collided only with the air in front of her—they didn't pass through her as the car had passed through Schuyler and Bookman. They found no resistance, yet he was unable to reach her. His perception of nearness, as though looking through a powerful telescope from great distance, with figures in clear view but untouchable, disoriented him. He lowered his arm. Though she said nothing, he was sure she heard him, heard something . . . words . . . sounds. He spoke, mélange of words and thoughts, unconcerned whether or not he babbled, trying to convey his admiration, his warning.

"Schuyler made it to . . . shouldn't say where, what if somehow. . . . Things happened, crazy things, but he got away . . . never knew what happened to you . . . didn't know about the steamboat. This ship? Your husband's? Your salvation—must not take the riverboat, no Hudson, no steamboat, sail, sail . . . California, Oregon, war in California soon, more territorial imperialism—"

He drew back, startled. Waves of fog devoured the ship and marched toward Madame Burgundy. The distance between

Lerner and Madame Burgundy expanded; the earth stretched and the fog clamped down.

Stampede of howling beasts, their screams deafening, their breath sour and furnace-hot. Sleek, armored bodies rampaged past him. Nowhere to hide, no way to survive their onslaught. He dove into a hollow where, moments ago, the riverbank had met the wharf. And landed on concrete, scraped, battered, inches from the onrush of cars on FDR Drive.

This time there was no Freed to happen by and patch his wounds. He stood and made his way to the overpass. At some point . . . on Delancey? . . . he waved down a taxi, but had no notion of where to go.

"Just drive," Lerner said, then after a block, "Oh . . . Geraty's. Drop me at Sixth and Charlton, Geraty's Tavern." He settled into the seat. Chilled . . . damp clothes—he should go home and change, but home . . . *alone* . . . he couldn't. He needed people, even strangers—the surrounding masses of the city. The cab stopped; he paid and went into Geraty's, to the restroom. Examined himself in the mirror. Face scraped, chin raw but not much blood, right forearm the same. He washed the injured places and dried them with a paper towel. One spot near his elbow seeped red. At the bar, he asked for band-aids and a shot of tequila: the universal cure for all but the most serious of injuries.

The drink prickled his scalp. He closed his eyes, letting the medicine spread. The bartender asked if he wanted another, but one was the proper dosage, followed by beer.

"Jacob!"

His name? Who knew him in this strange, foreign land? Barkeep! A pint of your best. But a hand gripped his shoulder, and Buddy Drake's face appeared, atop the body at the next bar stool. How had Buddy Drake found him, here, in Schuyler's nameless Eastern city of twisted lanes and human sacrifice?

"I just left you a message! The band broke up, big fight, falling out, whatever, so the tour ended early. We were in Amsterdam. I hung out for a while there with Mike, their drummer. Now I'm home. You look like hell!"

"It's great to see you, Buddy. Things have been strange here, very strange."

"Tell me about it. Let's go get some food. I ate some amazing Indonesian in Amsterdam the past few days—but what I want now is a dumb-ass American burger and onion rings."

Along the way to a hamburger place on Prince Street, Buddy Drake gave an account of the tour, England, Italy, Germany, tension rising to the final break-up between the co-leaders. "I have to say I liked Ray better, his songs and his personality. Nelson was more ambitious, or something, more into getting ahead. So now he can go do that on his own."

They talked about art and ambition, the necessity of both, in the proper balance. Not knowing where to start, what to tell Buddy Drake, Lerner described his current work for the autumn show. He didn't feel able to put a proper narrative together until they reached the restaurant.

"Remember that painting at Freed's? The woman in the red dress sitting, the man behind her in the doorway?" His throat constricted, filled with a jumbled mass of words, phrases, paragraphs, all straining to emerge at once; the force of their hunger clogged his mouth, sending a dull ache into his extremities and twisting his gut. "The painting. . . . " He willed the spirals in his stomach to unwind. Beer came, and he drank, swallowing the jumble of words, replacing them with a less contrary pattern.

"The painting. It got into my head. Not just composition, technique, execution . . . something inside it. I really felt the threat, that the man planned to hurt the woman. I did some research on the artist and eventually tracked down a journal he wrote when he was in New York, working on the painting." Lerner slipped the journal from his bag and laid it on the table. He told Buddy Drake about the first copy, finding the second, with its deletions and additions.

"Things kept happening . . . I met the woman who discovered the painting . . . noodle chef named Catherine Vanadis—she's got some of your photos in her house . . . the painting . . . walled up in a basement room on Bond Street. Tried to talk to the appraiser, but he pretended he'd never heard of the painting. Then those investment sisters made Freed sell it to them. And . . . I saw someone in the upstairs window of the Vanadis restaurant building.

"But read the journal first. Then we can talk."

From the restaurant they walked to Lerner's apartment, where he showered and cleaned his scrapes while Buddy Drake read the journal. How much to tell him immediately? Would he believe that Lerner was the man Schuyler saw from the window, and that Lerner had seen him too? The events, they multiplied, accumulated . . . from first sight of the painting and onward, a long, breathless plummet toward. . . .

Buddy Drake called out from his seat at the table: "Hey—when I was in Amsterdam I saw an exhibit of early photographs by a guy named Cornelis Steenkamp, stuff from the 1850s, really cool use of shadow, macro shots of architectural detail and such. Seems he'd done some botanical illustrations in Indonesia, then came back to Holland and learned photography." He held the journal toward Lerner.

"Remember? Right here, 're-christening myself Cornelis Steenkamp . . . letters from my parents . . . addressed to their "cousin" Cornelis'—it's him, back in Holland. He couldn't give up art. I've got the brochure from the exhibit at home. I'll get it for you. Says he died sometime in the 1860s, '67 maybe, can't remember from what. Nothing devious."

"Died?" Lerner sank to a chair.

"Let me finish reading," Buddy Drake said. "I've only gotten up to where he mentioned the name Steenkamp. So none of this Indonesian stuff was in the other copy?"

While he read, Buddy Drake fiddled with his earring, sliding the bead to his lobe one way, then the other. Lerner sat for a time, his head jammed with images, the Kreunens big as the sky, laughing down on him, crushing Schuyler's body with their tree-trunk fingers, plucking off arms and legs and flinging them into the ocean, aiming for Nooteboom's escaping ship. . . . He got up and filled his kettle with water, occupying himself with routine, unscrewing the tea jar lid and spooning Darjeeling leaves into the beautiful pot made by his friend Alicia Perkins. Schuyler's death needn't have been a result of Stuyvesant action. At least now Lerner knew what had happened to him. Not a bad life, experimenting with different forms, persevering. Perhaps he had married, had children . . . and somewhere, his descendants lived on. Did they know anything of their ancestor's past? Did they know Schuyler, or only Steenkamp? The kettle screeched; Lerner filled the teapot and carried it to the table.

Buddy Drake closed the journal. "I'd like to meet your noodle chef. She has taste, obviously, being a proud owner of the works of Buddy Drake."

Lerner brought out pastries from the refrigerator, custard tarts bought yesterday at a Chinese bakery. He poured milk into their cups and added tea through a strainer. The tea soothed his throat, warmed him. His elbow throbbed; it had stiffened, and he stretched it out on the table.

"There was this amazing little restaurant in Genoa," Buddy Drake said. "You think New York is full of great places to eat—"

"Buddy." Lerner grasped his friend's arm. "Buddy, listen to me. The dapper marionette has been here, my apartment. I've talked to it. Him."

Had Buddy Drake believed him? The words had forced their way out unbidden, bringing everything into the glare of reality. Lerner didn't believe in ghosts, magic, astrology, but Buddy Drake did: twice a year he visited Linda, a fortune-teller in Yonkers; he had often urged Lerner to accompany him. And he claimed that his apartment building on East 9th Street was haunted by the ghost of an old Puerto Rican woman named Soledad.

"It's not all as coincidental as it seems," Buddy Drake said. "Well, some of it anyway. If the dapper marionette had some grudge or whatever with the limbless octopi and their various worshippers around the world, he would've ended up in New York. How Schuyler connected with you and vice versa—who the fuck knows! But given that connection, the rest makes total sense. You've gotta give those Kreunens an ultimatum, tell them you know all about those limbless octopi fuckers. Show them you can't be manipulated like Freed."

The evening grew into night; Lerner lit several candles and put on side one of *S*, by Warsaw Lorca's band Section 32, letting its melodic whine fill the gaps in conversation.

"Weren't we sharing that dump on Avenue A when this came out?" Buddy Drake asked. "We both had to buy it but I can't remember who got it first. But I *can* picture everything else, the collapsing sofa . . . your new stereo!"

"Cheryl was there—haven't thought about her in ages. You and her were together . . . what? Three or four years?"

"I don't want to think about it. Crazy fucking bitch. Beautiful. Mesmerizing. Brilliant. But so fucked up by her John Birch family . . . those photos I took of her in the subway got me my first gallery."

"So you have to look at her face the rest of your life. I'm glad you didn't take pictures of Beth when we were married."

"Those Kreunens, Jacob, I don't think you're really in any kind of trouble. They don't know about the dapper marionette."

"They're just weird and wealthy. Maybe their group did some freaky shit in the past, but what do they do now besides buy and sell? Of course you can hurt lots of people doing that. They could buy this building and try to force me out."

Later, after Buddy Drake had gone, Lerner, not quite ready for bed, puttered in his studio, then turned on the TV and watched a sitcom rerun, allowing its numbing inanity to soothe him.

16
MAPS

Graceful ligatures bonded to surly engines, engines that creep along a landscape littered with shattered promises, worthless save as bitter compost to be built upon by later generations, degenerated beings with no concept of the wonders beneath their hovels. Future excavators find . . . but what if there is no future? No second chances? When everything is used up, expended, what remains will be devoid of life down to the smallest bacteria. Virtue locked in battle with expectation—once a nation reaches a certain point in its development, a corruption of wealth, power, and entitlement drives it to its doom (yes, it could be *virtuous* to *conserve* resources, but that would be contrary to the *fundamentals* of our way of life!). As technology increases, so does the energy consumed in death, and the energy that continues after death ensures further death. *The Finality of Lifelessness Equals Dust*. A fine title for his next piece—all he need do is live long enough to complete it.

As the days passed, Lerner found himself alternating between his two current projects. *Manhattan Greed* was farther along, necessarily so, but *Manhattan Green* had accelerated; he went out to a store that sold model-railroad supplies and browsed bags of trees, dyed straw, artificial grasses, gathering what he thought would be enough. At first, when confronting the variety before him, he worried about accuracy—how much of the Manhattan landscape had been deciduous, how much evergreen, but. . . . He stopped on his way to the cash register. The materials in his basket—their intended use, the accuracy of their design, specificity of purpose—these had no place in his studio. Configuring them into the shape of *Manhattan Green* would make an attractive object, but it would lack depth, subtext, it wouldn't excite, wouldn't convey the texture and emotion that he desired from his art.

He took another step toward the register. Re-imagining the entirety of his diorama . . . the effort involved . . . weariness descended, the weight of expectation, from Kreunens, the dapper marionette, himself . . . so much easier to proceed as planned. The result would serve the purpose, would it not? Though what *was* the purpose? *Not* to fulfill someone else's expectations. No, his art was *his*; what he sold, he sold because someone accepted and valued his vision. If his instinct told him that his current path was wrong, he had to follow its directive, or risk losing himself and his art.

Eyes closed, he rebuilt his city, casting aside the manufactured tools in his basket.

And later, in his studio, he worked. His plan was to create an uneven, but steadily rising surface (covered in trees, grass, and rocks) from the edge of the Dutch wall to its eventual ending at the canvas, which would continue the green and show the surrounding river. He was glad he had chosen to scale down his representation of the populated tip of Manhattan. He had his library book image of the Dutch Castello Plan enlarged, in color, to fit on an 11 x 17 inch sheet of paper. Then he applied plaster to a sheet of plywood to create an irregular surface, moistened the paper to make it more flexible, and glued it to the plaster. For this Dutch Manhattan he assembled two broken skyscrapers out of bronze strips.

The wall he made three-dimensional, papier mâché over wire

frame, to represent the wall's original timber and earthwork construction. The rest of the diorama? Another sheet of plywood to continue the island, from the Dutch wall onward. Scraps of wadded paper covered with clay to form the hilly terrain. Everything clay, trees, grasses . . . giving the suggestion of the unspoiled landscape. Later, after firing, he would join the two pieces.

The two works blended—he planted trees amongst the broken buildings of *Manhattan Greed*, as if to beautify the desolation, perhaps from a future perspective, like the nineteenth-century views of Italian ruins painted by young American artists on their European tours.

Frenzied activity pushed the days and nights forward. He worked early, he worked late. With his self-imposed deadline upset by Buddy Drake's premature return, outside influences reduced to minimal needs: eat, sleep, shit, piss. For a while, a part of him kept watch from a distance, prepared to step in lest his behavior become too manic, but the need to finish drove even that reserve into the fray.

The next external guidepost would be the opening party at Fresh Ginger, a decision reinforced when Catherine Vanadis stopped by his apartment. At first he ignored the sound of the buzzer, but his watchful self recommended a break, and he set aside his clay.

"I was in the neighborhood," she said, moving to embrace him.

He stepped back—"I don't think I showered today," he said. "Maybe not yesterday either. I probably stink." And he was still wary, still unsure. . . .

"There's a noodle factory on Walker I needed to check out. They've been open a year but I've been busy. Good products." She held up a bag. "I could whip something up for lunch. If you've got any decent ingredients." She pushed toward the kitchen, but stopped at his incomplete diorama.

"Jacob—this is fucking amazing!"

"Trying to finish by your opening party. My deadline. It's

gotten in the way of my other thing." He gestured toward *Manhattan Greed*. "They go together, but the other one is for my show in November and this one isn't. More of a personal obsession. When it's finished, this part, the Dutch settlement and the diorama, it'll have painted canvas on the back and sides. Box around the whole thing, glass on top and in the front . . . the sides . . . either plywood attached to the backs of the canvases, painted black, or a lighter-weight material, plastic of some sort. Whatever. Something that won't distract from what's inside."

"The metaphors," she said. "Nature transformed, city spreading, taking over the land . . . and your clay, bringing earth back to the city." She picked up an air-dry clay pine tree and waved it over *Manhattan Green*. "I want to buy it for the restaurant. We can unveil it at my party."

Allowing Catherine reign over the kitchen, Lerner tended to his hygiene. He washed his hands and put on a shirt that he thought might be clean. A streak of dried clay marked his temple, but he left it for later. After finishing his day's work, he would wash himself, would wash all of his clothes.

Catherine's suggestion appealed to him. The site of her restaurant was a nexus. But the Kreunens would likely be attending . . . the thought of their presence, witnesses at the unveiling of his piece . . . snarling vultures, fangs dripping with bloody remnants of their last victim; engorged, they expanded, ballooned in size until their bulk filled the sky . . . leathery wings spread wide, they darkened the cityscape, and with the sun banished, frigid winds blew snowdrifts over cars and doorways—Lerner cried out as the dapper marionette flung the small acrobat woman at the towering bulk of the Kreunens, who furled their wings to form a shield, and in doing so allowed the lonely sun to shine again, melting the ice into a steam-cloud that reduced the Kreunens to their former proportions.

Had Catherine Vanadis heard his cry? The dull clang of spoon on pan sounded from the kitchen. Time to release his mania: the sisters were nothing more than representatives of the common species of money-worshipping Manhattanites, whatever rites and sacrifices their predecessors may have engaged in.

"Okay, I'm mostly clean," he said when he rejoined her. "What's for lunch?"

"You didn't have much. A little gnarled stub of ginger. Some cabbage. A tired carrot. Good thing you've got chili paste and good soy sauce. Go grocery shopping today, okay? You can't spend your whole time working. You need to eat. At least when *I'm* overworking, I'm surrounded by food!"

The triangle formed where Walker met Canal housed assorted fruit and vegetable stands, and across the street on the downtown side there were several fish markets. Life intruded: buy produce, fish for tonight (perhaps a soy sauce braise), and cans of Yeo's Singapore Curry Gravy for quick meals. What had he been eating the past few weeks? His body didn't appear to be any thinner than normal. He must have gone out to pick up food. Grand Sausages . . . he was sure he had been there once or twice, and if not there, one of the other Chinese window-food places. And an emptying of his refrigerator and cabinets. Time to replenish. Good thing Catherine had showed up. Not healthy letting things go, and look at his neighborhood—food everywhere! All he need do is venture out.

Now that he had torn himself from work, broken free of his studio prison, he wished to savor the afternoon, despite the heat and humidity.

A return to his apartment only to deposit groceries, then out again, downtown, toward Manhattan's tip. But what would he find? His last visit to the edge of the island had conjured Madame Burgundy.

In all his years living here, he had never gone down to Battery

Park, or Castle Clinton, into the congested heart of the city's oldest districts (though the park was built on landfill, off the edge of what had been the original Dutch settlement). There, the past lay in shallow graves, watchful, resentful of usurpers, even though they, too, would soon enter graves of their own. Is time a string stretched between two points, with a person bound to follow from one end to the other? Or does it have many entries and exits scattered along a twisted, looping cord with no beginning or end?

Down Broadway, past nondescript wholesalers and discount stores, pale remnants of what had once been the fashionable shopping district. The hotel where Dickens and Schuyler had stayed, long-gone, its rubble scattered to expand the island (valuable real estate!). Lerner concentrated on exit-points, desiring a glimpse of . . . if not the Dutch city then Schuyler's. Viscous bloody rivers cascaded from the buildings . . . but that was the other city. Poor Schuyler, lost in that unnamed place until, rescued by the dapper marionette, he found freedom and returned home to a new identity as the photographer Cornelis Steenkamp.

Block by block, backward in time, though little remained of the past. Recent history—here an apartment building that had been converted from offices during an economic downturn; Lerner had attended a party there, a couple—Mark and Marc—who ran a company that built models for use in advertisements. They had offered Lerner work, model-making, if he ever needed money, and he had spent a week there constructing a medieval castle that was supposed to serve as a platform for displaying watches . . . considering the money he had been spending on *Manhattan Green,* he might need to call them. Bending his art to the thrall of advertising . . . he had seen the effects of that kind of money. Buddy Drake had worked as a photographer for a series of magazines, each paying him more than the previous. Being frugal, like Lerner, he had been able to save a lot to live on later, when he quit, but there had been others from art school who remained in their secure positions, fueling the economy with their spending.

Ahead, a glint drew Lerner's attention, sunlight refracting through reddish glass. The dapper marionette? A crimson glow spread over the street, parked cars, pedestrians; it thickened, grew darker, encasing everything it touched. Then, as quickly as it had appeared, the glow passed.

He hadn't seen the dapper marionette since the iguana parade. And before, all that stuff about the city model, water, trees and green—well, Lerner was making his own model now, his own green for the city's concrete landscape. Perhaps his art could have an effect on the future development of Manhattan.

The rosy glint reappeared on Fulton Street. A sharp red framed the doorway of the Strand bookstore, giving it the appearance of a portal leading to unimaginable realms, places reached along pathways of crimson light.

Scent of books, rich and musty like the interior of a cave—stacks marched onward into the store's depths. Words floated out to greet him, letters bound and unbound, syllables teeming with energy. He recalled the caretaker of books and hidden water who granted him his first viewing of Schuyler's journal. Webs of ink and paper drew him onward, clinging, pulling him into the store. Ahead, lightning, dazzling flashes of red. Towers of ruby crystal rose to insane heights and shattered; glass rain fell, coating the streets with red dust that burned flesh and concrete. Through new apertures the hidden water . . . geysers, whale spouts . . . the hidden water ascended to reclaim its realm, stronger now after years of conserving itself, placating desire, patient, so patient its flow had more the aura of a caress than a slap, but that was always water's strength, its serene evolutionary drip, construction by destruction, stripping layers to reveal inner forms. What fabulous sculptures! Hidden in subterranean realms they called with soft melodies and liquid notes, danced a glistening dance of mineral drip. Immeasurable caverns existed, filled with complex civilizations, lifetimes spent outside the boundaries of human knowledge and perception, observed, if at all, only as dream images that fade on awakening.

Pages appeared, colorful covers splashed along the horizon, portending the inevitable dance of change, energetic new partners calling their greetings. The world contracted, surrounding walls of words, suffocating in their need for sustenance. Lerner gagged for breath amongst the constricting pages. Collapsing letters, released from fibrous prisons, drizzled soft and dark. A tangled mass accumulated. Lerner swam, thrashing to keep his head above the heaving, shifting pile. The current pulled, and he swam with it. A landing appeared, against which the viscous alphabetic sea cleaved, throwing out a gibberish wave. Lerner grasped the rail, clinging tight to wrestle the current's force. He pulled himself out. The lettered flow released him with a sucking tear that left his legs raw and stinging. Cold steel railing bordered a staircase made of books, their spines illegible in the darkened air. He climbed blindly, step after step spiraling upward. His legs became an inferno of wheezing muscle, then a frigid darkness engulfed them. Unable to sense their movement, he concentrated on the *idea* of movement.

Periodic flashes of red cut the darkness, rotations like those of a lighthouse. After a time, after much blind, legless climbing carried him beyond all imaginable heights, beyond the paths between stars and back again, the slope leveled, passing through a forest of books, scattered stacks, shelves coming clear as murk decreased. One book appeared atop a stack, presented at such an angle it proved impossible to ignore. He veered toward it, took it into his hands, and fled.

Brightness . . . humidity . . . heat . . . onrush of life . . . the sidewalk carried him along, driftwood in the city's flow. Ahead, the overhanging bulk of FDR Drive, and past it, despite the gloss of chain clothing stores, stood buildings from a more solid era, buildings Schuyler would have passed after disembarking from his ship. But the ships docked today were floating museums, and the piers, home to nautical-themed restaurants.

Lerner took a seat in one and ordered a beer, which he drank down in a swift, satisfying gulp. It wasn't until after he had ordered another, and a bowl of seafood chowder, that he became aware of the book resting in his lap.

Manhattan in Maps. The cover showed a map of lower Manhattan and surrounding water, then below, a painting of ships in the harbor. He opened the book. The city, his city, evolving on paper from 1527 on, gorging and growing with unbelievable speed. The foreword: "a book that is destined to have a profound and positive influence on twenty-first-century New York." But how could a map, a picture, be expected to have such an influence? Indeed. (His artist-self laughed at him.) " . . . the British Headquarters Map . . . delineates . . . every stream, pond, swamp, marsh, elevation, and contour of shoreline that then existed on Manhattan."

And more: "Because the gigantic Headquarters Map does not hang in a place of honor in the City Hall rotunda . . . under the notorious waffle-iron influence of a second map, the 1811 Commissioners' Plan, Manhattan was squashed, flattened, dried, de-greened, and gridded with right-angle streets and avenues . . . In this two-dimensional vision of the city, every marsh and stream was a receptacle waiting to be smothered by a displaced hilltop. New York was placed in the artificial position of creating an economy and a society that had almost no connection to the underlying environment. . . . "

Lerner flipped pages to reach the Headquarters Map, and he was there! Immersed in *Manhattan Green,* fingers deep in soil, toes cooling in every brook. The trees! The trees bent to whisper secrets, and he deferred to their wisdom, gained through contact with earth and sky. Green fluttered around him, green of uncountable shades and hues. Green infused his lungs, filled his mouth, his eyes. Each particle of green sent tendrils deep, granting him vitality, the unopposable force of steady natural growth (the true growth that the gods of economy try so feebly to imitate), and in return, he pledged his support.

If, with his art, he could evoke even the slightest movement in a few individuals, movement toward . . . a greener consciousness? . . . but that wasn't it exactly, not in a strict environmental sense, though the environment was of course connected—more of a softening of the nation's psyche, where art or learning might be more appreciated, rather than the current stampede in which people wore their ignorance with pride, speaking and voting with ignorance as their escort. This ignorance warred with the rest of the world. How long before ignorance dominated? Some nations resisted, but so much of the world emulated what happened here, desiring fast-food homogeneity and the false comfort it provides.

A virus of art, an art so strong, so deep-rooted that nothing could expel it. A democratic art to reverse the tide of ignorance. Could he do that? He must. He must.

17
WILLING CATALYST

Tonight, the petrified city drowned under fevered, sweeping rain, a downpour that washed the streets of grime, scouring the summer's accumulations—not the renewal of spring, nor the annunciation of summer's death: that wasn't expected for another week or two, but still, magnificent...furious purple sheets churned, collecting their kin, a flow recalling that of the island's long-forgotten long-buried streams. The homeless found what refuge they could, doorways, awnings, cash-machine alcoves. From one side of Broadway the other vanished, consigned to memory. Those few, those secret few who fished for blind catfish from streams accessed in downtown basements known only to the members of their club, stood ready, poles in hand to see what new oddities the rain and upwelling water might bring. If the downpour persisted, how long before it filled basements, crumbled and swept away foundations? But this is the city that ignores disaster, incorporating calamity into new mythos, new construction.

Choices. Simple ones. Ones of great complexity. Rafts of them floated on the horizon, carried along by the rainwater current; obelisks of choices marked the seven directions. Some choices are basic: leave bed at 7:00, or wait another half hour. Some involve the fate of the world. Savage doom-wielders meet in the halls of power, dividing everything into easily digestible grids while stupefied populations watch and cheer. In the future there will be no war, no hunger, no jealousy. Or perhaps there will be more of it, as hyenas and vultures scramble for smaller and smaller portions.

The future promised to Lerner's generation was to be a modern and enlightened age. The century turned, but where were the jetpacks and moon bases? Somewhere, somewhen, choices had been made, paths entered, paths that diverged from progress and back to fear and the embrace of ignorance. What shaped these paths—collective indifference, or the machinations of the fear-mongers, the religious conservatives who saw education as a threat to their hegemony? Both, likely. Far easier to accept one's condition than work to change it.

Which paths did the Kreunens choose? Stability and steady growth—if any group tilted the world too far in one direction, the Kreunens and their ilk would take control. Sometimes though, unexpected disaster caused even *their* plans to veer awry.

But other worlds exist, worlds of air and art, where agents of ignorance dwell only in small, amorphous clusters that float at random, unable to remain anywhere long enough to corrupt. Each shape Lerner formed, each line drawn, was an attempt to find such a place. And what progress thus far? A studio filled with scraps of dreams, scattered fragments of a puzzle so vast he could work a lifetime without matching two contiguous pieces.

Outline of parts, separation of matter, numbers, colors, transitional elements, alchemist's delight—brightness dulled by repetition, but each day, each sunrise, gives hope for change. One chance, one happy accident can alter the flow of inexorable currents, continent-spanning escalations that crumble, slices dispersing through the atmosphere to reconfigure in new and surprising relationships. No more massed-army conflagrations, no more gentleman's war, both sides evenly matched, feinting, probing, slashing at exposed weakness then withdrawing for a respectable period of regrouping. What savages, those who decline to follow such time-honored rules! Hiroshima and Nagasaki gave their answers.

Blood dripped onto the clay hillside: Lerner, distracted, had nicked his finger while cutting up an apple for breakfast. He held his hand over a grove of clay trees, using his blood to darken the crowns in places.

"I really put myself into my art," he said, and laughed.

And then, like all the pieces that came before, failed pieces, pieces that continued to thrill him, *Manhattan Green* was finished and delivered, via Savage, to Catharine Vanadis. Aside from the usual rumination over minor details (Could it use another few clumps of tall grass? A grouping of conifers? A more definite link to the British Headquarters Map?), its final appearance satisfied him. The Headquarters Map had been a great aid to his painting of the backdrop. Someday he hoped to do more than approximate: like the 1846 Miniature City now hidden in the Kreunens' private gallery, he could craft a scale model. That would require a team of assistants, money — but why not? He could apply for grants, divert his sculpture seminar. . . .

The Headquarters Map had to have been an eighteenth-century anti-Stuyvesant attempt that failed. Lerner swore that *his* would succeed.

Today he had worked on *Manhattan Greed* without significant progress. Bits and pieces, no consistent flow. But he had time. The show didn't open till the second week of November. Though if he didn't finish soon, his work would be interrupted. He was going to Amsterdam! Buddy Drake had dropped off the brochure from the Steenkamp/Schuyler exhibit — it ended in September. Lerner's departure date was eight days after the restaurant opening. If necessary he could finish *Manhattan Greed* when he returned.

Lerner tidied his studio, then himself. He had decided to go out for a late lunch. But on exiting his building, he stopped. A black limousine sat at the curb. Its rear door swung open and darkness poured out; cold and oblong claws dug into his arms before he could flee. Walls of darkness erupted around him, squeezing him toward the limousine. A seat claimed him, a seat opposite the Kreunens.

"The value of that property will double in two years. Hold till then . . . plastic shelving manufacture . . . of course mining equipment . . . " and on, a litany of income-producers for the upper classes, spoken into twin headset mobile phones.

Then they turned their attention to him.

"There he is, the sculptor Jacob Lerner."

"A meeting conducted, yet no conclusion of business."

"Shares are available, Jacob Lerner. Properties. A check to secure your position."

"Savage says your next piece."

"Savage allowed us to purchase in advance."

"For our personal collection."

"We find ruins intriguing."

"When one property is destroyed, another gains value. The economy moves upward."

"Art is always a willing catalyst."

Similar statements followed, spoken in that same enervating tone. Their voices assumed such a structure of sameness that there could easily have been one speaker. From time to time, their names would pop out, sparks in the blackness, and Lerner wondered what kind of fuel it would take for those sparks to ignite and sear off their darkness. *Manhattan Green,* he knew, was a key, the antidote to their desire for *Manhattan Greed.*

Without any apparent communication from them to the driver, the car stopped. The door hissed open. Darkness propelled Lerner from his seat and onto the sidewalk outside the Flatiron building. Still hungry, he walked toward the Puerto Rican cafeteria on 18th.

Wolves prowled the distant hills, whose wooded slopes— branches bare with the advent of autumn—gave precarious shelter. But he, caretaker of this land, could walk without fear from beasts, even on cold, candle-lit nights such as this. Blessed shadows sang sweet trills that told him not to mistrust the snaking path, and at the top of the hill he came upon a ring of straight-trunked pines standing apart from the rest, the lesser trees of the preceding slopes. Among the tall pines, elements of light cascaded through the air, scattering particles like glowing snowflakes that revealed the essence of nighttime.

In the middle of the ring was the stump of what had been a tree more massive than any of those surrounding it, sheared to form a flat surface, a stage on which the dapper marionette danced with the naked acrobat woman.

Lerner tried to superimpose the Headquarters Map onto the neighborhood. He saw no sign of the spring-fed creek that had emerged where 22nd Street passes behind the Flatiron building.

The dance of the dapper marionette and the acrobat woman formed a pattern, a tracery of bluish light that flowed from their heels, growing more complex with each movement. Lerner focused on the movements, soaring along the light-stream like a raptor on currents of air; blue currents led him higher, too high to risk looking down, but that was a ridiculous fear—nothing could hurt him, not the distance or the wolves. He opened his eyes, seeing the congested sewer that had once been his city, and the surrounding nation grew ever more layers of concrete skin, occasionally shedding them to mold a thicker layer. Rain hissed as it fell, marking the concrete with an acid kiss, tracing abstract designs in its surface, designs that Lerner had at first taken for markings of brand identity, advertising billboards to comfort air travelers disoriented by the trackless sky.

For what is more comforting than the familiar logo of a favorite product?

But *this* rain only produced torment; gone was its restorative magic. Even if logos had been painted on the concrete surface, the caustic rain would have long since obliterated them. Too late, now, for an eruption of green to save this barren land, too late. Lerner's tears mixed with the rain, creating a lacy curtain that hid the desolation, and the dancers twirled out into the darkness of space.

Cataclysms of air and earth, spawning dark creatures that shat out noxious, sulfuric lumps. Building blocks of the future or backfill for mass graves? Waves of extinction are not unique—why must humanity claim special status? Iguanodon died too, but at least its death helped to fuel later generations (that same fuel contributing to later deaths as well, in colliding metal shells and invisible emissions—what you can't see has no meaning!).

When Lerner first viewed Schuyler's painting he became ensnared in a succession of events. Had Schuyler's journal even existed before the painting captured Lerner, or was it brought into being by the force of his obsession and the will of the endless struggle?

Manhattan Greed versus *Manhattan Green*, and which would be the victor?

But Lerner wasn't a believer in extremes. *His* Manhattan would have to accommodate both. Though the Kreunens represented that which he shunned, and the dapper marionette the side he chose, it didn't mean he would *always* choose one and shun the other. Life was more complex than that. Humanity, he hoped, was more complex.

18

BLISTERED SKY

Aftermath of Lerner's encounter with the Kreunens—his body harbored a zone of coldness somewhere inside his chest, a zone that he couldn't seem to banish but could sometimes ignore. The next time he saw them, he feared the zone would become overwhelming. And so, for the party at Catherine Vanadis's new restaurant, he invited an army to shield him: Simon Hoff and his partner, Dr. Randolph the ant biologist; Tansy; Buddy Drake; and half a dozen others. Savage, of course. Their presence would deliver enough strength for him to persevere.

Freed would of course be there. They had talked since Freed's return from Italy but hadn't met. Lerner wasn't sure what to think about Freed anymore. They had known each other since boyhood, but Freed's entanglement with the Kreunens . . . though now look at his own situation . . . encircled . . . sinking into their miasma.

The night preceding the party, Lerner imagined a scene in which he briefed his troops, giving them the dual-edged weapon of art and hope to combat the Kreunens' chill. His brain spun wilder and wilder incarnations of the evening's possible events, from the bland to the horrific.

"The dapper marionette will know what to do," he said to his assembled company.

But what of the dapper marionette? Surely he would make an appearance soon.

Lerner felt sick at the thought of the Kreunens possessing

Manhattan Greed—his statement *against* economic cruelty co-opted by those responsible for it. Normally, once he sent a work off into the world, it ceased to exist; whoever bought it didn't concern him (the dilemma of the artist—those who could purchase art were likely the same materialists he disdained). If the Kreunens were merely benign bullies, the thought of his work sharing space with Schuyler's painting would thrill him. But the history behind their collection . . . its role in twisting the city's development . . . he couldn't allow his art to join that. And his art *had already* shared space with the painting, his immature sculpture at Freed's, before the Kreunens carried the painting off to their private gallery. Perhaps he wouldn't bother finishing the piece. Savage would have to return the money (something he would *hate* to do, and he would be extremely angry with Lerner over it, might even drop Lerner from his roster—these relationships were always delicate).

Working one morning, he dampened an ink drawing of Madame Burgundy and glued it to one of the streets, then painted over it, a buried charm to hinder the Kreunens.

As the time for Catherine's party approached, he distracted himself with deliberations over his wardrobe, eventually choosing lightweight denim pants, black, with a light-blue ribbed tee-shirt, and sturdy boots: handsome clothing plus his stamina and determination would be his weapons. Ready to leave, he stood in his doorway observing the street—no Kreunens in sight—then continued uptown.

City blocks descended, concrete and brick landscape creating its own climate, a way of life to which some adapted but many didn't, though they continued, for years they continued—most would never admit that their lives might be better elsewhere, a place where kindness grew in greater supply, where everyone could breathe and sing, no guarded glances, no cocoon of distance from neighbors, no lack of green. But so much here he needed . . . the mix of people on the street—there, the emaciated model passing a pair of women whose thick, lined faces could have been transported from twelfth-century Latvia . . . stores, oddities, bars, museums . . . this city fueled his art. Could he find inspiration elsewhere?

He had only talked to Tansy briefly since her return from the Shakespeare festival. She had mentioned the possibility of moving to Western Massachusetts to teach at a college there. He wondered if such a path would work for him. Only two hours away by train—no wide distances to cross—but awakening in the city was an essential element of his work. What he wanted . . . somehow a combination, the softness of life elsewhere but the immanence of here.

A dank and sluggish wind tugged at Lerner's sleeve. Notes sounded, a series of guitar-shaped bells in a minor key—they formed a conduit to safety but he couldn't find the entrance. Splashes of bloody evening light stained the sidewalk. He sagged into the blank wall that faced what remained of once-grand Colonnade Row. How had he gotten here? Walked on, past Bond Street where he should have turned to reach the restaurant, his body unwilling to revisit the site of Schuyler's imprisonment. He hadn't been there since the place was a construction zone, soon after he first saw the painting of Madame Burgundy and began his search for Schuyler . . . *and when he saw the Schuyler apparition in the window, mirrored by Schuyler in his journal as a sighting of Lerner, resident of the phantom city that overlapped Schuyler's time.*

The phantom city—Lerner's New York—had supported Schuyler's escape; perhaps Schuyler's city would appear tonight to aid Lerner.

Across the front of the building a sign glowed FRESH GINGER in neon red. Inside, the place burned with too much light, which reflected off the metal tabletops and counters. Nowhere to hide, in this brightness. Whom would that better serve, himself, or the light-swallowing Kreunens? At the entrance, the sideboard from the basement tomb, rescued and refinished, with Lerner's *Homage to the Fallen Deities of Commerce* displayed on top. He had forgotten it now resided here. Its presence reassured him; his art would provide a shield.

No Kreunens yet.

The restaurant's walls were bare of art, their color and texture serving as both border and decoration; a rough faux-plaster painted in variegated browns and reds that evoked warmth, or would have in a gentler light. Counters lined both sides, with another in the back, that one set up like a sushi bar, with a glass case behind which figures stood, ready to assemble requested noodle specialties. Lerner sat at a side counter, from which he could observe new arrivals. Small square tables, some pushed together to form long seating arrangements, some separate, occupied the space between the counters. A waitress approached, offering wine. He took a glass and sipped. Freed, followed by his girlfriend, Stephanie, emerged from the kitchen. Likely Catherine was back there, showing guests the features. Wishing to examine the crowd for Kreunen allies, Lerner deferred going to offer Catherine his congratulations.

The artificial atmosphere of the gathering, the cleanliness of the new restaurant, fueled his watchfulness. Those assembled were not a random crowd of restaurant-goers. All had been picked with care to grant the most favorable attention to the new establishment. Which ones sided with the Kreunens? Though he tried to ignore the street door, whenever it opened he looked up. But what would he do when the Kreunens arrived? At that dinner party he had been able to function in their proximity, had escaped safely, but their later visit, away from Catherine's warm presence. . . . Responding to his thoughts, his doubts, the inner coldness stretched and throbbed.

A group of two women and a man stopped nearby, blocking his view of the door. One of them said: "The last time my portfolio looked this good when I invested in that chicken processing company."

The statement gave Lerner a clear vision of what the city represented to so many people, and what his life might have been without art, without his stubbornness at keeping to the plan, living his simple-yet-full life while surrounded by excess. Portfolio indeed. *This* was the alternative, wearing the latest fashions (gray linen appeared to be in), driving stylish new cars to parties, complaining about parking, talking money . . . a kind of character death in which bland actors waltzed in unison to cloying symphonies of waste and gluttony. He observed this from the safe distance of his resolve, resolve in turn strengthened by the observation, and the coldness receded.

The restaurant space, interior walls dismantled and replaced by steel support pillars, had once been the ground floor of Bookman's house, where Lilley had brought Schuyler for his forced labor and incarceration. Above Lerner: the room where Schuyler met the garrotter and incorporated him into the painting. But something was off—the stairs, they should have been near the door . . . he got up, went to the entrance, and looked out. The building appeared to have been modified; the original row house door remained, but walled off from the restaurant space, which had its own, newer door.

Exiting Fresh Ginger, Lerner approached the original door, which bore the usual signs of a residential building: buzzer/intercom outside, and in the entryway, six mailboxes, then an inner door. Each floor was likely divided into two apartments (he had been in many such apartments, throughout the city). The upstairs rooms . . . rentals.

The building had to be owned by the Kreunens. He would not ask *them* for permission to look around.

"Hey, Jacob!"

A hand touched his shoulder and he turned to welcome Tansy, a much-changed Tansy: long red hair now cropped close, skin of arms and shoulders—bare under black tank-top—covered in a riot of green.

They embraced, and he stepped back to examine her.

"Different, huh?" she said, laughing, and twirled around to show her back.

Both arms, from elbows up, and continuing along her back and shoulders, were filled with tattoos of vines, flowers, and trees, like a mad Rousseau painting. Along her spine water bubbled from a spring, its flow hidden by the fabric of her shirt.

"The green! Wait till you see my installation. I wish I could paint half as well as you look."

"I'll show you more, later, if you like," she said in a husky tone, then laughed again. "It doesn't go much further than what you see. For now"—she turned back to face him—"I met a tattoo artist up in Massachusetts. He was helping paint some scenery backdrops for *As You Like It*. Really beautiful stuff. We got to talking . . . and. . . . "

"Something is percolating," Lerner said. Nature trying to compensate for all this traffic and concrete, preparing to break free." Lerner ran a finger up the trunk of a tree, rough on her soft skin, and a multitude of scents arose, a spicy conglomeration of green. A damp breeze stirred grassy plains, but the tree-stump stage was empty—the dapper marionette and partner, gone. A branch fell, thumping to the ground, then another, and a crack sounded from one of the sentinel trees. Lerner jerked his hand back, and the sidewalk solidified beneath his feet.

"We're using a lot of interchangeable ingredients, but not so much that everything ends up tasting the same. Each type of noodle dish has a separate core spice family. Then of course there'll be seasonal variations. . . . Oh—there's Jacob!"

Lerner and Tansy had joined the back of a group touring the kitchen and noodle assembly line with Catherine. He had been hoping for anonymity, waiting till she was free so he could congratulate her.

"Jacob's sculpture is by the door, and later we'll have an unveiling of his brand-new work."

She weaved through the tour group to embrace him, pressing her body close. She wore a tapered faux-apron dress that bared her back and shoulders. Her cheeks were flushed, and she spoke with what seemed a forced enthusiasm—what he called Important Voice—a phenomenon he had seen in others at various art openings, as others had likely seen in him as well.

"The place looks fabulous," Lerner said. "I'm sure you're frazzled, but stop and look around. Savor it!"

She kissed him, and he introduced Tansy. They shook hands; Tansy commented on the design, praising the colors. Catherine thanked her, then turned back to the group. "The only problem with this kind of food is that it's too sloppy for standing around and eating, so we're going to have to sit." She waved them all to the seating area.

Lerner's friends had arrived; he sat beside Buddy Drake, with Tansy shielding his right. Freed and Stephanie sat opposite— Lerner hoped he wouldn't be weakened by their presence.

The Kreunens had also arrived, and now perched at the assembly counter. He was glad their backs were to him.

"That's them, the investment sisters," he said to Buddy Drake, leaning toward his ear and speaking low.

"They look harmless from here," Buddy Drake said.

Tansy told Simon Hoff and Dr. Randolph about the summer's productions (they had attended one, Lerner discovered, suddenly filled with guilt at having missed everything during his all-consuming submergence in his work). The noise level, voices bouncing off metal surfaces, made conversation difficult. Catherine would need to modify something to reduce the noise. Did she want feedback? This was the maiden voyage of a new restaurant; she was likely aware that changes would be needed. And the noise would be obvious . . . though Lerner knew from his own art openings that a curtain descends, everything merges, all detail becomes lost.

A succession of small bowls arrived, filled with cold noodles, crispy noodles, made from wheat, rice, liang fen . . . some with a sweet dipping sauce, some with bits of duck, vegetables, pork belly, lobster . . . and Lerner found, as at that dinner with the Kreunens, he was able to separate from his surroundings, eat, converse, but remain watchful.

Catherine roamed, checking in at every table. While Lerner introduced her around, she rested a hand on his shoulder. He felt self-conscious with Tansy beside him, for whom, he forced himself to admit, he had lost most of his desire long before they agreed to discontinue their physical relationship. But this new Tansy radiated a tropical heat that Lerner welcomed, a foil for the lurking cold. Compared to her, Catherine Vanadis appeared insignificant, and what was she anyway but a willing tool of the Kreunens? Her food though, the perfumes and flavors — those spoke of a deeper sensibility, not one decimated by materialism.

"I want to show *Manhattan Green* after everyone has finished eating," she said. "I was thinking we'd move the tables aside and wheel it out on a cart. Savage can unveil it — but I haven't seen him — "

"He never gets to anything on time," Lerner said. "Sometimes not even his own openings."

Catherine turned to Buddy Drake and said she would like to hire him to photograph the restaurant's food and décor, for use in advertising. Lerner's attention receded, replaced by the jumble that usually infected him at openings — *Manhattan Green* debuting here, soon . . . in the Kreunens' presence, in the building where Schuyler had painted. . . .

Needing to be alone, he got up to find the restroom, downstairs, the basement. The magnitude of the evening spread before him, an accretion of meetings and events that created suffocating layers, layers that soon acquired weight and substance. The room that had contained Schuyler's painting erupted gray mist, trapping him. Millennia of sediment pressed down. Immobile, he lay with arms outstretched beneath a dome of blood-colored rock. Tendrils dangled everywhere, flexible stalactites of myriad thickness and color. They taunted him with the promise of safety. From afar came the trill of water dancing over stone.

As long as water flows unrestrained, hope can never be banished.

He struggled to sit up, forcing the sediment to recede, outgoing tide a wave at a time, until his torso lifted free of the weight. Crawling, he made his way toward the nearest of the dangling ropes. But which would be the most likely guide? The first crumbled at his touch, leaving a sticky residue clinging to his palms.

Sounds emerged from a far-off corridor, the clack of stone on stone . . . drawing closer. The next rope, pale and thicker than the first, stretched and stretched, so that no matter how far he thought he climbed—pulling himself arm over arm—his feet never lifted from the floor.

A muffled thump joined the stone-claw sounds, and in the cavern's dim distance a large, spiny shape appeared.

Lerner bit through the thick, stretchy rope and wrapped it around his waist and shoulders, then looped it over a group of thin, lacy strands. He lunged, and the strands held taut. Sliding the thick loop up and weaving his feet into the strands, he climbed, a desperate lunging that carried him higher and higher. Far below, the group of tendril-ropes swayed, as though gripped by something huge and heavy. Faster he climbed, ignoring the pain in his legs, the ragged breathing that tore his throat.

Light shone above, a glowing rectangle that expanded with each lunge. He stood at the top of the stairs that led to the restaurant's basement, looking out at the tables and diners. The basement depths sucked at him, but he pushed forward, emptying the door frame.

The harsh lights of the restaurant had been dimmed, replaced by candles on each table. And the tables had been moved to the sides, leaving an open space in the center of the room. Defying the urge to flee, Lerner found his table's new location. Buddy

Drake and Tansy had faced the chairs toward the center. He sat. A waitress poured coffee and he held the cup, savoring its warmth and aroma.

Buddy Drake leaned toward him. "Hey—I can't wait to see the finished piece. I'm glad you did *something* useful with your summer."

From the other side Tansy squeezed his arm. Their presence, and that of his other friends, formed armor that no foe could penetrate. Now that his chair pointed toward the Kreunens, he met their blank, passive faces with his determination.

Savage and his young imp assistant emerged from the back wheeling a cart on which *Manhattan Green* hid, its glass case submerged beneath a bronze-colored cloth. Their languid movements lulled him, and he had to concentrate on the business of watchfulness. All around rose the hum of happy conversation.

" ... buying a place on Lake Como," Freed said. "It should be ready by next summer. Everybody's welcome. Maybe I can even convince Jacob to come." And from farther off, fragmentary voices of others: "broken" "ironic" "like a fright-night *West Side Story*, gangs with fangs ... " a din that took on the form of musical accompaniment to Savage's preparations.

While Savage stood at one end of the cart, head bowed slightly toward the covered artwork, his assistant placed a series of four metal stands, each holding a slim candle, then returned with a fifth, this one's candle as thick as the other four combined.

"Five into one," Lerner said.

He rose from his chair, but Tansy's resinous grip pulled him back down. The green across her arms and shoulders writhed in the flicker of the candles. "You have to stay," she said, with a voice that was no longer hers.

The assistant held a long match to the candles, starting to the left of the larger one and moving counter-clockwise, lighting the large one last. When the thick candle flared to light, Savage turned from the cart and spoke.

"Buried water, buried earth, where dormant life lingers. ... "

Savage's odd chant—totally out of character for the pragmatic gallery owner—silenced the crowd. Near the ceiling, a hint of movement in the dim light, a reddish movement: the dapper marionette hovered, suspended on nonexistent strings, lips moving in time to Savage's words. Several feet behind the cart, barely visible under dancing candlelight shadows, stood the naked acrobat woman.

The crowd's silence became a wall against which Savage's words pushed, probing into fissures and sliding around edges.

"From below to above, once above all-encompassing. . . . "

The dapper marionette had drugged Schuyler to help him escape from the bloody city, a drug that allowed the dapper marionette to control him, the way he now controlled Savage.

Darkness gathered. The Kreunens merged, pulpy body shifting, writhing, lashing toward Savage with ice-bound invisible tentacles, and within Lerner, the coldness answered, attempting to stretch out to meet them . . . but Tansy's tropical heat bound the cold as tightly as it bound Lerner to his chair.

"Branch of tree, branch of river. . . . "

The dapper marionette darted across the tentacles' path, distracting their pursuit of Savage. Tentacles spread, probing for an opening, and the dapper marionette, anticipating the trajectory of each tentacle, flitted out of range before it could strike him. The dance continued, but the Kreunen-body grew, spreading their tentacles farther, aiming for the dapper marionette from multiple directions. One icy thrust wrapped the dapper marionette and slammed him into a wall. The acrobat woman flung herself into the center of the Kreunens' icy mass, and shattered, screaming.

Black dust obscured the Kreunens' side of the room. The dapper marionette, freed by his partner's sacrifice, stood and limped toward Savage.

"Banished water concrete suffocation encircled unleashed unencumbered. . . . "

His chant ended, Savage threw off the dark cloth, and *Manhattan Green* emerged, glowing in the candlelight bath.

People gathered before *Manhattan Green*, even the Kreunens, their energy to resist apparently spent. Airborne again, the dapper marionette hovered over them. The crowd circled *Manhattan Green*, a counter-clockwise movement. Tansy pulled Lerner along. The finger he had cut while working on the piece tingled, then burned, shooting currents of fire up his arm and also out, at his art. Fissures appeared on the papier mâché Dutch wall, fissures that spread into the Castello Plan map. One of the bronze-strip buildings toppled. As the last person circled past *Manhattan Green*, the head of the line turned toward the door and filed out onto Bond Street.

Which split wide. Water erupted, a magnificent sparkle, thrusting cars and pedestrians into a chaotic mass. The rupture continued, running out into Broadway, then downtown and up. Shimmering air cloaked the sides of the rupture, distorted ozone ripples. The building opposite Fresh Ginger crumpled, floors disappearing into the warped air. Along the rupture trees sprang up, grasses, shrubs, a dense profusion through which deer and beaver roamed. And the schism grew, expanding outward in a green wave.

Howls from the Kreunens pushed at Lerner, an enraged cry at the disappearance of the city that their ancestors had created, reclaimed by the nature from which they had taken it.

The ancient water exhaled, dissolving concrete, brick, glass, asphalt. Blisters cracked the sky, expelling more water, burning water that bathed the onlookers in a sickly pink light. A woman near Lerner melted. A man screamed, seeking shelter under an awning, but it collapsed, succumbing to the attack from above. Lerner, followed by the Kreunens, backed into Fresh Ginger. Buddy Drake and Tansy came in after. Tansy's clothes had dissolved. Her leafy tattoos sent shoots out into the air and entwined her arms and torso.

The building containing Fresh Ginger remained stable in the onslaught, protecting *Manhattan Green*. From the windows they watched the expanding chaos. Simon Hoff and a few others staggered into the restaurant, claiming refuge. The Kreunens drooped, buried by realization of their failure. Somewhere, the dapper marionette conducted a symphony of dancing earth and singing water.

Lerner picked up a bar stool and carried it toward *Manhattan Green*.

The dapper marionette plopped down to confront him. "No you fucking won't."

The force of the dapper marionette's words thrust Lerner back. Buddy Drake and Simon pushed their way between the dapper marionette and Lerner, giving him a path. He drove himself forward and hoisted the stool, crashed its base through the glass top of *Manhattan Green*. Shards flew out into the restaurant. He raised the stool again. Strong arms, arms of coarse ivy, wrapped his body from behind, lifting him, but he swung the chair, crunching through the landscape. He raised the stool a third time. The dapper marionette leaped to grab his left arm and pulled him up to the ceiling. Bone cracked, and he screamed, releasing the stool, which landed amongst his shattered trees and hills.

The plain extended much farther than anyone could have anticipated, requiring a daunting series of steps to achieve the crossing. No clouds, no breeze, sky the color of dead foliage. No sun, yet some form of illumination caressed the landscape. None of them spoke. Staring forward, concentrating on the grass ahead, or a companion's back, they trudged. No sounds emerged but the muffled tread of boot on grass. Seventeen of them set out, but the agony of unchanged day and the effort of slogging through the stiff knee-high grass wilted resolve. First one, then, as they continued, others would stop, kneel, prostrate themselves. How many who came before them had suffered a similar fate? The grass hid all signs.

Nothing penetrated the sculptor Jacob Lerner's consciousness but the plain before him and the vague shapes of his companions. His sense of self—a core made up of the entirety of his life— lay hidden behind a wall that could only be breached by not wavering from the journey.

At some point, the one remaining figure ahead of him stopped, surrendering to the grass.

Fog draped the horizon, a thickness that obscured everything but basic sensations: warmth, cold, hunger, pain. For centuries, the fog lingered, preventing ships from leaving the harbor, shutting out the sun so that all plants withered. Life, reduced to its bacterial essence, lay in wait for a catalyst.

Lerner ran, knowing that he risked the fate of his companions. And what of them? He strained to hear steps following, but nothing penetrated the din of his own movements.

The plain gave way to a soft landscape of white sand. He slowed, feet dragging in the yielding sand. Nothing grew here, yet the sand gave off no sense of desolation. Tiring, he lay down. The sand welcomed his weary body, and he slept. Several times he woke, too comfortable to rise and continue, and each time he awakened, he thought he heard faint, birdlike murmurings, the sandy landscape apparently not devoid of life after all. The murmurings grew louder, prompting him to open his eyes. Sunlight shone through a window, and the white landscape assumed the shape of a hospital bed.

19

PHOTOGRAPHY EXHIBIT

The Cornelis Steenkamp photography exhibit was in a former merchant's house on the Keizergracht Canal. Lerner had been in Amsterdam for several days before he looked for it. He had spent his first day wandering, learning the neighborhood around where he was staying, in the Eastern Canal District apartment of one of Savage's patrons, a man who owned two pieces of Lerner's as well as a multitude of paintings and other artwork, an apartment that Lerner was thrilled to be able to use at a time of year when hotels in this city were full *and* expensive. Jetlagged, the first night, he pulled out Schuyler's journal, which he had packed as a last-minute impulse. But after he touched the binding, he had felt disinclined to open it.

His arm still ached, especially in the damp weather that welcomed him to Amsterdam, but just before his departure the plaster cast shielding his cracked radius had been replaced by a removable fiberglass one. His other injuries had faded: the bruises on his hip and thigh from when the dapper marionette dropped him, and the back of his head—struck by something that left it lumpy, tender, and concussed. He had awakened in the hospital with a fragmentary memory of the night's events, memories quite different from those of the other attendees. Explanations of gas main explosion . . . bursting pipes . . . falling beam that destroyed *Manhattan Green.* As to which version of the night was the true one, it mattered little. The differing perceptions didn't grant validity to one over another.

Tansy had suffered the most. Burned everywhere her tattoos had been, even the memory of them burned away. Lerner had visited her hospital room as soon as they allowed him to get up. One doctor had remarked on the odd pattern of Tansy's burns, but more important: they would heal without much scarring. As would Catherine Vanadis's restaurant. Perhaps the attention would be good for business.

Lerner wondered if any trace of the green eruption remained, but had avoided the area.

An unpleasant side-effect—his actions had aided the Kreunens. He didn't obliterate their New York. What repercussions would result . . . each decision in life, each act, bore a consequence. The Kreunens could return to their office, conduct their business of rape and greed, but others would balance, and perhaps, as the new century progressed, forces would shift the world toward something more benign. Had the dapper marionette's plan reached its full unfolding, had the vengeful landscape reclaimed the island . . . what would have prevented new speculation in real-estate, new development of the transformed island? There were many who would not mourn New York's passing.

Despite his injuries, he had forced himself to finish *Manhattan Greed* before leaving for Amsterdam, knowing that the interruption would prevent him from ever returning to it, for he had lost all interest in the piece, if not the thoughts that fueled its creation. He had accepted the fact of the Kreunens' impending ownership—but as an acknowledgment from them of what he had done, they granted two conditions: that they hire someone to paint out the garrotter from Madame Burgundy's painting and return it to Freed, a minor healing to reinforce his hoped-for tide of progress.

Lerner visited the Rijksmuseum and the Van Gogh Museum. Other days followed, languid days without responsibility. He would often sit and pull out his sketchbook, working to keep his fingers active. And now, here he was: Keizergracht. He entered the building and bought a ticket. The Steenkamp exhibition occupied the 2nd floor.

Stairs led to a suite of three rooms laid out along a hallway. The first contained the earliest photographs, shots of canals, bridges, and buildings, even a shot of the house in which the exhibit now hung. Other rooms contained, as Buddy Drake had said, close-ups, a profusion of architectural detail, textures of brick and stone. There were no portraits, and Lerner wondered whether that resulted from a continuing desire for anonymity, to keep anyone from connecting Steenkamp to Schuyler.

Most of the time, he had the exhibit to himself. Two men passed through together, a fleeting browse before moving on. Lerner was standing in the hallway before a photograph of a plain brick wall with a curved shadow along one side, when a woman entered. She glanced at Lerner as she came into the first room; he smiled and nodded.

He moved to the next photograph, lingering in the hallway while the woman viewed the early works. Was she Dutch? A fellow tourist? Farther down was a bench. He sat. He had talked to few people since the night at Fresh Ginger, hadn't felt much like being with others, not even his friends, and had begun this trip straight after completing *Manhattan Greed.* Alone in a foreign city, he had regained some desire for social interaction. Many natives spoke perfect English, and there were tourists everywhere, from Britain, the U.S., Australia . . . in the Rijksmuseum he had spoken to a couple, a man and woman, writers from Brisbane, but mostly, he wanted to be on his own.

The woman was tall, with short, dark hair and a slim build; watching her, an interest . . . lust—dormant since the night of the opening—awakened. He wanted to talk to her but wasn't sure how.

She passed through the hall and into the second room. He got up and walked into the third room. A few minutes later, she joined him.

"Excuse me—do you speak English?" she asked.

He thought she spoke with some kind of British accent. "I'm from New York," he said. "So the answer to your question depends on your definition of English."

She laughed, a soft sound that healed one of his many scars.

"I hope I'm not disturbing you, but I . . . being here . . . I need to share with someone."

He liked the shape of her face, her milk-chocolate eyes. "I don't mind," Lerner said. "I had just been thinking about talking to *you*." He smiled, trying to read her expression.

"I've been researching my family. My grandparents and my mother happened to be in England when the Nazis invaded Holland. They stayed even after the war; my mother barely remembers it here, and she married an Englishman."

Time, particle after particle, filled the room, seeping out of the walls and shadows. A chorus of years, of connections, intersected with the photographs of Schuyler/Steenkamp.

"This is where the family line ends . . . or starts. Before Cornelis Steenkamp it's like a blank wall, nothing about his family, where he came from. The exhibit was happening—I had to come, see if I felt some, something from the past. I've been coming here the last three days, hoping to—I don't know—learn where I come from."

All around, land reclaimed from the sea over centuries, walls built, brick upon brick, lives lived in lost detail. Choruses of voices from the past whispered, ghosts of buildings, a swirling mass of remnants, and in Lerner's bag, sharing space with his sketchbook, a physical artifact.

"I might be the only person in the world who can help you," Lerner said. He extracted Schuyler's journal and held it out for her. "Take it. Keep it. I don't need it anymore."

She took the book from him and stared at the stained, worn cover. He pulled a card from his wallet and wrote the art collector's phone number on it. His Madame Burgundy sketch smiled her gentle smile at him as he closed the wallet. "When you've read it, call me. I'll be here a few more days, then I'm heading back to New York."

The chorus continued, flowing down the streets and canals of the ancient fishing village turned colonial power, birthplace of Schuyler, birthplace of New York. Up, up, up, the chorus danced, crescendos reverberating across the sea, carried on muscular winds that encircled the globe.

ACKNOWLEDGMENTS

Thanks to Steve Connell of Verse Chorus Press and The Visible Spectrum for making this new edition possible; his perceptive edits have made this a much better book.

For the 2009 PS Publishing edition, thanks to: Cornelis Alderlieste for translation from Dutch of information on Franz Wilhelm Junghuhn; E. M. Beekman for describing Junghuhn's route from the Dutch East Indies (Indonesia) to Europe; Kirk H. Witmer for Charles Dickens's date of departure from New York; Amy Korpieski for help with research on New York row houses; the late Mike Simannoff for links and help with the New York Public Library's Art and Architecture Collection website; the Yellow Springs and Antioch College libraries for excessive interlibrary loans; Christopher Garcia for advice on ceramic sculpture. Many people helped with feedback at various stages . . . Richard Bowes, Darin Bradley, Dan Dixon, Kristopher O'Higgins, John Klima, Alexander Lamb, Deborah Layne, Nancy Jane Moore, Jeff VanderMeer, Richard Wadholm, and of course Rebecca Kuder.

Many thanks to Jeffrey Ford for the introduction to the PS edition, Pete and Nicky Crowther of PS for publishing, and Nick Gevers for editorial guidance.

I read a good bit of New York history, books on art, etc, in the course of this work. Finding the right book is always a challenge;

I was looking for more than information. I needed an essence, an essence that I couldn't identify until I saw it.

Here are some that I found helpful. *American Notes*, by Charles Dickens; *The Columbia Historical Portrait of New York: an Essay in Graphic History in Honor of the Tricentennial of New York City and the Bicentennial of Columbia University*, by John Atlee Kouwenhoven; *Low Life: Lures and Snares of Old New York*, by Luc Sante; *The Island at the Center of the World*, by Russell Shorto; *Fugitive Dreams: An Anthology of Dutch Colonial Literature*, edited and translated by E. M. Beekman; *The Architecture of New York City*, by Donald Martin Reynolds; *New York Moves Uptown* and *Bricks and Brownstone: The New York Row House 1783–1929*, by Charles Lockwood; *New York New York, A History of the World's most Exhilarating and Challenging City*, by Oliver E. Allen; *Art and the Empire City: New York, 1825–1861*, edited by Catherine Hoover Voorsanger and John K. Howat; *Fifth Avenue: A Very Social History*, by Kate Simon; *Manhattan in Maps*, by Paul E. Cohen and Robert T. Augustyn; *What Painting Is*, by James Elkins; *The Artist's Assistant: Oil Painting Instruction Manuals and Handbooks in Britain 1800–1900 with Reference to Selected Eighteenth-Century Sources*, by Leslie Carlyle; various stories of Edgar Allen Poe (re-read and newly read, especially "The Narrative of Arthur Gordon Pym of Nantucket" and "The Journal of Julius Rodman, Being an Account of the First Passage across the Rocky Mountains of North America Ever Achieved by Civilized Man"; and *Incidents of Travel in Yucatán*, by John Lloyd Stephens.

Made in the USA
Monee, IL
03 April 2023